TALES FROM THE CRYPT®

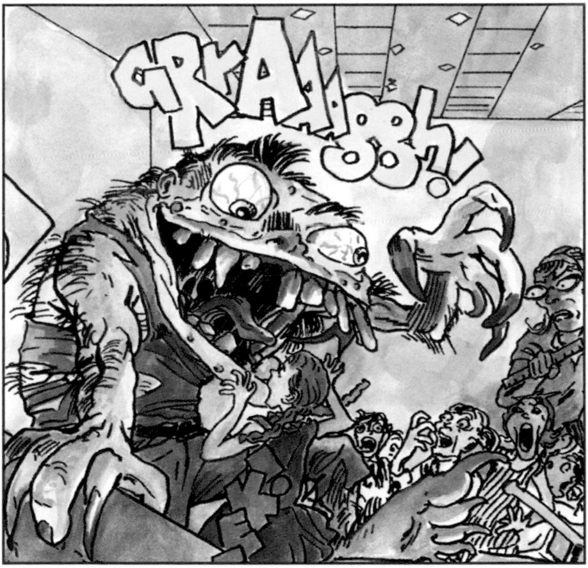

PAPERCUTZ™

TALES FROM THE CRYPT®

Graphic Novels Available from Papercutz

ALL-NEW STORIES! FULL-COLOR GRAPHIC NOVEL!
TERROR
NO. 1
TALES FROM THE CRYPT
FEATURING...

ALL-NEW STORIES! FULL-COLOR GRAPHIC NOVEL!
TERROR
NO. 2
TALES FROM THE CRYPT
FEATURING...

ALL-NEW STORIES! FULL-COLOR GRAPHIC NOVEL!
TERROR
NO. 3
TALES FROM THE CRYPT
FEATURING...
PAPERCUTZ

ALL-NEW STORIES! FULL-COLOR GRAPHIC NOVEL!
TERROR
NO. 4
TALES FROM THE CRYPT
FEATURING...
PAPERCUTZ

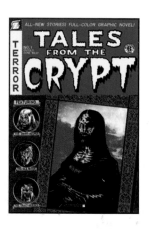

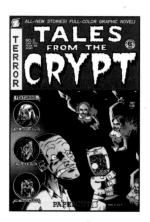

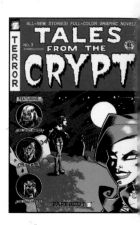

Graphic Novel #1
"Ghouls Gone Wild!"

Graphic Novel #2
"Can You Fear Me Now?"

Graphic Novel #3
"Zombielicious"

Coming July 2008: Graphic Novel #4
"Crypt-keeping it Real"

$7.95 each in paperback, $12.95 each in hardcover. Please add $3.00 for postage and handling for the first book, add $1.00 for each additional book.
Send to: Papercutz, 40 Exchange Place, Suite 1308, New York, NY 10005 • www.papercutz.com

TALES FROM THE CRYPT ®

NO. 3 – *Zombielicious!*

NEIL KLEID	CHRIS NOETH
MARC BILGREY	MR. EXES
ROB VOLLMAR	TIM SMITH 3
JARED GNIEWEK	JAMES ROMBERGER
JIM SALICRUP	RICK PARKER
Writers	Artists

MR. EXES
Cover Artist

Based on the classic EC Comics series.

PAPERCUTZ ™
New York

"EXTRA LIFE"
NEIL KLEID — Writer
CHRIS NOETH — Artist
MARK LERER - Letterer

"THE QUEEN OF THE VAMPIRES"
MARC BILGREY — Writer
MR. EXES — Artist
MARK LERER — Letterer

"GRAVEYARD SHIFT AT THE TWILIGHT GARDENS"
ROB VOLLMAR — Writer
TIM SMITH 3 — Artist
MARK LERER — Letterer
DIGIKORE — Colorist

"KID TESTED, MOTHER APPROVED"
JARED GNIEWEK — Writer
JAMES ROMBERGER — Artist
MARK LERER — Letterer
MARGUERITE VAN COOK — Colorist

GHOULUNATIC SEQUENCES
JIM SALICRUP - Writer
RICK PARKER - Artist, Title Letterer, Colorist
MARK LERER - Letterer

PREVIEW OF "JUMPING THE SHARK"
ARIE KAPLAN - Writer
MR. EXES - Artist
MARK LERER — Letterer

JOHN McCARTHY
Production

JIM SALICRUP
Editor-in-Chief

ISBN 10: 1-59707-090-4 paperback edition
ISBN 13: 978-1-59707-090-4 paperback edition
ISBN 10: 1-59707-091-2 hardcover edition
ISBN 13: 978-1-59707-091-1 hardcover edition

10 9 8 7 6 5 4 3 2 1

THE CRYPT OF TERROR

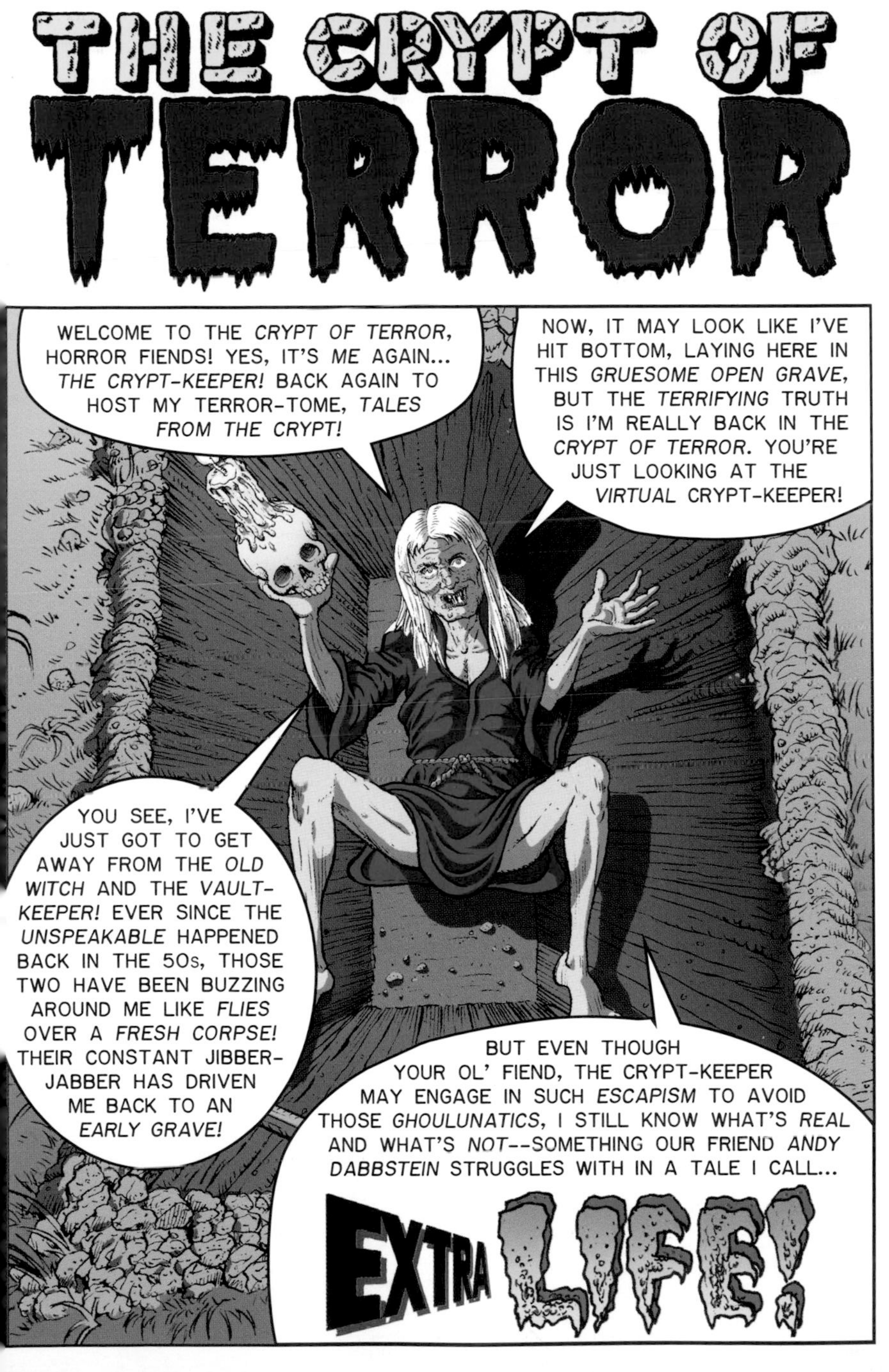
WELCOME TO THE CRYPT OF TERROR, HORROR FIENDS! YES, IT'S ME AGAIN... THE CRYPT-KEEPER! BACK AGAIN TO HOST MY TERROR-TOME, TALES FROM THE CRYPT!
NOW, IT MAY LOOK LIKE I'VE HIT BOTTOM, LAYING HERE IN THIS GRUESOME OPEN GRAVE, BUT THE TERRIFYING TRUTH IS I'M REALLY BACK IN THE CRYPT OF TERROR. YOU'RE JUST LOOKING AT THE VIRTUAL CRYPT-KEEPER!
YOU SEE, I'VE JUST GOT TO GET AWAY FROM THE OLD WITCH AND THE VAULT-KEEPER! EVER SINCE THE UNSPEAKABLE HAPPENED BACK IN THE 50s, THOSE TWO HAVE BEEN BUZZING AROUND ME LIKE FLIES OVER A FRESH CORPSE! THEIR CONSTANT JIBBER-JABBER HAS DRIVEN ME BACK TO AN EARLY GRAVE!
BUT EVEN THOUGH YOUR OL' FIEND, THE CRYPT-KEEPER MAY ENGAGE IN SUCH ESCAPISM TO AVOID THOSE GHOULUNATICS, I STILL KNOW WHAT'S REAL AND WHAT'S NOT--SOMETHING OUR FRIEND ANDY DABBSTEIN STRUGGLES WITH IN A TALE I CALL...
EXTRA LIFE!

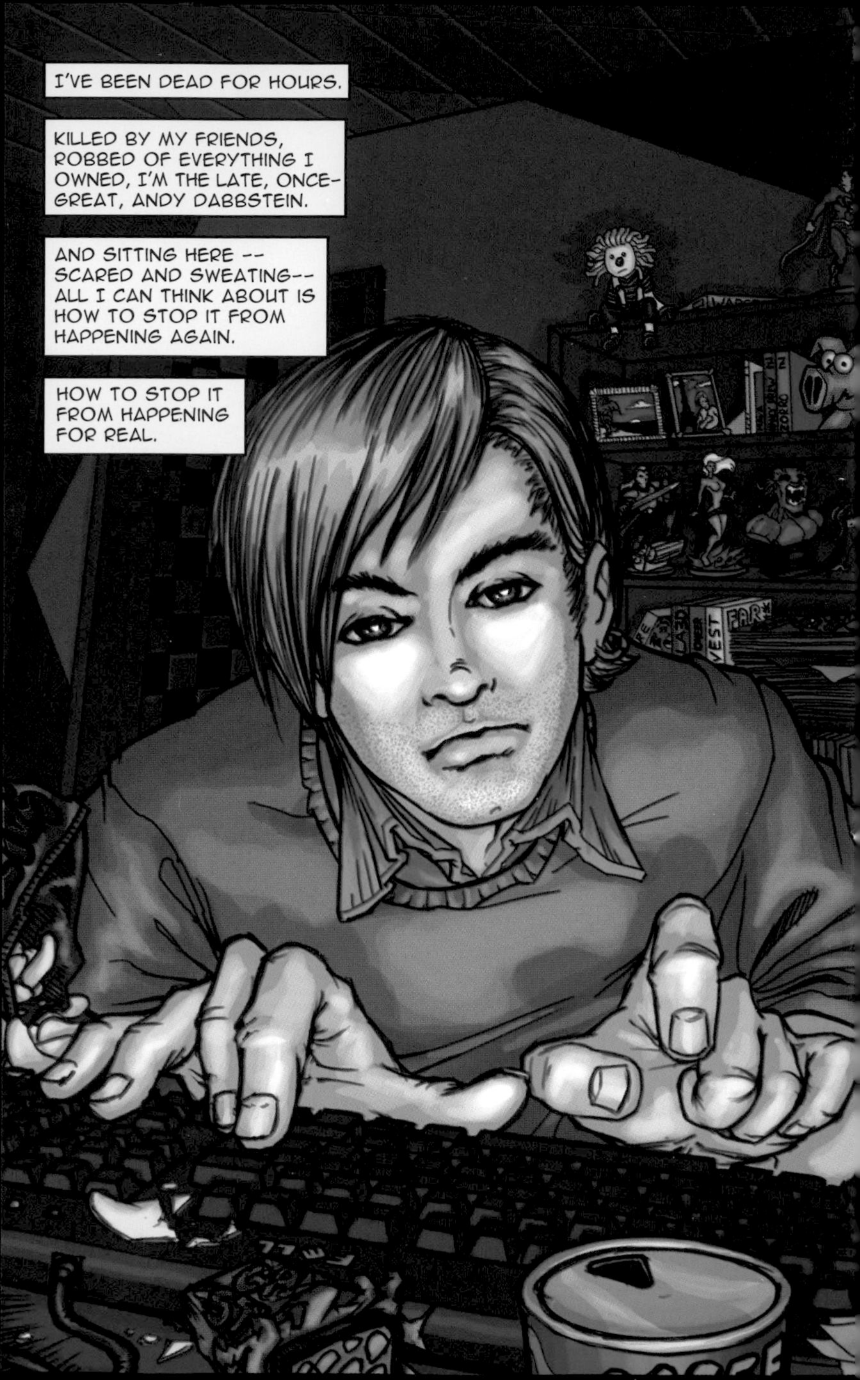
I'VE BEEN DEAD FOR HOURS.
KILLED BY MY FRIENDS, ROBBED OF EVERYTHING I OWNED, I'M THE LATE, ONCE-GREAT, ANDY DABBSTEIN.
AND SITTING HERE -- SCARED AND SWEATING-- ALL I CAN THINK ABOUT IS HOW TO STOP IT FROM HAPPENING AGAIN.
HOW TO STOP IT FROM HAPPENING FOR REAL.

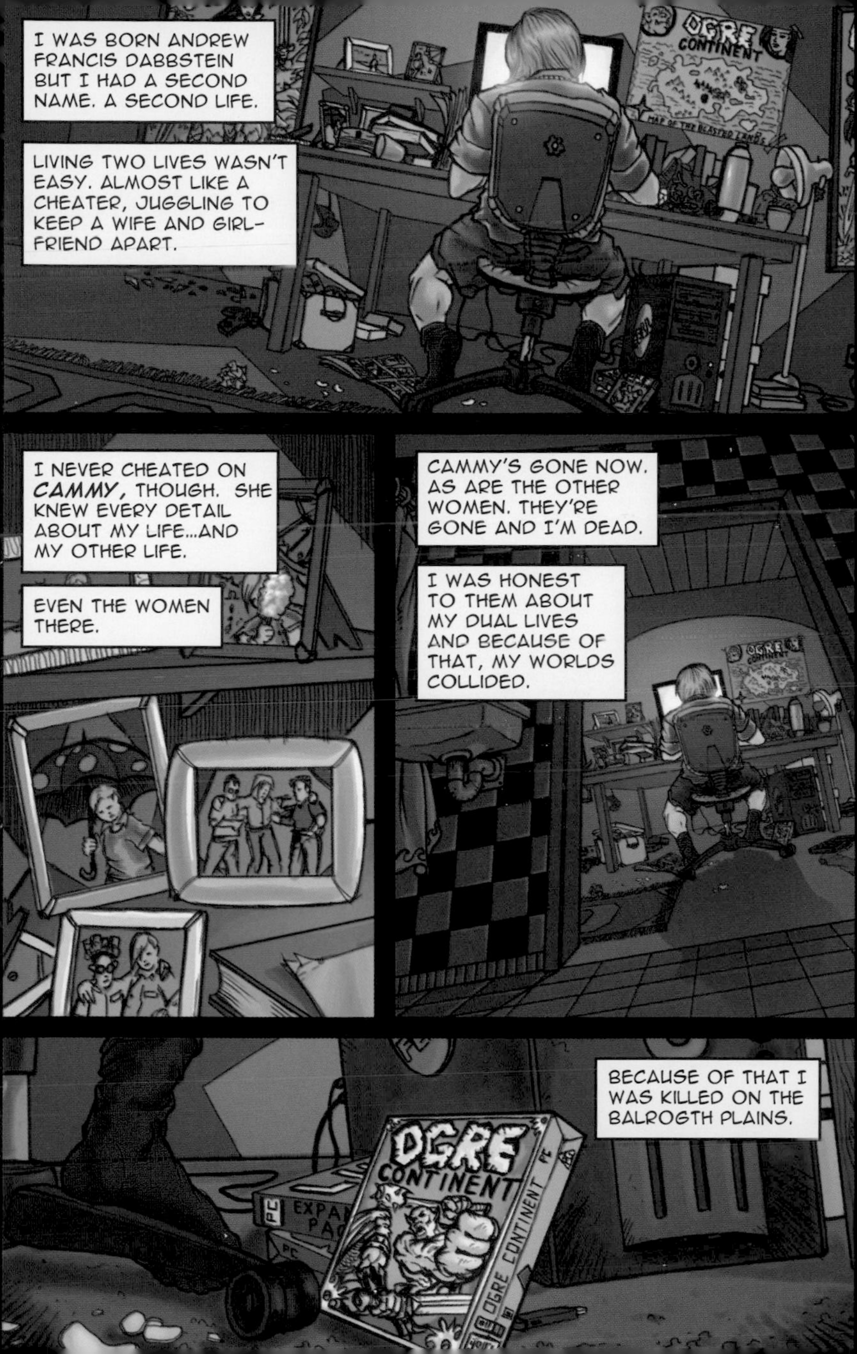
I WAS BORN ANDREW FRANCIS DABBSTEIN BUT I HAD A SECOND NAME. A SECOND LIFE.
LIVING TWO LIVES WASN'T EASY. ALMOST LIKE A CHEATER, JUGGLING TO KEEP A WIFE AND GIRL-FRIEND APART.
OGRE CONTINENT
MAP OF THE BLASTED LANDS
I NEVER CHEATED ON *CAMMY,* THOUGH. SHE KNEW EVERY DETAIL ABOUT MY LIFE...AND MY OTHER LIFE.
EVEN THE WOMEN THERE.
CAMMY'S GONE NOW. AS ARE THE OTHER WOMEN. THEY'RE GONE AND I'M DEAD.
I WAS HONEST TO THEM ABOUT MY DUAL LIVES AND BECAUSE OF THAT, MY WORLDS COLLIDED.
BECAUSE OF THAT I WAS KILLED ON THE BALROGTH PLAINS.
OGRE CONTINENT
PC
OGRE CONTINENT

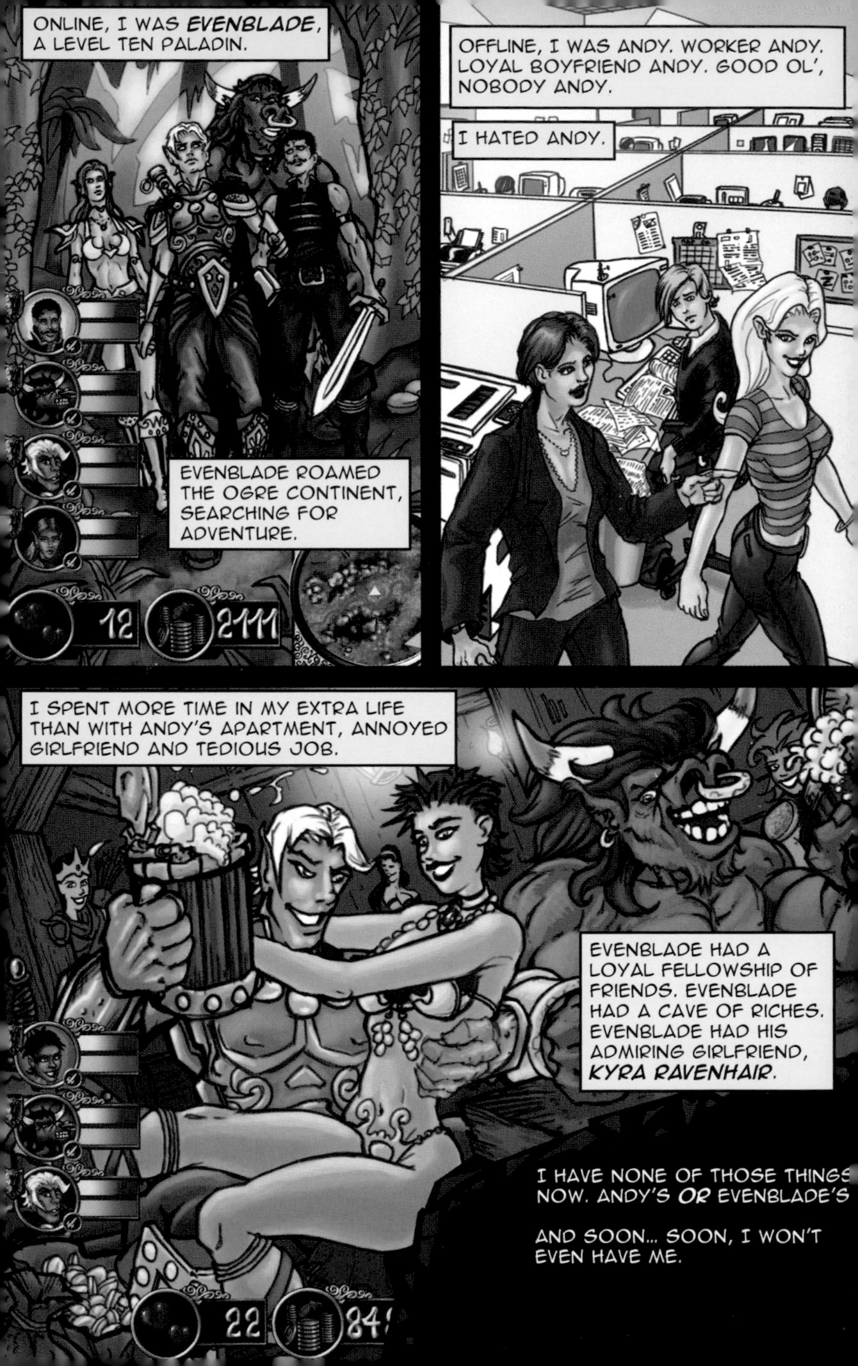
ONLINE, I WAS EVENBLADE, A LEVEL TEN PALADIN.
EVENBLADE ROAMED THE OGRE CONTINENT, SEARCHING FOR ADVENTURE.
12
2111
OFFLINE, I WAS ANDY. WORKER ANDY. LOYAL BOYFRIEND ANDY. GOOD OL', NOBODY ANDY.
I HATED ANDY.
I SPENT MORE TIME IN MY EXTRA LIFE THAN WITH ANDY'S APARTMENT, ANNOYED GIRLFRIEND AND TEDIOUS JOB.
EVENBLADE HAD A LOYAL FELLOWSHIP OF FRIENDS. EVENBLADE HAD A CAVE OF RICHES. EVENBLADE HAD HIS ADMIRING GIRLFRIEND, KYRA RAVENHAIR.
22
I HAVE NONE OF THOSE THINGS NOW. ANDY'S OR EVENBLADE'S.
AND SOON... SOON, I WON'T EVEN HAVE ME.

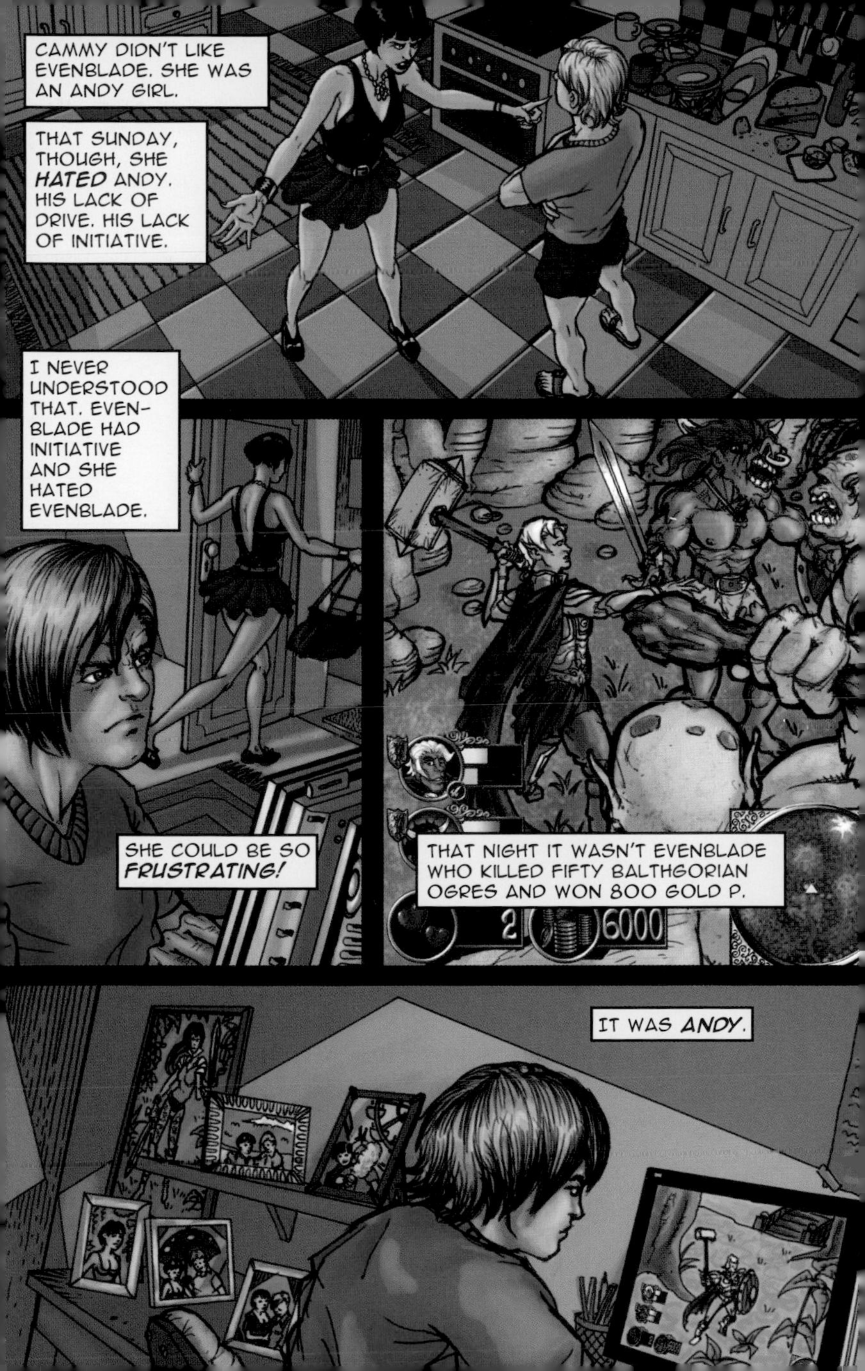
CAMMY DIDN'T LIKE EVENBLADE. SHE WAS AN ANDY GIRL.
THAT SUNDAY, THOUGH, SHE *HATED* ANDY. HIS LACK OF DRIVE. HIS LACK OF INITIATIVE.
I NEVER UNDERSTOOD THAT. EVEN-BLADE HAD INITIATIVE AND SHE HATED EVENBLADE.
SHE COULD BE SO *FRUSTRATING!*
THAT NIGHT IT WASN'T EVENBLADE WHO KILLED FIFTY BALTHGORIAN OGRES AND WON 800 GOLD P.
2
6000
IT WAS *ANDY*.

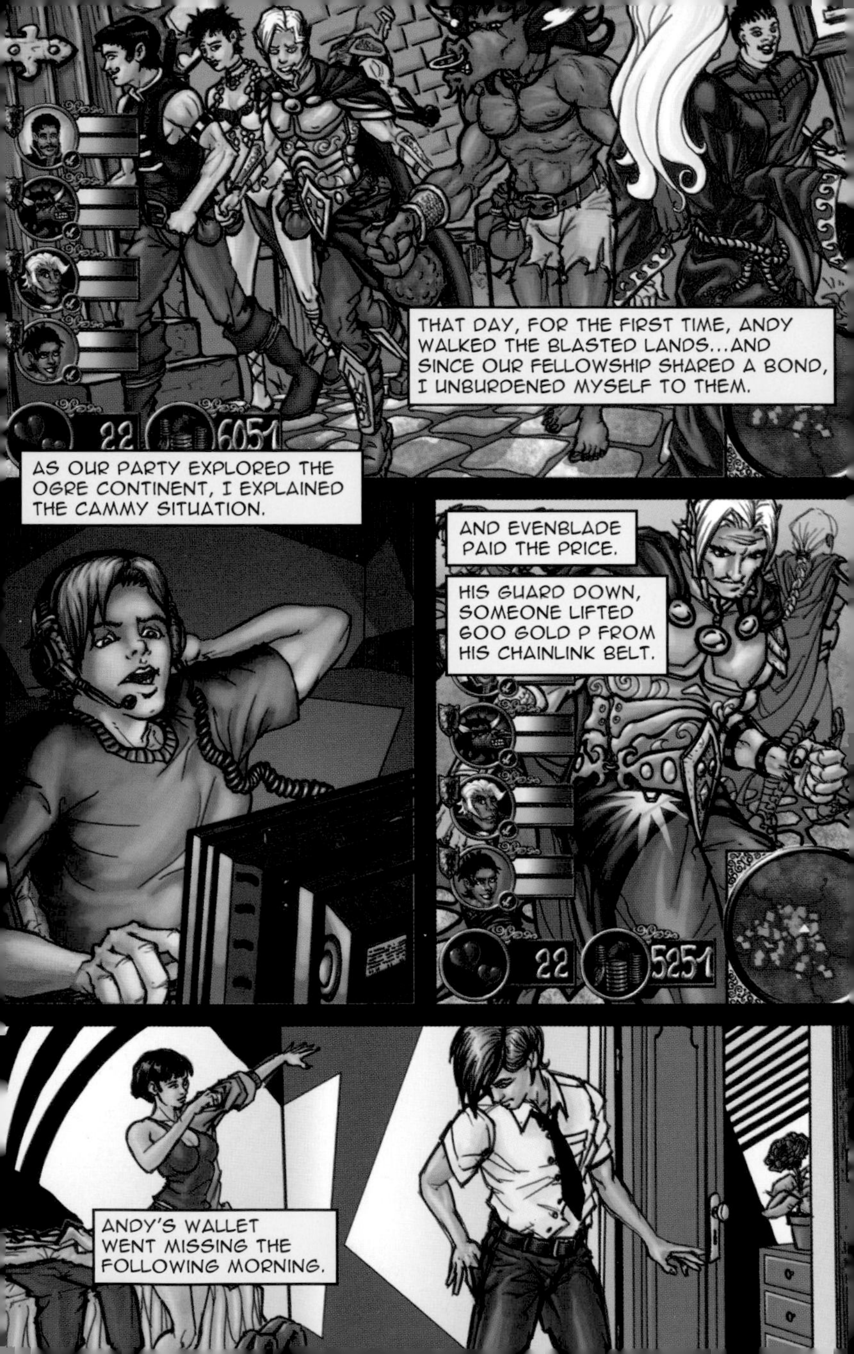
22
6051
THAT DAY, FOR THE FIRST TIME, ANDY WALKED THE BLASTED LANDS...AND SINCE OUR FELLOWSHIP SHARED A BOND, I UNBURDENED MYSELF TO THEM.
AS OUR PARTY EXPLORED THE OGRE CONTINENT, I EXPLAINED THE CAMMY SITUATION.
AND EVENBLADE PAID THE PRICE.
HIS GUARD DOWN, SOMEONE LIFTED 600 GOLD P FROM HIS CHAINLINK BELT.
22
5251
ANDY'S WALLET WENT MISSING THE FOLLOWING MORNING.

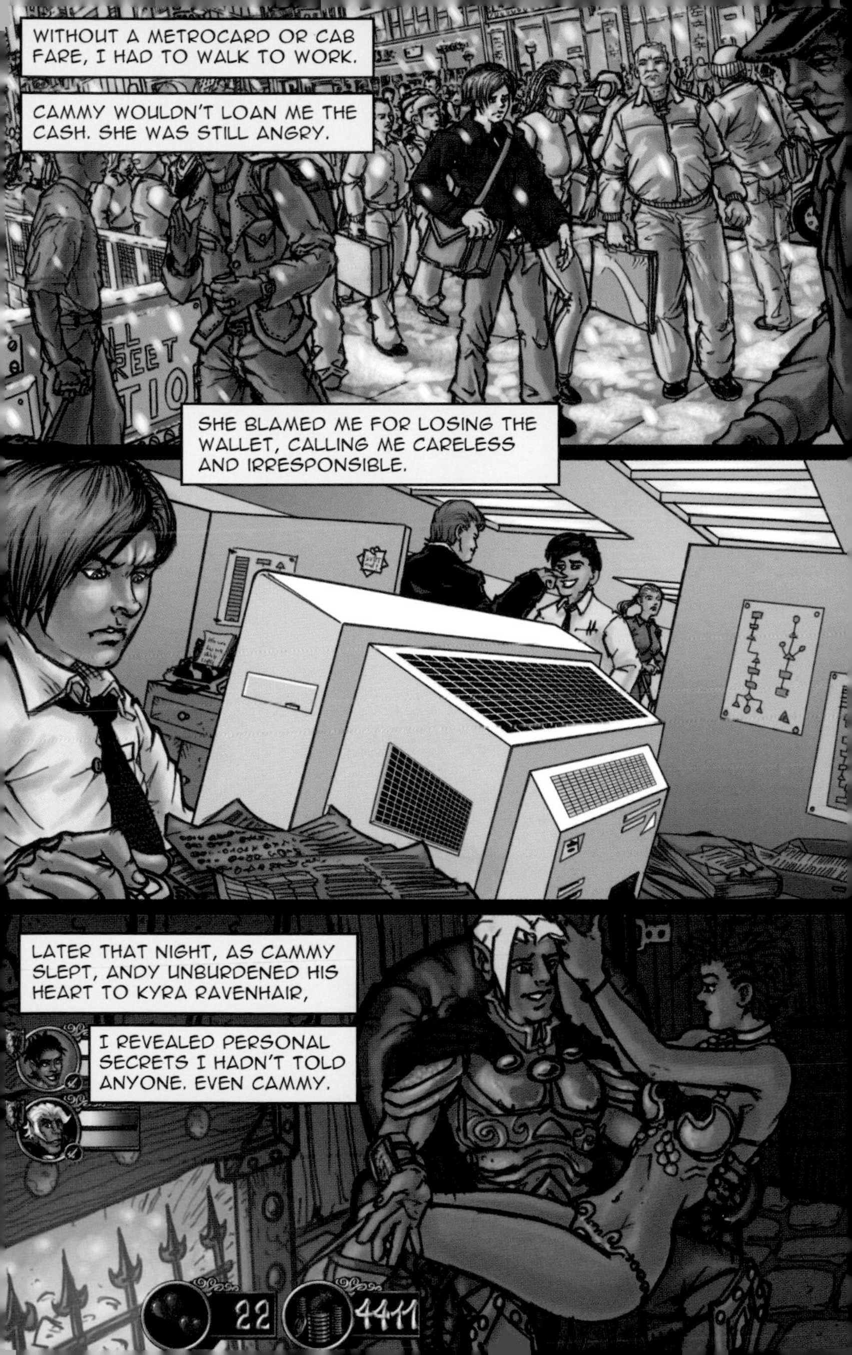
WITHOUT A METROCARD OR CAB FARE, I HAD TO WALK TO WORK.
CAMMY WOULDN'T LOAN ME THE CASH. SHE WAS STILL ANGRY.
SHE BLAMED ME FOR LOSING THE WALLET, CALLING ME CARELESS AND IRRESPONSIBLE.
LATER THAT NIGHT, AS CAMMY SLEPT, ANDY UNBURDENED HIS HEART TO KYRA RAVENHAIR,
I REVEALED PERSONAL SECRETS I HADN'T TOLD ANYONE. EVEN CAMMY.
22
4411

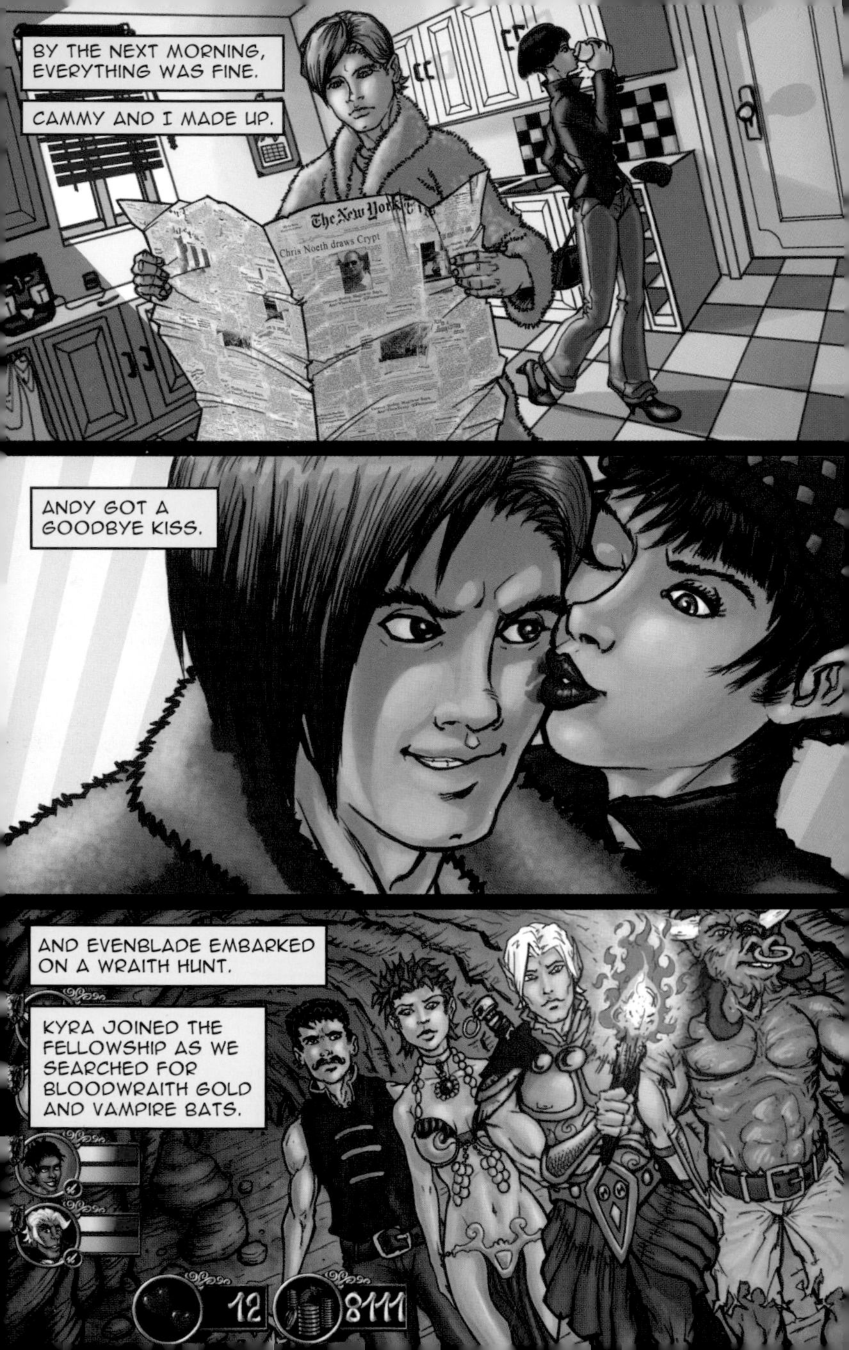
BY THE NEXT MORNING, EVERYTHING WAS FINE.
CAMMY AND I MADE UP.
The New York Times
Chris Noeth draws Crypt
ANDY GOT A GOODBYE KISS.
AND EVENBLADE EMBARKED ON A WRAITH HUNT.
KYRA JOINED THE FELLOWSHIP AS WE SEARCHED FOR BLOODWRAITH GOLD AND VAMPIRE BATS.
12
8111

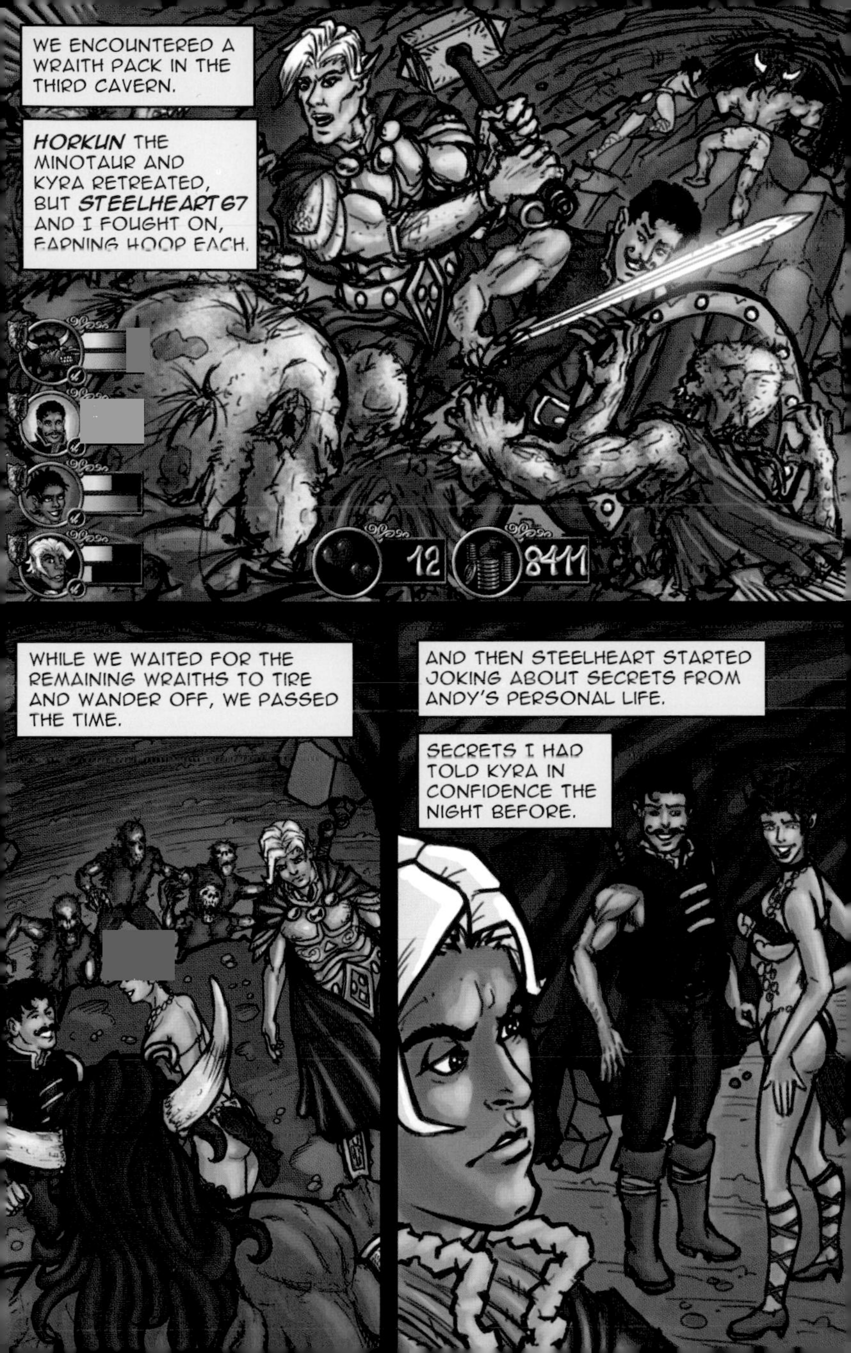
WE ENCOUNTERED A WRAITH PACK IN THE THIRD CAVERN.
HORKUN THE MINOTAUR AND KYRA RETREATED, BUT STEELHEART67 AND I FOUGHT ON, EARNING 100GP EACH.
12
8411
WHILE WE WAITED FOR THE REMAINING WRAITHS TO TIRE AND WANDER OFF, WE PASSED THE TIME.
AND THEN STEELHEART STARTED JOKING ABOUT SECRETS FROM ANDY'S PERSONAL LIFE.
SECRETS I HAD TOLD KYRA IN CONFIDENCE THE NIGHT BEFORE.

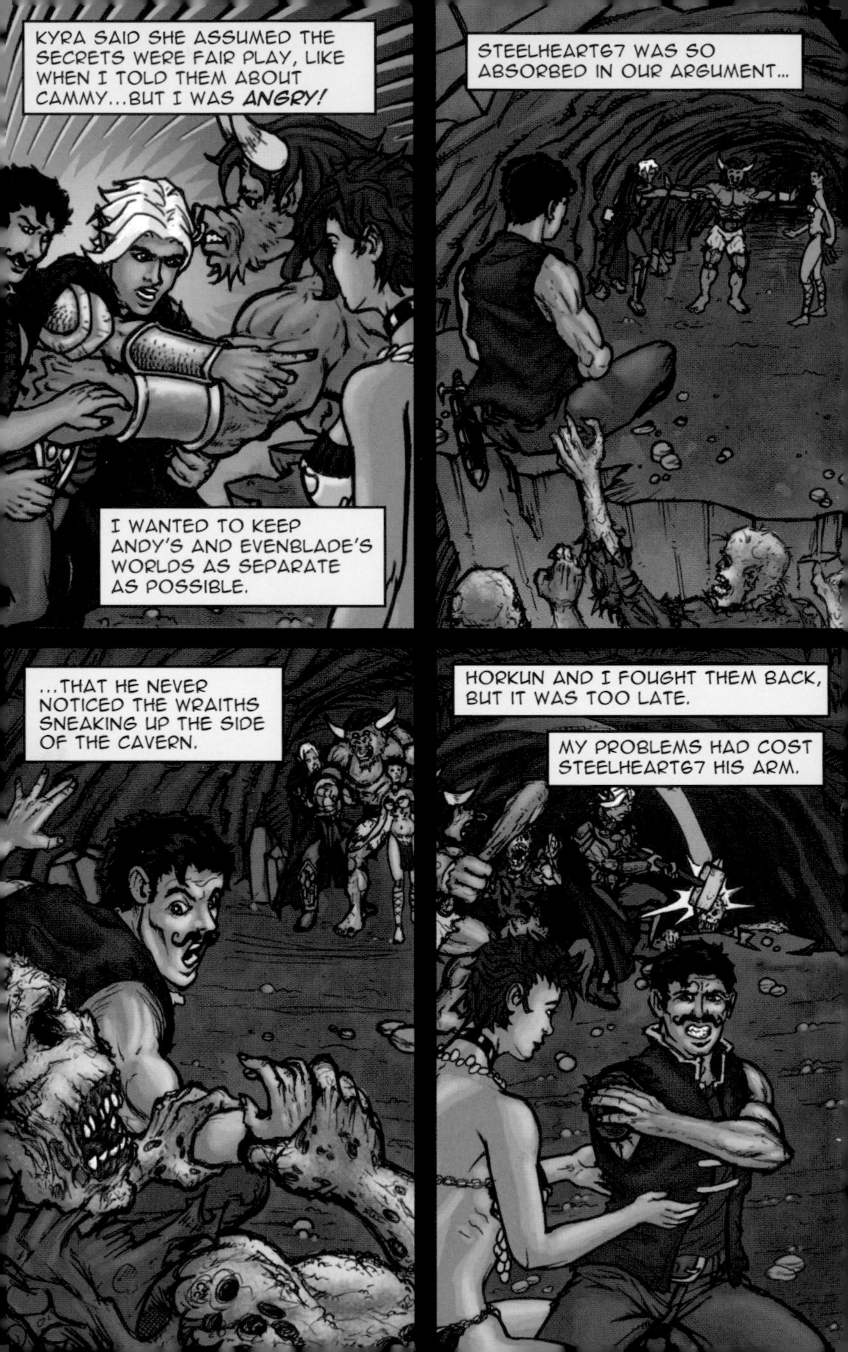
KYRA SAID SHE ASSUMED THE SECRETS WERE FAIR PLAY, LIKE WHEN I TOLD THEM ABOUT CAMMY...BUT I WAS ANGRY!
I WANTED TO KEEP ANDY'S AND EVENBLADE'S WORLDS AS SEPARATE AS POSSIBLE.
STEELHEART67 WAS SO ABSORBED IN OUR ARGUMENT...
...THAT HE NEVER NOTICED THE WRAITHS SNEAKING UP THE SIDE OF THE CAVERN.
HORKUN AND I FOUGHT THEM BACK, BUT IT WAS TOO LATE.
MY PROBLEMS HAD COST STEELHEART67 HIS ARM.

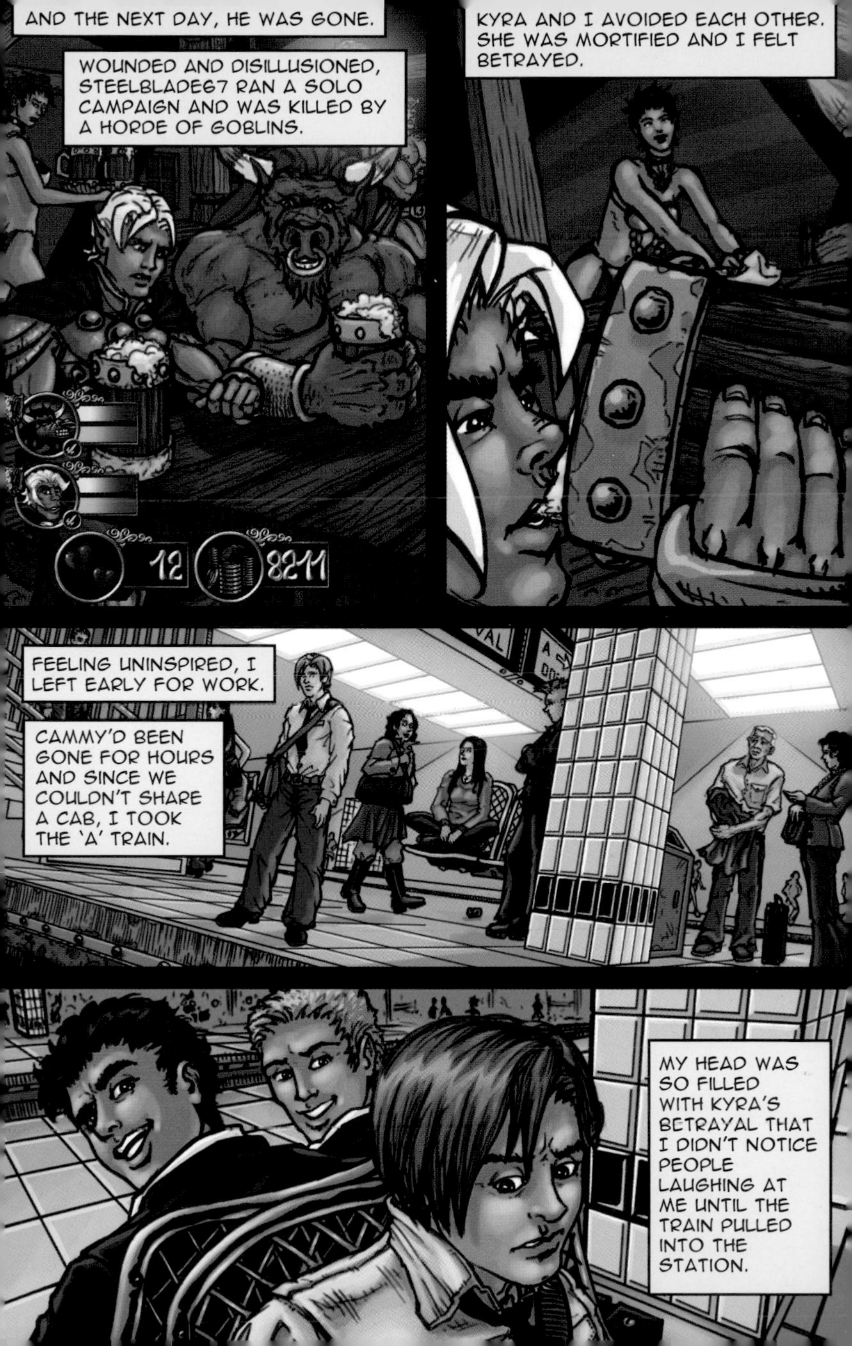
AND THE NEXT DAY, HE WAS GONE.
WOUNDED AND DISILLUSIONED, STEELBLADE67 RAN A SOLO CAMPAIGN AND WAS KILLED BY A HORDE OF GOBLINS.
12
8211
KYRA AND I AVOIDED EACH OTHER. SHE WAS MORTIFIED AND I FELT BETRAYED.
FEELING UNINSPIRED, I LEFT EARLY FOR WORK.
CAMMY'D BEEN GONE FOR HOURS AND SINCE WE COULDN'T SHARE A CAB, I TOOK THE 'A' TRAIN.
MY HEAD WAS SO FILLED WITH KYRA'S BETRAYAL THAT I DIDN'T NOTICE PEOPLE LAUGHING AT ME UNTIL THE TRAIN PULLED INTO THE STATION.

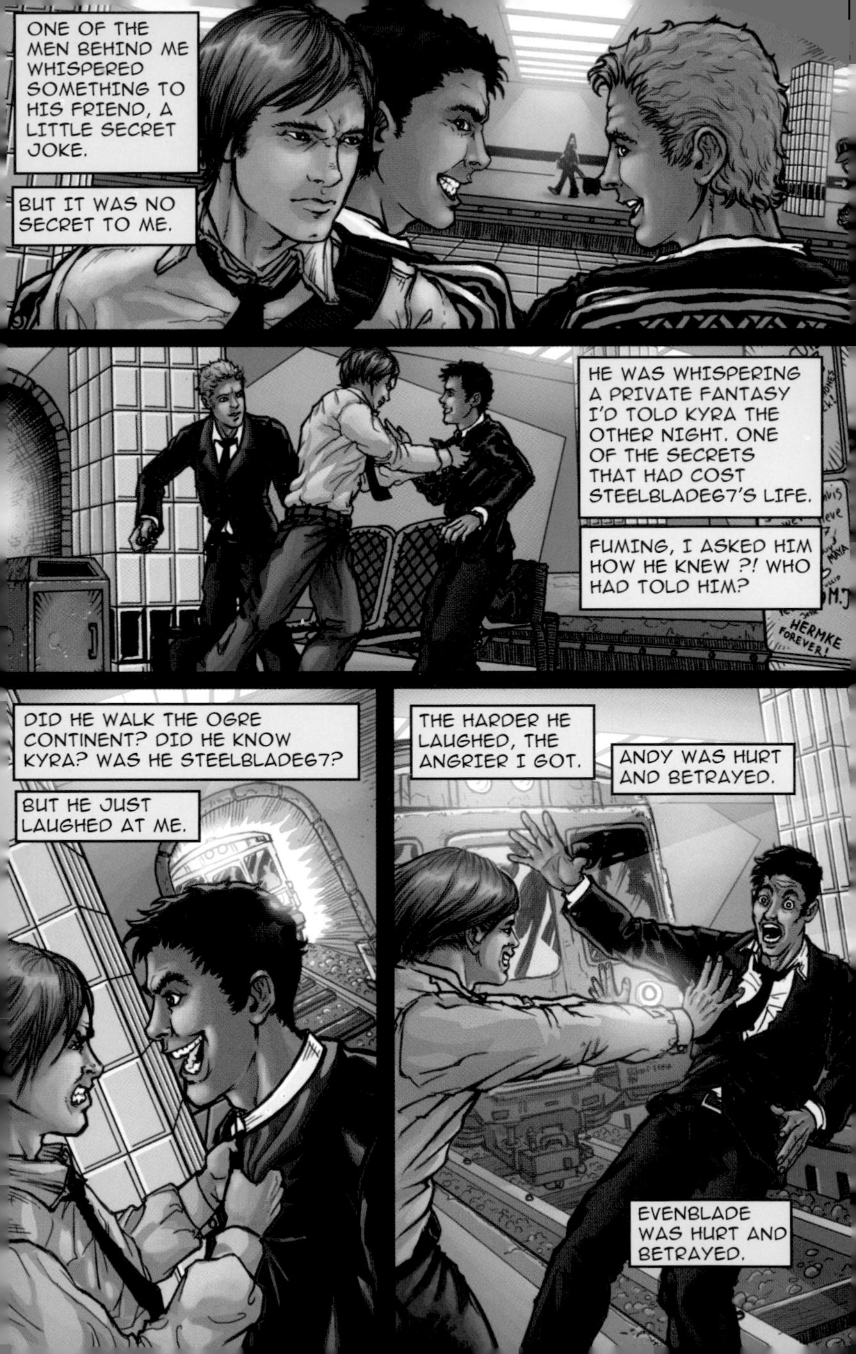
ONE OF THE MEN BEHIND ME WHISPERED SOMETHING TO HIS FRIEND, A LITTLE SECRET JOKE.
BUT IT WAS NO SECRET TO ME.
HE WAS WHISPERING A PRIVATE FANTASY I'D TOLD KYRA THE OTHER NIGHT. ONE OF THE SECRETS THAT HAD COST STEELBLADE67'S LIFE.
FUMING, I ASKED HIM HOW HE KNEW ?! WHO HAD TOLD HIM?
HERMKE FOREVER!
DID HE WALK THE OGRE CONTINENT? DID HE KNOW KYRA? WAS HE STEELBLADE67?
BUT HE JUST LAUGHED AT ME.
THE HARDER HE LAUGHED, THE ANGRIER I GOT.
ANDY WAS HURT AND BETRAYED.
EVENBLADE WAS HURT AND BETRAYED.

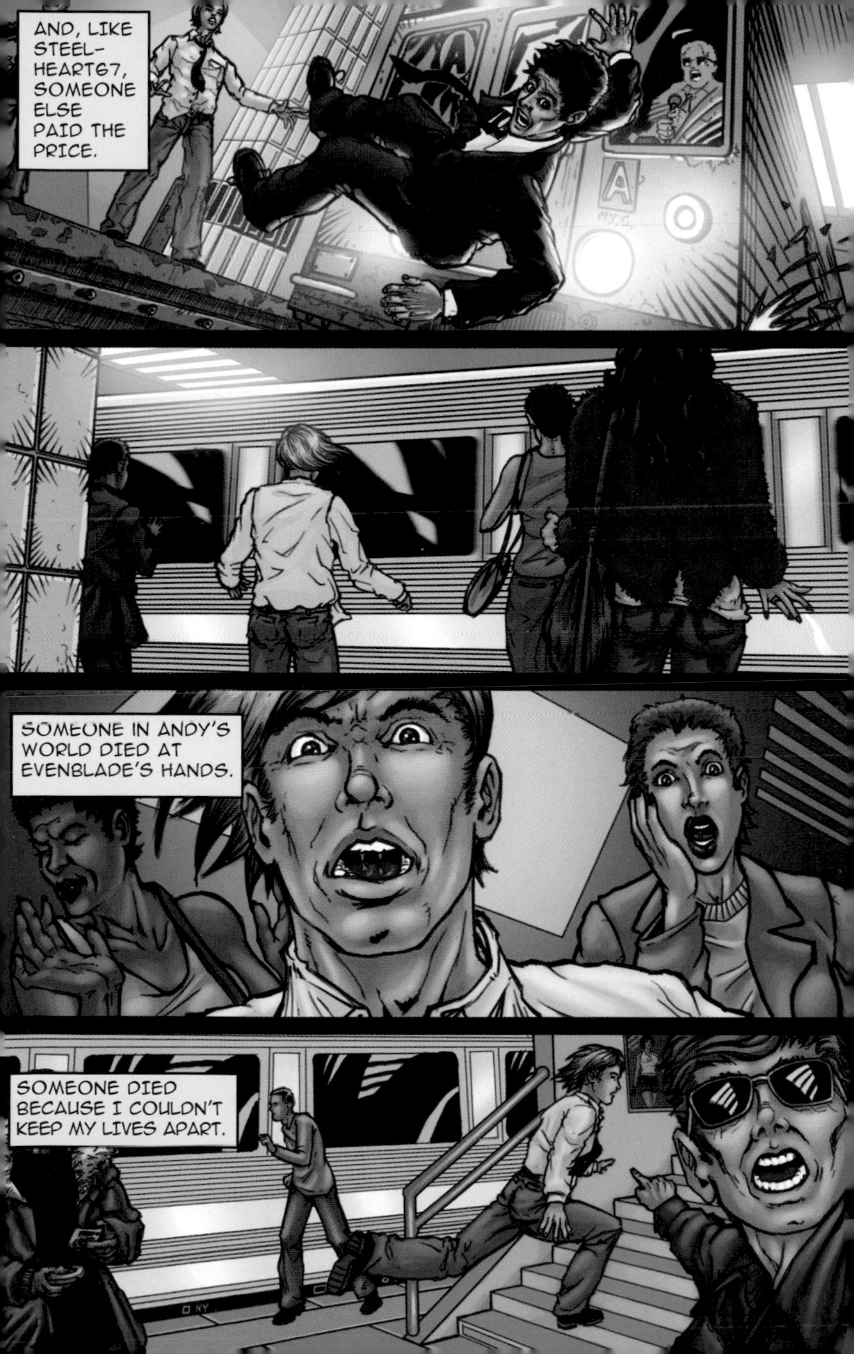
AND, LIKE STEEL-HEART67, SOMEONE ELSE PAID THE PRICE.
SOMEONE IN ANDY'S WORLD DIED AT EVENBLADE'S HANDS.
SOMEONE DIED BECAUSE I COULDN'T KEEP MY LIVES APART.

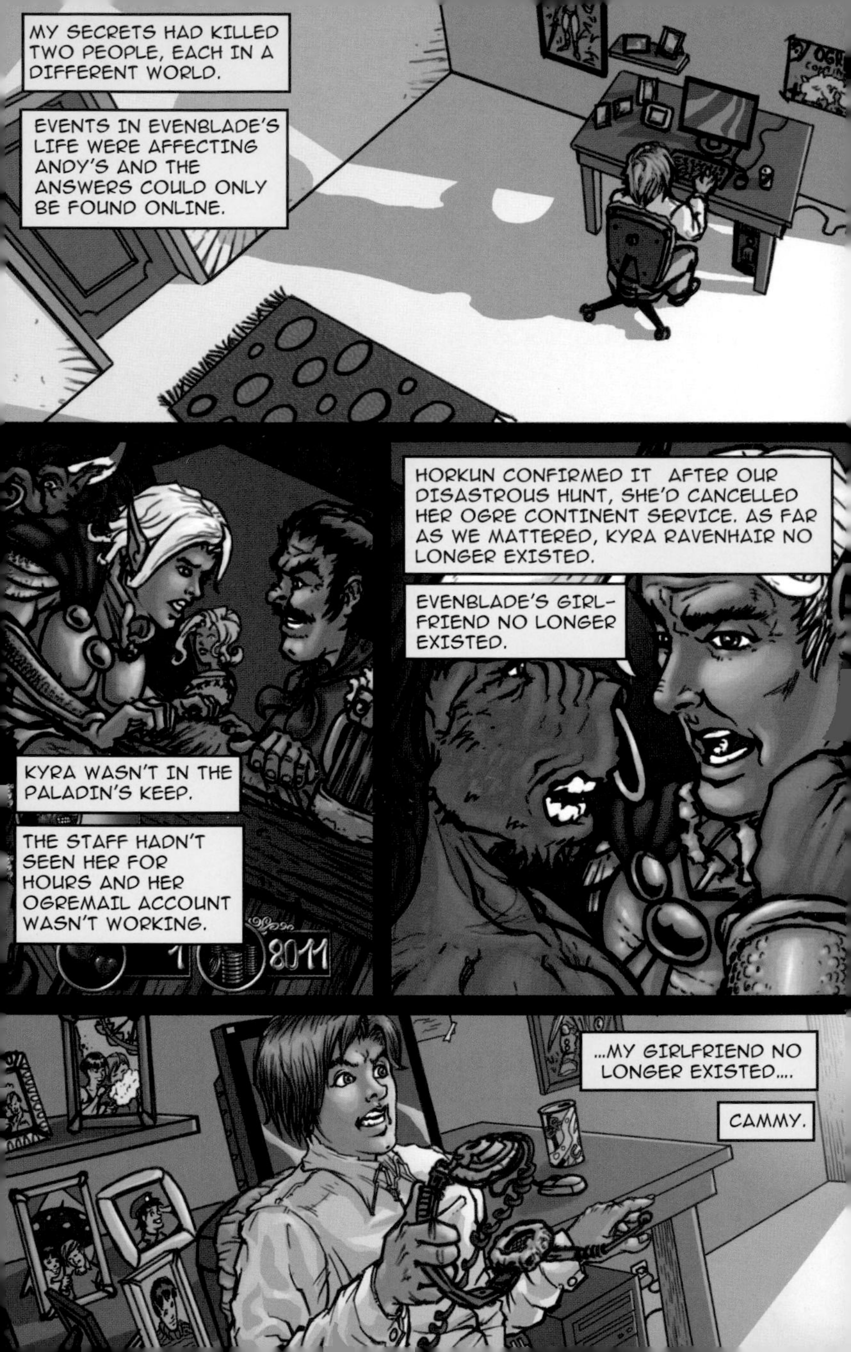
MY SECRETS HAD KILLED TWO PEOPLE, EACH IN A DIFFERENT WORLD.
EVENTS IN EVENBLADE'S LIFE WERE AFFECTING ANDY'S AND THE ANSWERS COULD ONLY BE FOUND ONLINE.
KYRA WASN'T IN THE PALADIN'S KEEP.
THE STAFF HADN'T SEEN HER FOR HOURS AND HER OGREMAIL ACCOUNT WASN'T WORKING.
1
8011
HORKUN CONFIRMED IT AFTER OUR DISASTROUS HUNT, SHE'D CANCELLED HER OGRE CONTINENT SERVICE. AS FAR AS WE MATTERED, KYRA RAVENHAIR NO LONGER EXISTED.
EVENBLADE'S GIRLFRIEND NO LONGER EXISTED.
...MY GIRLFRIEND NO LONGER EXISTED....
CAMMY.

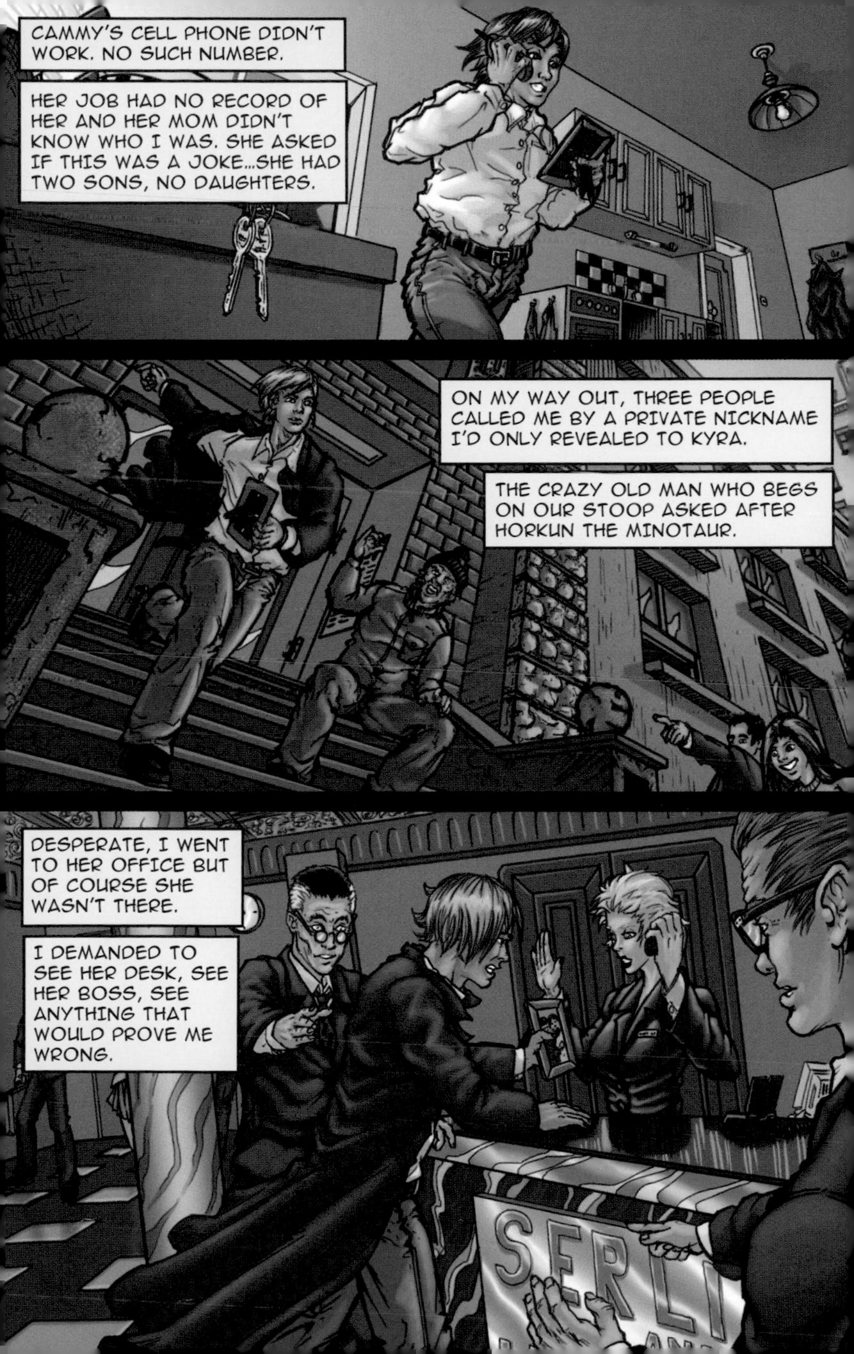
CAMMY'S CELL PHONE DIDN'T WORK. NO SUCH NUMBER.
HER JOB HAD NO RECORD OF HER AND HER MOM DIDN'T KNOW WHO I WAS. SHE ASKED IF THIS WAS A JOKE...SHE HAD TWO SONS, NO DAUGHTERS.
ON MY WAY OUT, THREE PEOPLE CALLED ME BY A PRIVATE NICKNAME I'D ONLY REVEALED TO KYRA.
THE CRAZY OLD MAN WHO BEGS ON OUR STOOP ASKED AFTER HORKUN THE MINOTAUR.
DESPERATE, I WENT TO HER OFFICE BUT OF COURSE SHE WASN'T THERE.
I DEMANDED TO SEE HER DESK, SEE HER BOSS, SEE ANYTHING THAT WOULD PROVE ME WRONG.

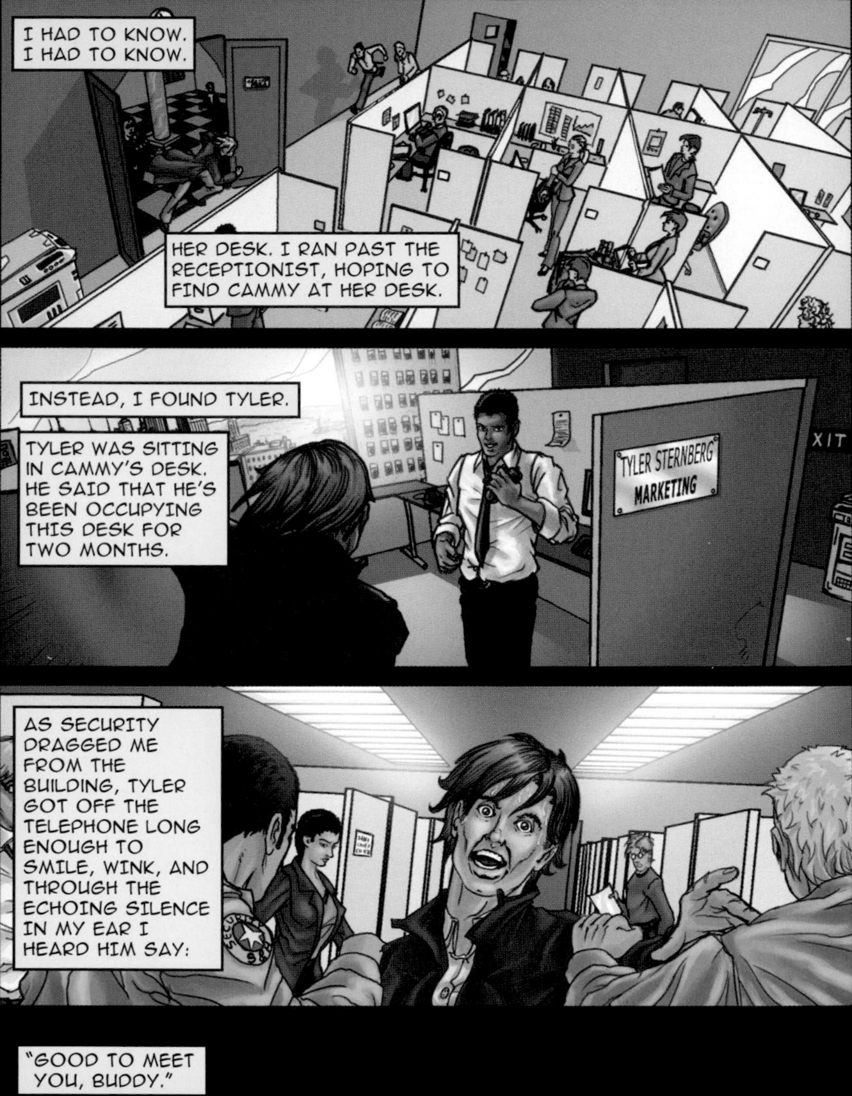
I HAD TO KNOW. I HAD TO KNOW.
HER DESK. I RAN PAST THE RECEPTIONIST, HOPING TO FIND CAMMY AT HER DESK.
INSTEAD, I FOUND TYLER.
TYLER WAS SITTING IN CAMMY'S DESK. HE SAID THAT HE'S BEEN OCCUPYING THIS DESK FOR TWO MONTHS.
TYLER STERNBERG
MARKETING
XIT
AS SECURITY DRAGGED ME FROM THE BUILDING, TYLER GOT OFF THE TELEPHONE LONG ENOUGH TO SMILE, WINK, AND THROUGH THE ECHOING SILENCE IN MY EAR I HEARD HIM SAY:
"GOOD TO MEET YOU, BUDDY."

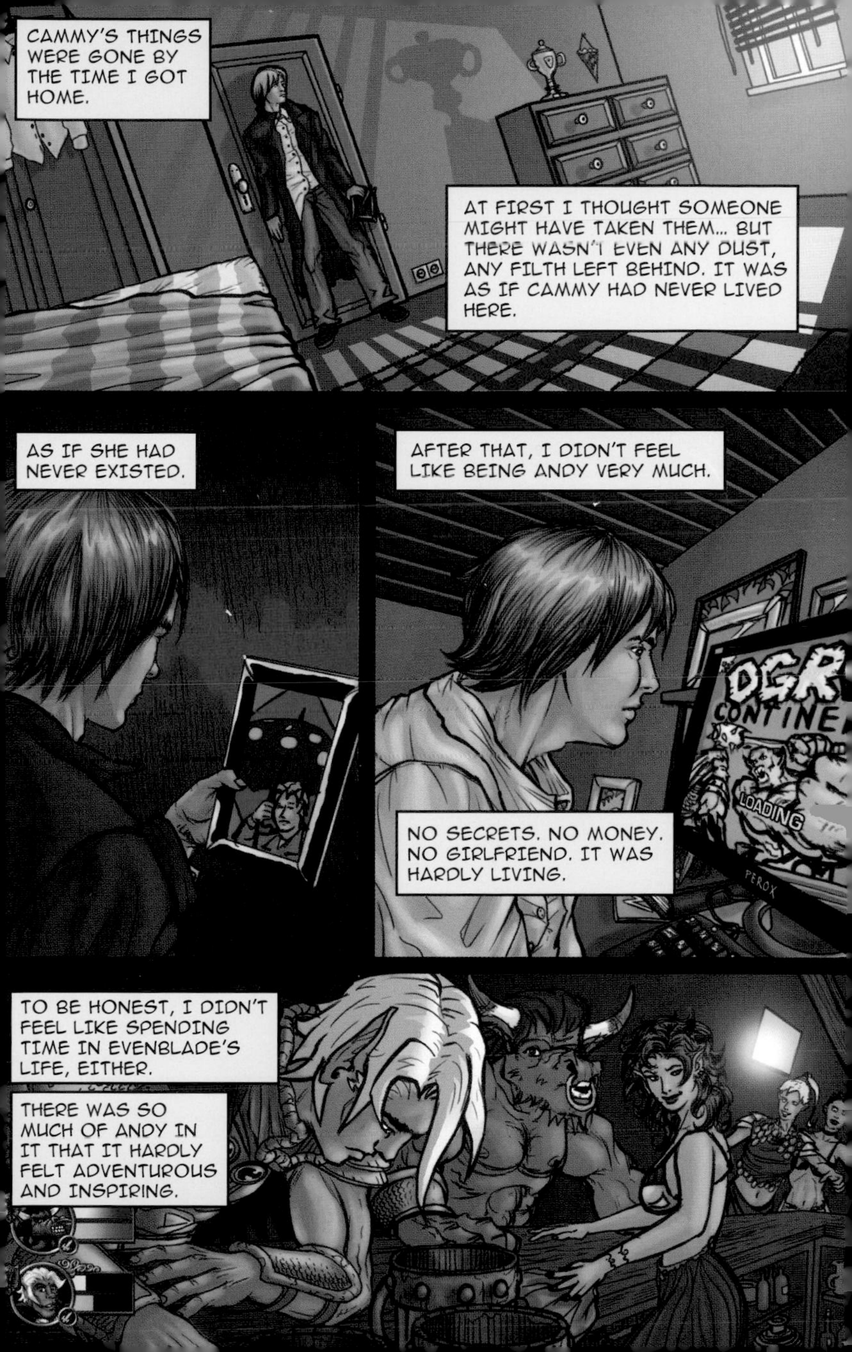
CAMMY'S THINGS WERE GONE BY THE TIME I GOT HOME.
AT FIRST I THOUGHT SOMEONE MIGHT HAVE TAKEN THEM... BUT THERE WASN'T EVEN ANY DUST, ANY FILTH LEFT BEHIND. IT WAS AS IF CAMMY HAD NEVER LIVED HERE.
AS IF SHE HAD NEVER EXISTED.
AFTER THAT, I DIDN'T FEEL LIKE BEING ANDY VERY MUCH.
LOADING
NO SECRETS. NO MONEY. NO GIRLFRIEND. IT WAS HARDLY LIVING.
PEROX
TO BE HONEST, I DIDN'T FEEL LIKE SPENDING TIME IN EVENBLADE'S LIFE, EITHER.
THERE WAS SO MUCH OF ANDY IN IT THAT IT HARDLY FELT ADVENTUROUS AND INSPIRING.

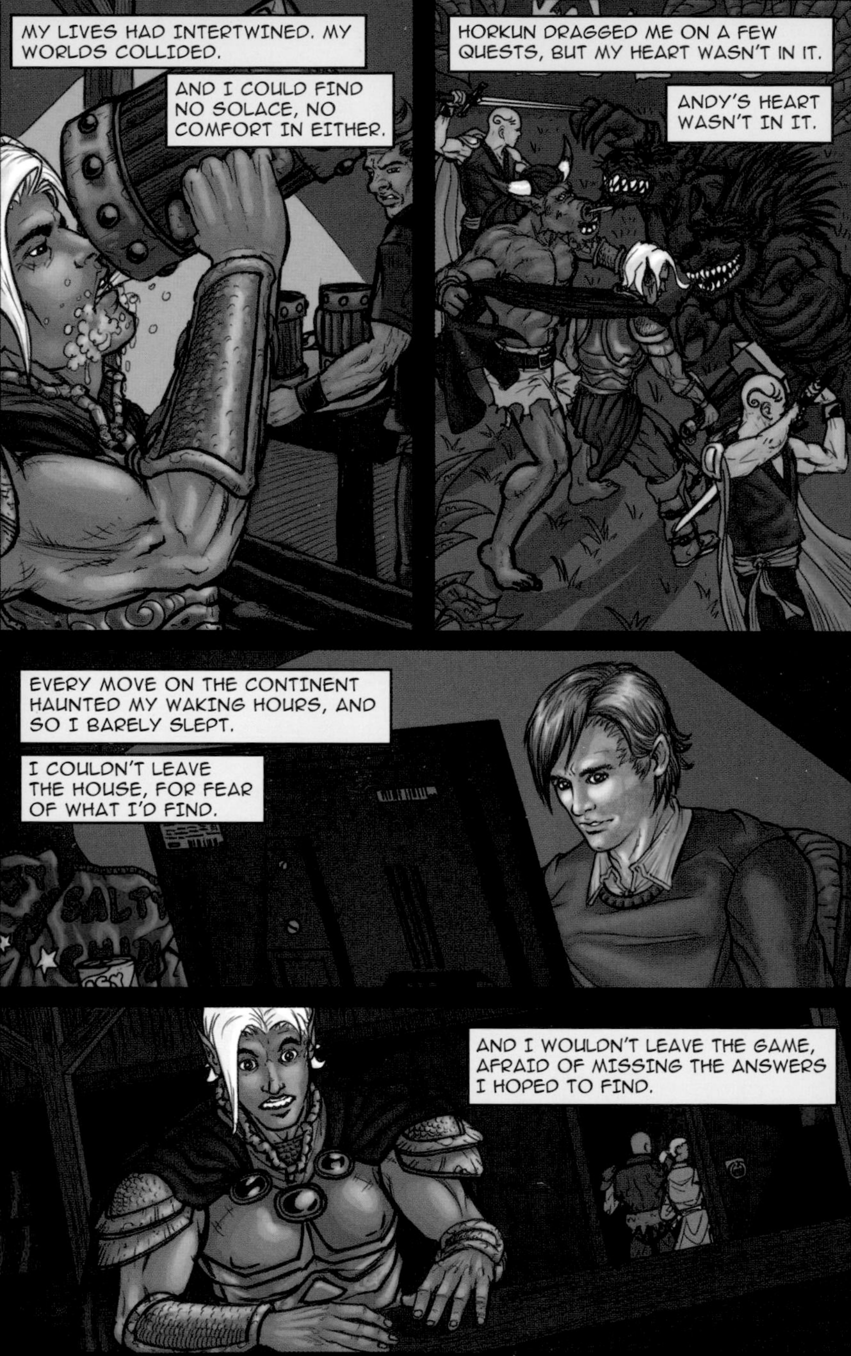
MY LIVES HAD INTERTWINED. MY WORLDS COLLIDED.
AND I COULD FIND NO SOLACE, NO COMFORT IN EITHER.
HORKUN DRAGGED ME ON A FEW QUESTS, BUT MY HEART WASN'T IN IT.
ANDY'S HEART WASN'T IN IT.
EVERY MOVE ON THE CONTINENT HAUNTED MY WAKING HOURS, AND SO I BARELY SLEPT.
I COULDN'T LEAVE THE HOUSE, FOR FEAR OF WHAT I'D FIND.
AND I WOULDN'T LEAVE THE GAME, AFRAID OF MISSING THE ANSWERS I HOPED TO FIND.

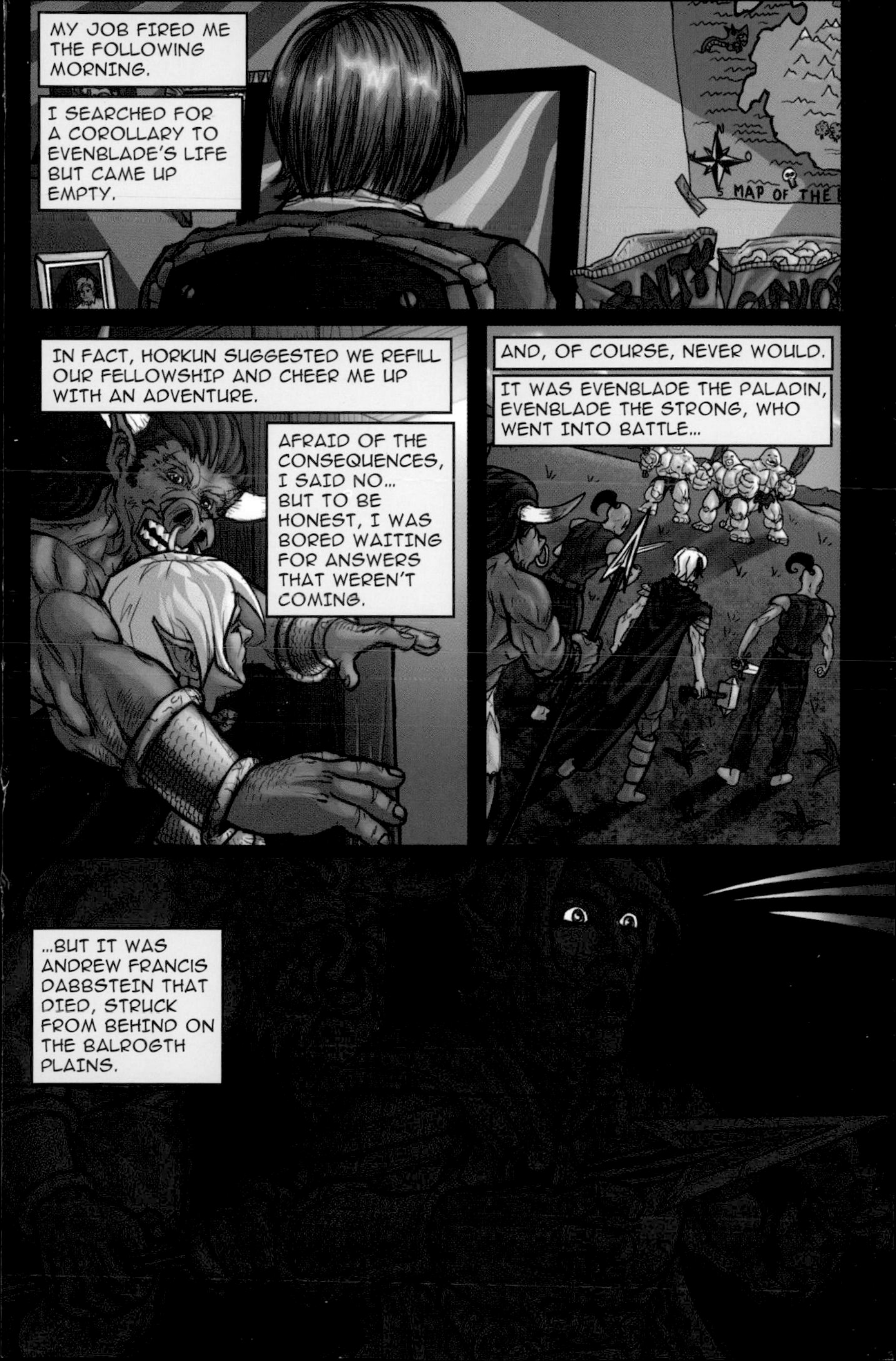
MY JOB FIRED ME THE FOLLOWING MORNING.
I SEARCHED FOR A COROLLARY TO EVENBLADE'S LIFE BUT CAME UP EMPTY.
MAP OF THE
IN FACT, HORKUN SUGGESTED WE REFILL OUR FELLOWSHIP AND CHEER ME UP WITH AN ADVENTURE.
AFRAID OF THE CONSEQUENCES, I SAID NO... BUT TO BE HONEST, I WAS BORED WAITING FOR ANSWERS THAT WEREN'T COMING.
AND, OF COURSE, NEVER WOULD.
IT WAS EVENBLADE THE PALADIN, EVENBLADE THE STRONG, WHO WENT INTO BATTLE...
...BUT IT WAS ANDREW FRANCIS DABBSTEIN THAT DIED, STRUCK FROM BEHIND ON THE BALROGTH PLAINS.

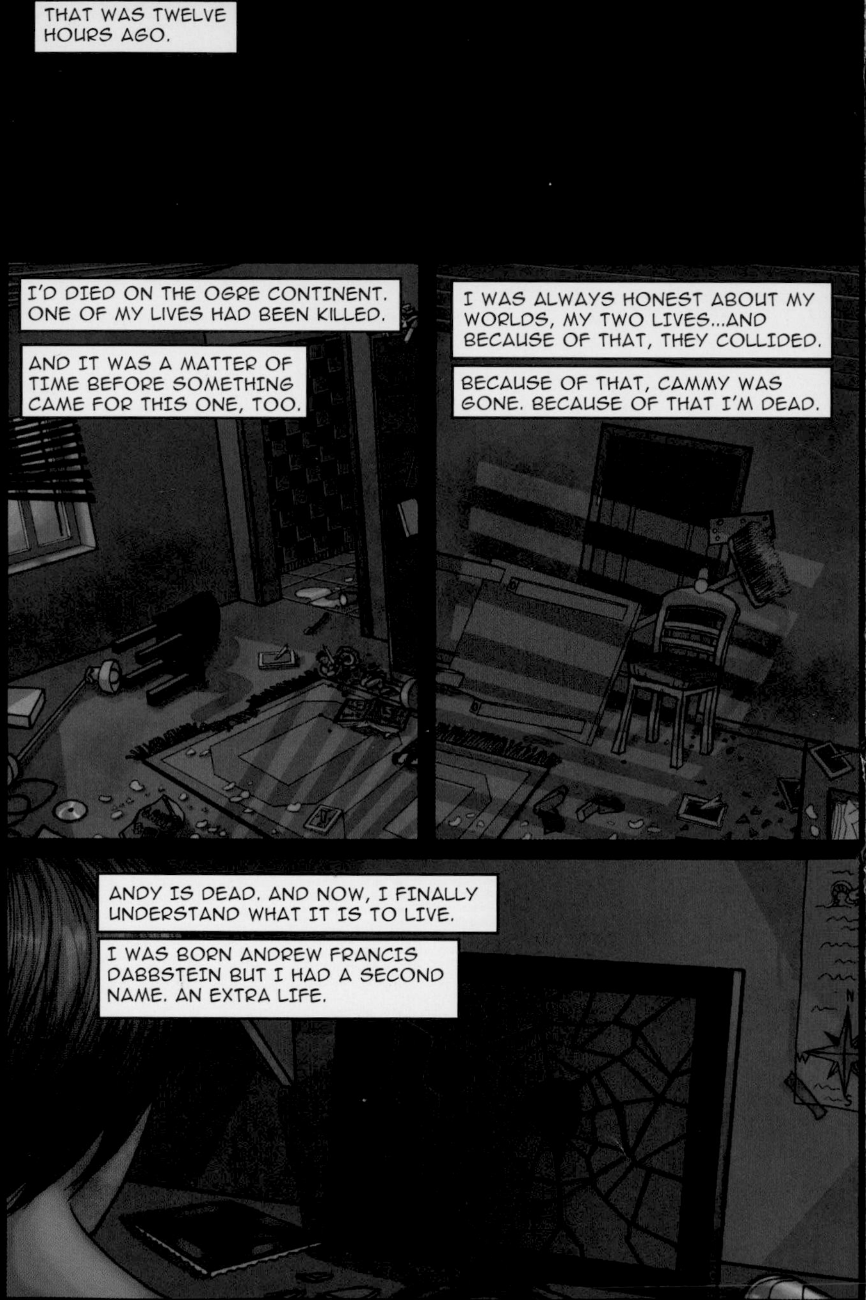
THAT WAS TWELVE HOURS AGO.
I'D DIED ON THE OGRE CONTINENT. ONE OF MY LIVES HAD BEEN KILLED.
AND IT WAS A MATTER OF TIME BEFORE SOMETHING CAME FOR THIS ONE, TOO.
I WAS ALWAYS HONEST ABOUT MY WORLDS, MY TWO LIVES...AND BECAUSE OF THAT, THEY COLLIDED.
BECAUSE OF THAT, CAMMY WAS GONE. BECAUSE OF THAT I'M DEAD.
ANDY IS DEAD. AND NOW, I FINALLY UNDERSTAND WHAT IT IS TO LIVE.
I WAS BORN ANDREW FRANCIS DABBSTEIN BUT I HAD A SECOND NAME. AN EXTRA LIFE.

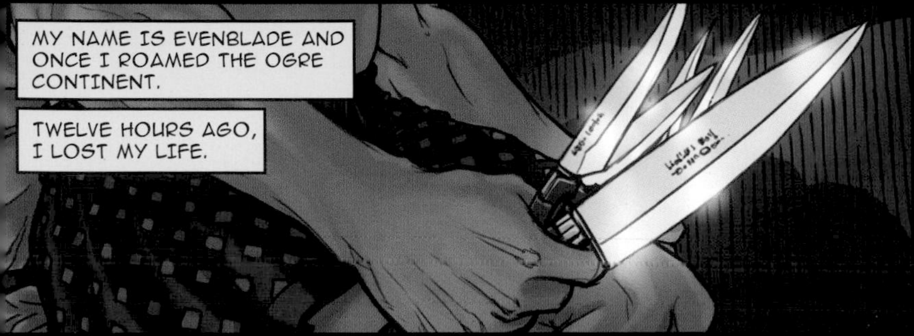
MY NAME IS EVENBLADE AND ONCE I ROAMED THE OGRE CONTINENT.
TWELVE HOURS AGO, I LOST MY LIFE.

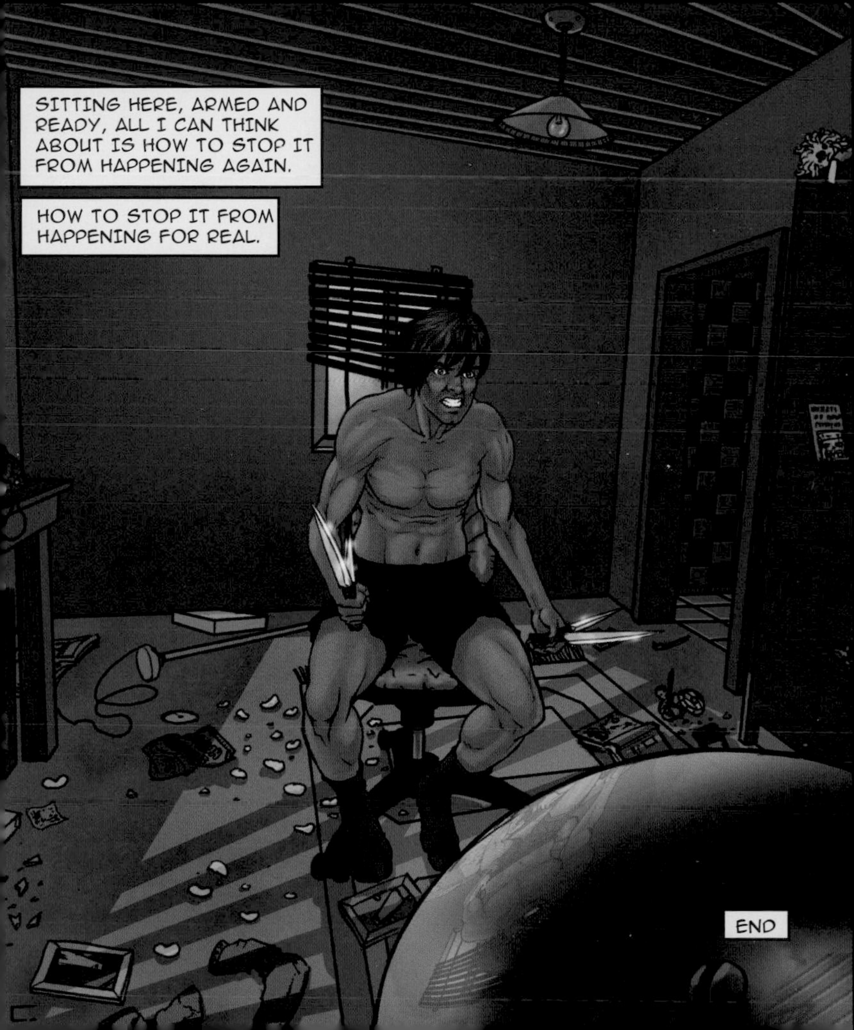
SITTING HERE, ARMED AND READY, ALL I CAN THINK ABOUT IS HOW TO STOP IT FROM HAPPENING AGAIN.
HOW TO STOP IT FROM HAPPENING FOR REAL.
END

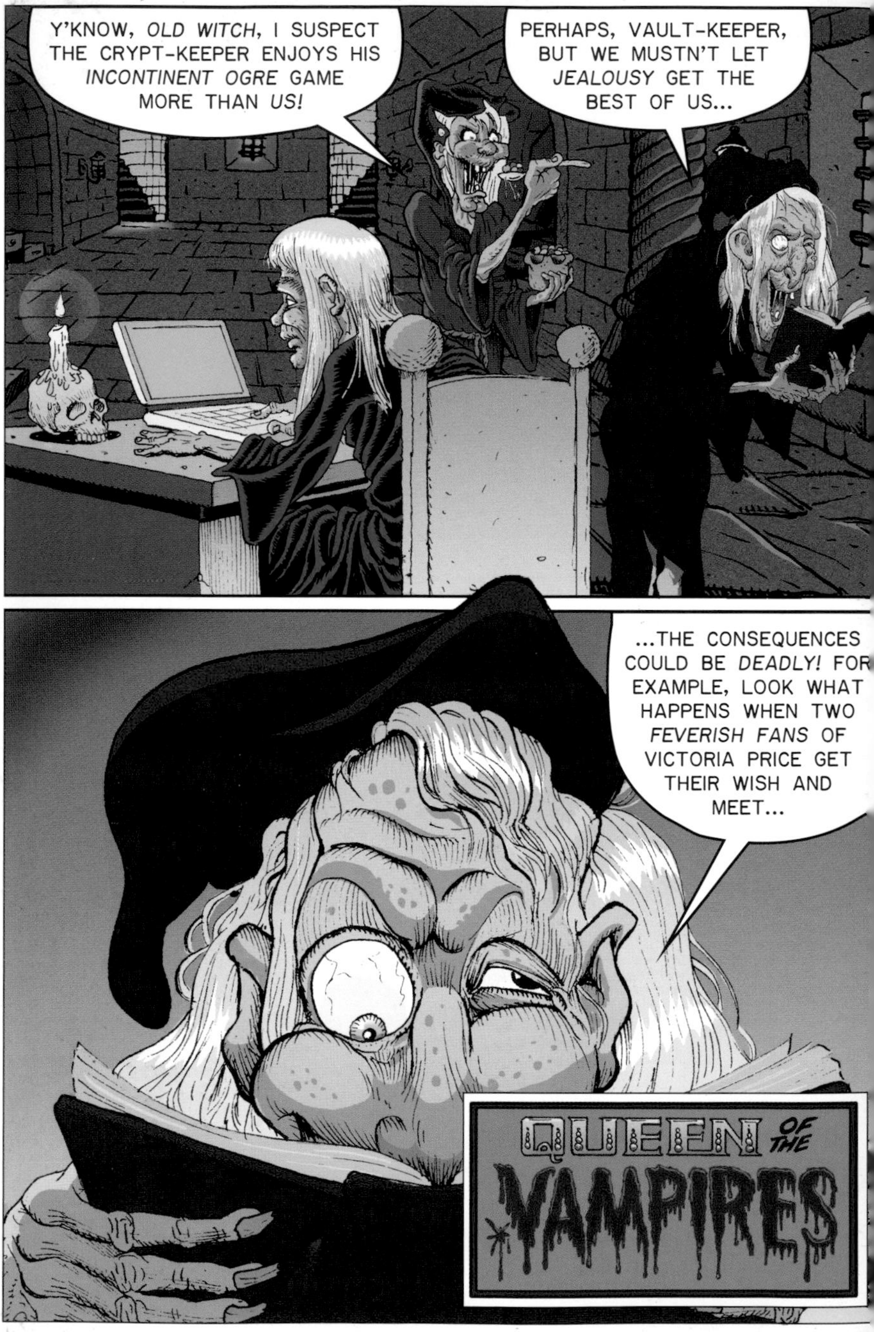

Y'KNOW, *OLD WITCH*, I SUSPECT THE CRYPT-KEEPER ENJOYS HIS *INCONTINENT OGRE* GAME MORE THAN *US!*
PERHAPS, VAULT-KEEPER, BUT WE MUSTN'T LET *JEALOUSY* GET THE BEST OF US...
...THE CONSEQUENCES COULD BE *DEADLY!* FOR EXAMPLE, LOOK WHAT HAPPENS WHEN TWO *FEVERISH FANS* OF VICTORIA PRICE GET THEIR WISH AND MEET...
QUEEN OF THE VAMPIRES

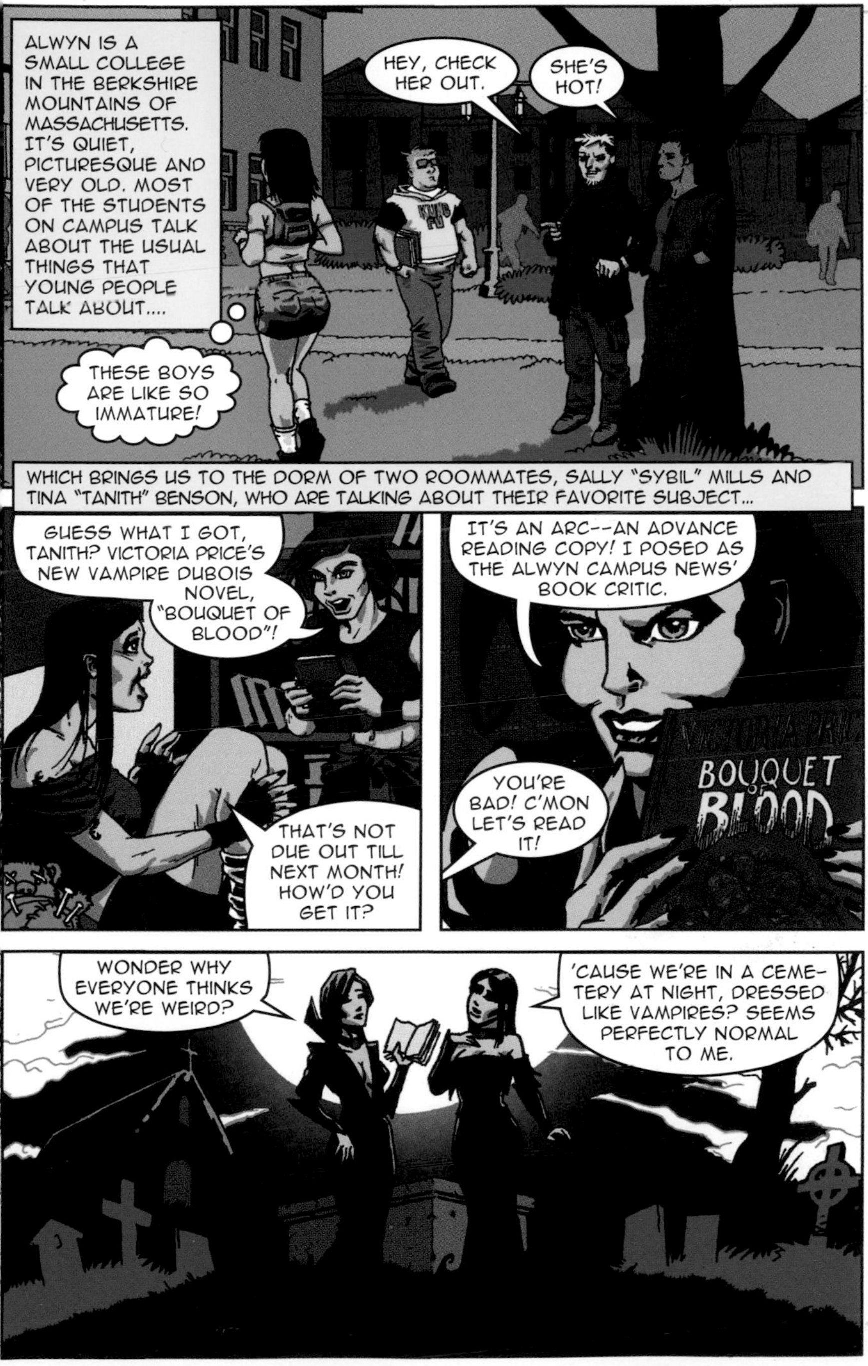
ALWYN IS A SMALL COLLEGE IN THE BERKSHIRE MOUNTAINS OF MASSACHUSETTS. IT'S QUIET, PICTURESQUE AND VERY OLD. MOST OF THE STUDENTS ON CAMPUS TALK ABOUT THE USUAL THINGS THAT YOUNG PEOPLE TALK ABOUT....
HEY, CHECK HER OUT.
SHE'S HOT!
THESE BOYS ARE LIKE SO IMMATURE!
WHICH BRINGS US TO THE DORM OF TWO ROOMMATES, SALLY "SYBIL" MILLS AND TINA "TANITH" BENSON, WHO ARE TALKING ABOUT THEIR FAVORITE SUBJECT...
GUESS WHAT I GOT, TANITH? VICTORIA PRICE'S NEW VAMPIRE DUBOIS NOVEL, "BOUQUET OF BLOOD"!
THAT'S NOT DUE OUT TILL NEXT MONTH! HOW'D YOU GET IT?
IT'S AN ARC--AN ADVANCE READING COPY! I POSED AS THE ALWYN CAMPUS NEWS' BOOK CRITIC.
BOUQUET OF BLOOD
YOU'RE BAD! C'MON LET'S READ IT!
WONDER WHY EVERYONE THINKS WE'RE WEIRD?
'CAUSE WE'RE IN A CEMETERY AT NIGHT, DRESSED LIKE VAMPIRES? SEEMS PERFECTLY NORMAL TO ME.

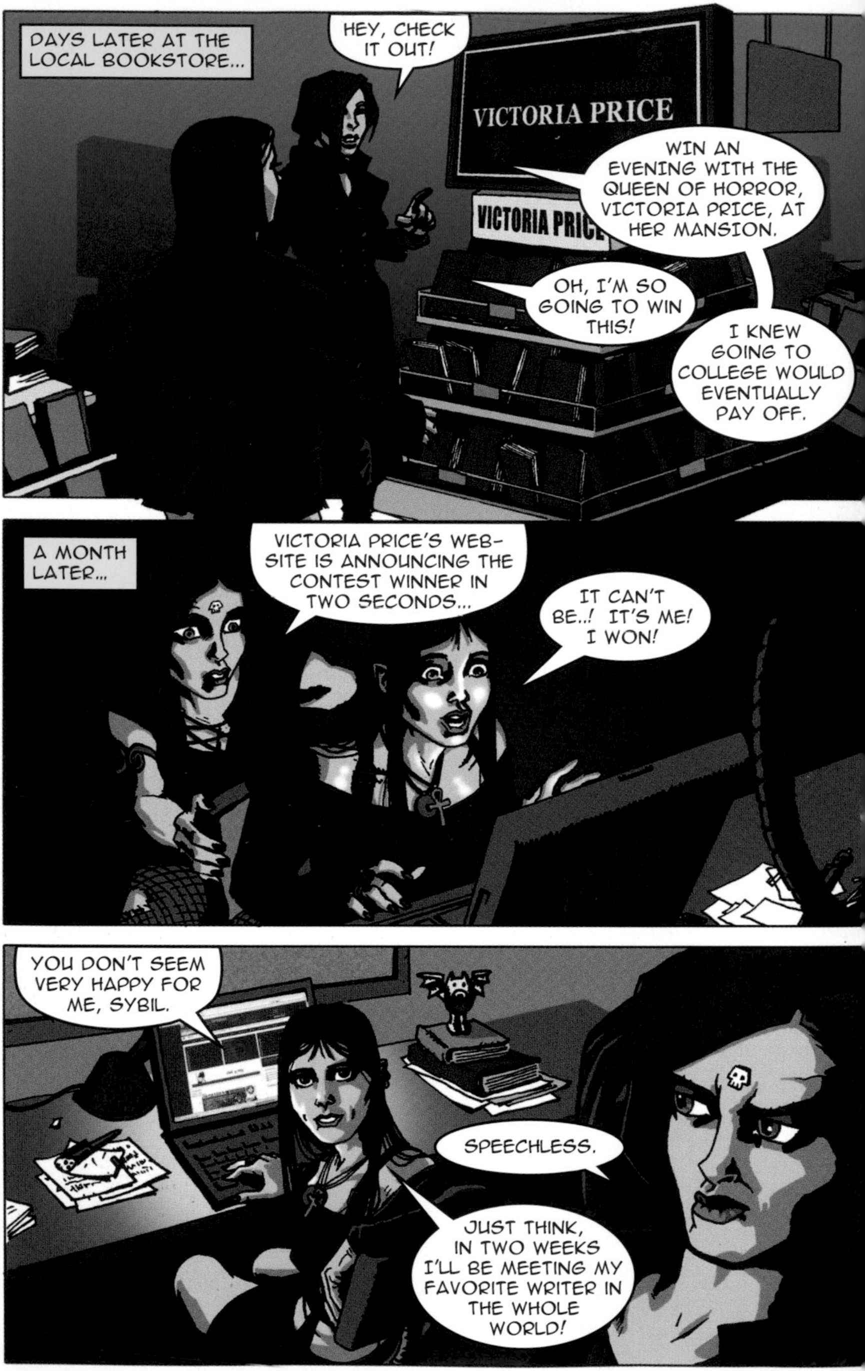

VICTORIA PRICE
VICTORIA PRICE
DAYS LATER AT THE LOCAL BOOKSTORE...
HEY, CHECK IT OUT!
WIN AN EVENING WITH THE QUEEN OF HORROR, VICTORIA PRICE, AT HER MANSION.
OH, I'M SO GOING TO WIN THIS!
I KNEW GOING TO COLLEGE WOULD EVENTUALLY PAY OFF.
A MONTH LATER...
VICTORIA PRICE'S WEB-SITE IS ANNOUNCING THE CONTEST WINNER IN TWO SECONDS...
IT CAN'T BE..! IT'S ME! I WON!
YOU DON'T SEEM VERY HAPPY FOR ME, SYBIL.
SPEECHLESS.
JUST THINK, IN TWO WEEKS I'LL BE MEETING MY FAVORITE WRITER IN THE WHOLE WORLD!

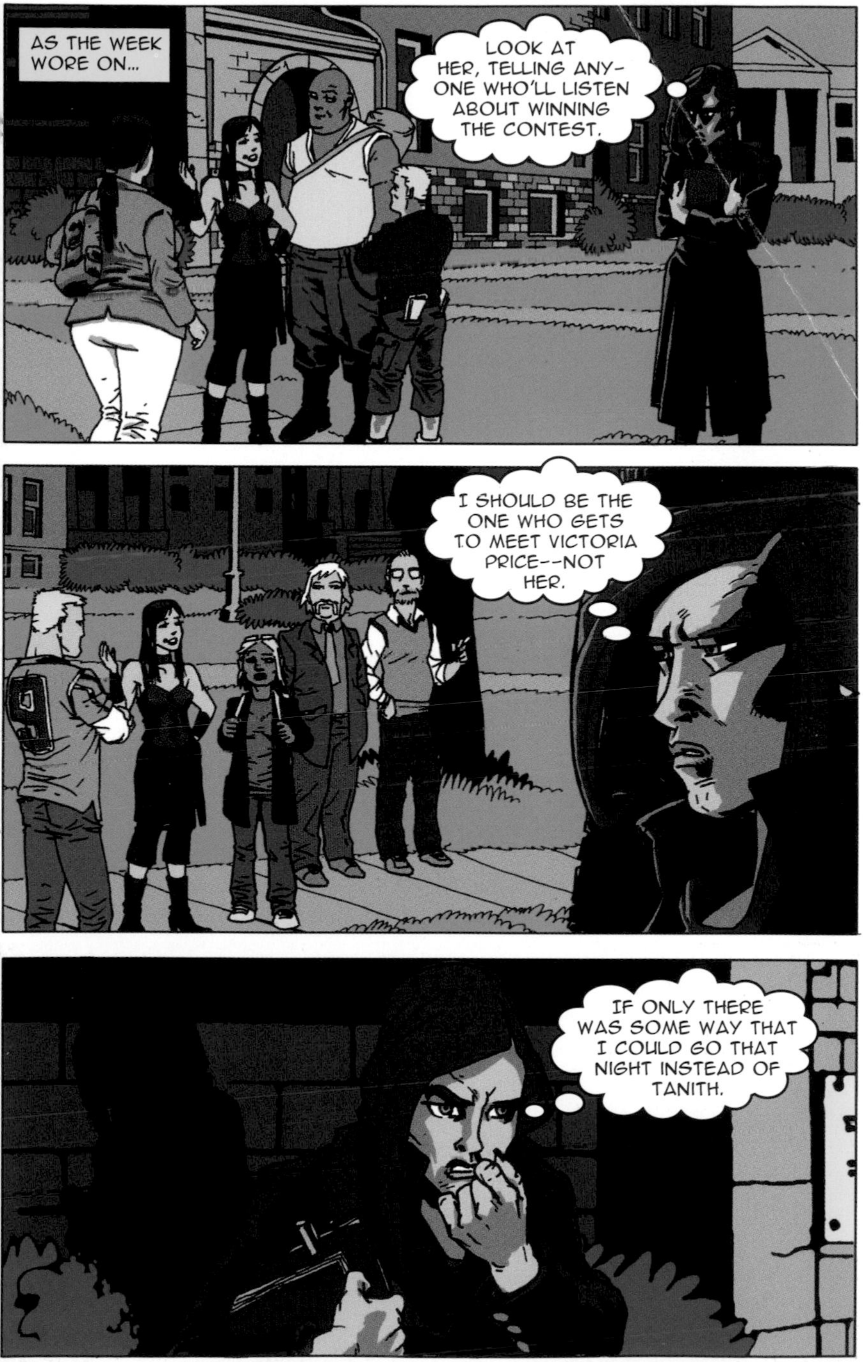
AS THE WEEK WORE ON...
LOOK AT HER, TELLING ANY-ONE WHO'LL LISTEN ABOUT WINNING THE CONTEST.
I SHOULD BE THE ONE WHO GETS TO MEET VICTORIA PRICE--NOT HER.
IF ONLY THERE WAS SOME WAY THAT I COULD GO THAT NIGHT INSTEAD OF TANITH.

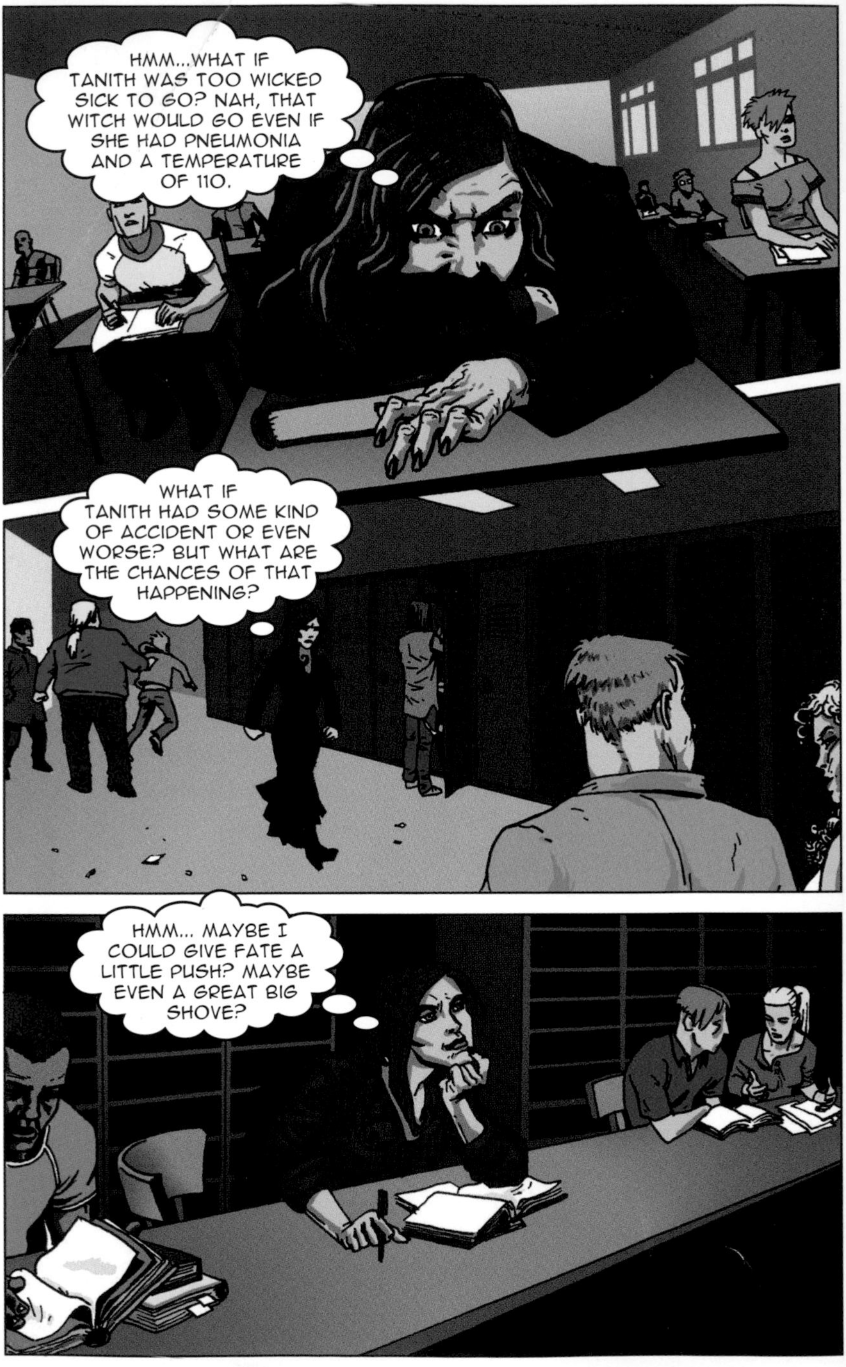
HMM...WHAT IF TANITH WAS TOO WICKED SICK TO GO? NAH, THAT WITCH WOULD GO EVEN IF SHE HAD PNEUMONIA AND A TEMPERATURE OF 110.
WHAT IF TANITH HAD SOME KIND OF ACCIDENT OR EVEN WORSE? BUT WHAT ARE THE CHANCES OF THAT HAPPENING?
HMM... MAYBE I COULD GIVE FATE A LITTLE PUSH? MAYBE EVEN A GREAT BIG SHOVE?

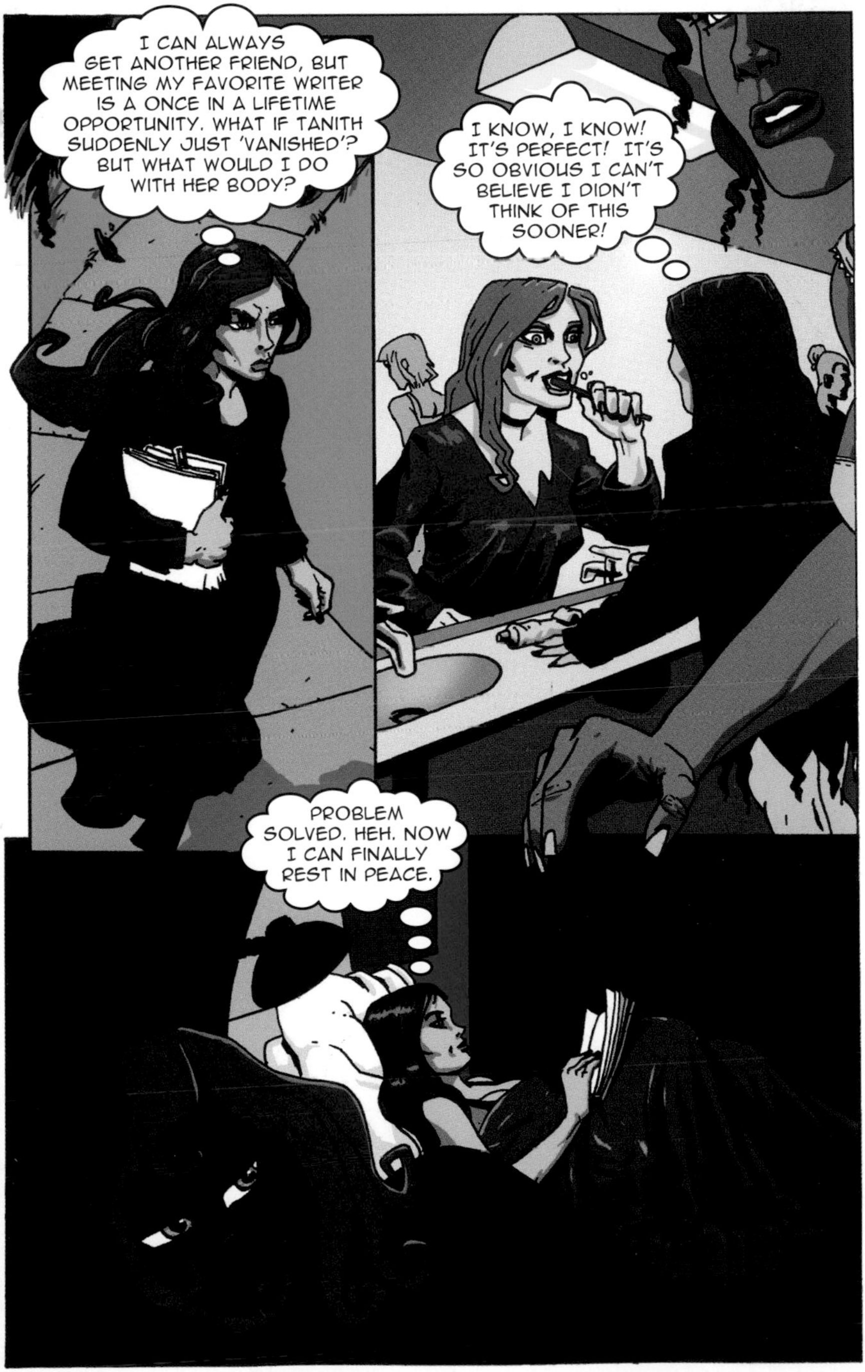
I CAN ALWAYS GET ANOTHER FRIEND, BUT MEETING MY FAVORITE WRITER IS A ONCE IN A LIFETIME OPPORTUNITY. WHAT IF TANITH SUDDENLY JUST 'VANISHED'? BUT WHAT WOULD I DO WITH HER BODY?
I KNOW, I KNOW! IT'S PERFECT! IT'S SO OBVIOUS I CAN'T BELIEVE I DIDN'T THINK OF THIS SOONER!
PROBLEM SOLVED. HEH. NOW I CAN FINALLY REST IN PEACE.

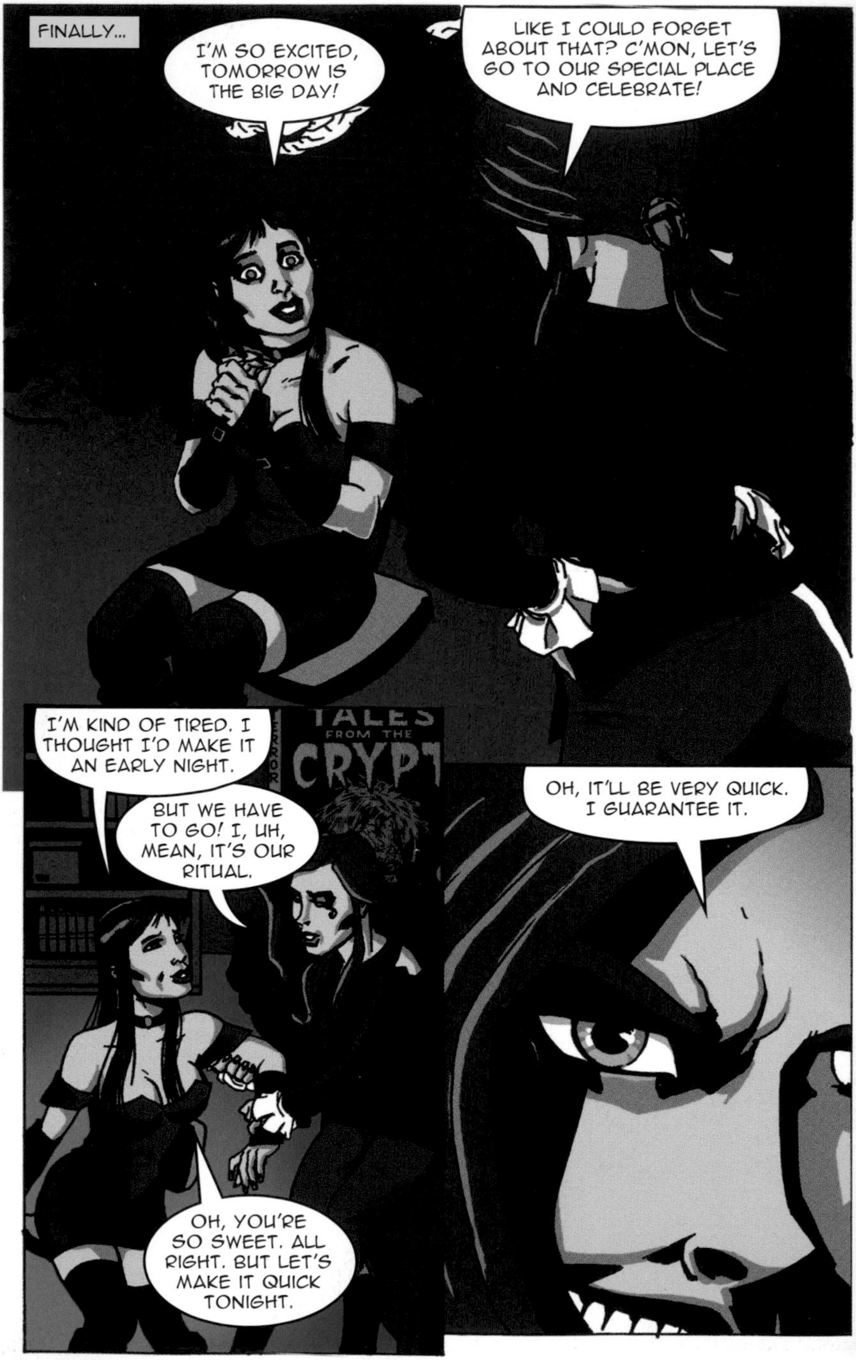
FINALLY...
I'M SO EXCITED, TOMORROW IS THE BIG DAY!
LIKE I COULD FORGET ABOUT THAT? C'MON, LET'S GO TO OUR SPECIAL PLACE AND CELEBRATE!
I'M KIND OF TIRED. I THOUGHT I'D MAKE IT AN EARLY NIGHT.
TALES FROM THE CRYPT
BUT WE HAVE TO GO! I, UH, MEAN, IT'S OUR RITUAL.
OH, YOU'RE SO SWEET. ALL RIGHT. BUT LET'S MAKE IT QUICK TONIGHT.
OH, IT'LL BE VERY QUICK. I GUARANTEE IT.

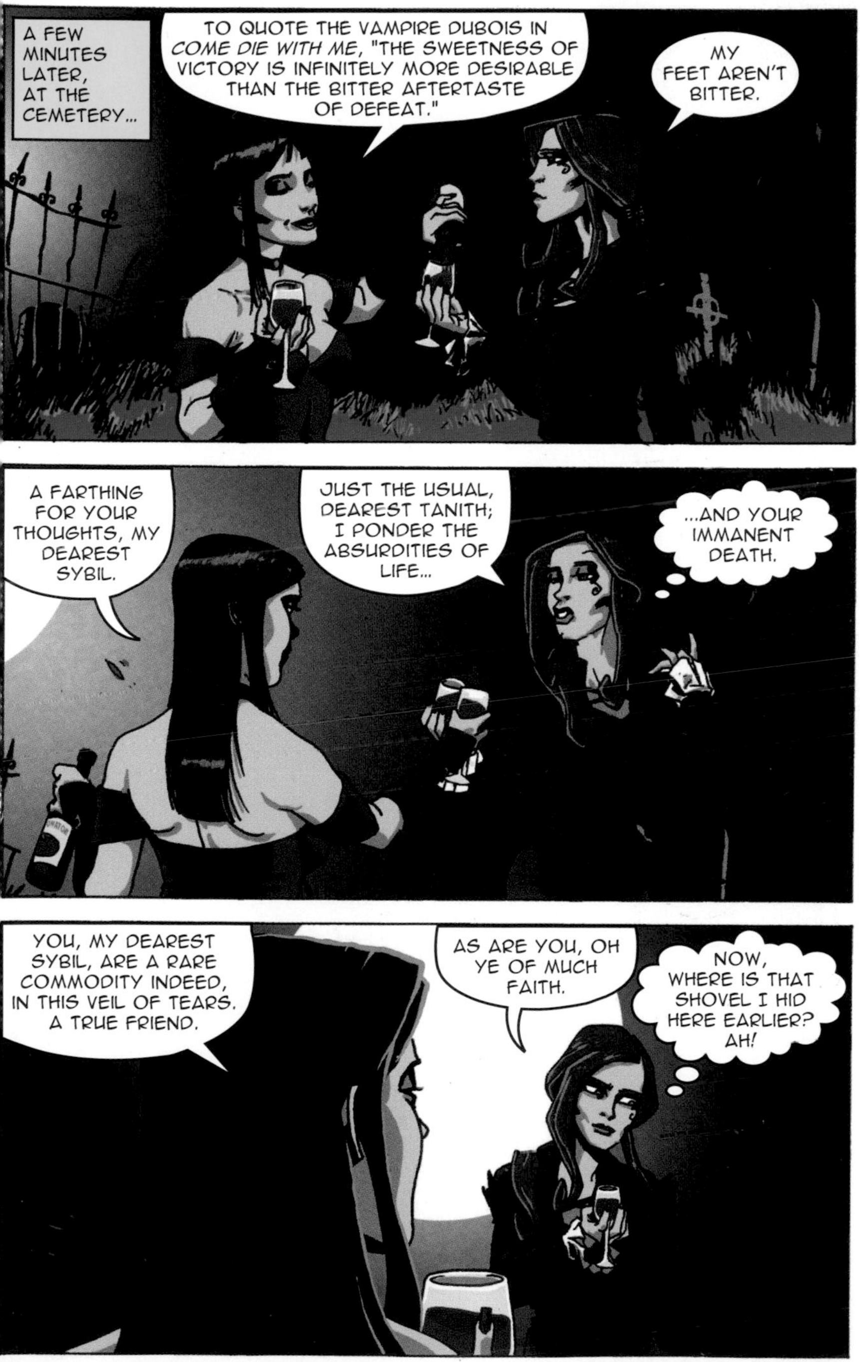
A FEW MINUTES LATER, AT THE CEMETERY...
TO QUOTE THE VAMPIRE DUBOIS IN *COME DIE WITH ME*, "THE SWEETNESS OF VICTORY IS INFINITELY MORE DESIRABLE THAN THE BITTER AFTERTASTE OF DEFEAT."
MY FEET AREN'T BITTER.
A FARTHING FOR YOUR THOUGHTS, MY DEAREST SYBIL.
JUST THE USUAL, DEAREST TANITH; I PONDER THE ABSURDITIES OF LIFE...
...AND YOUR IMMANENT DEATH.
YOU, MY DEAREST SYBIL, ARE A RARE COMMODITY INDEED, IN THIS VEIL OF TEARS. A TRUE FRIEND.
AS ARE YOU, OH YE OF MUCH FAITH.
NOW, WHERE IS THAT SHOVEL I HID HERE EARLIER? AH!

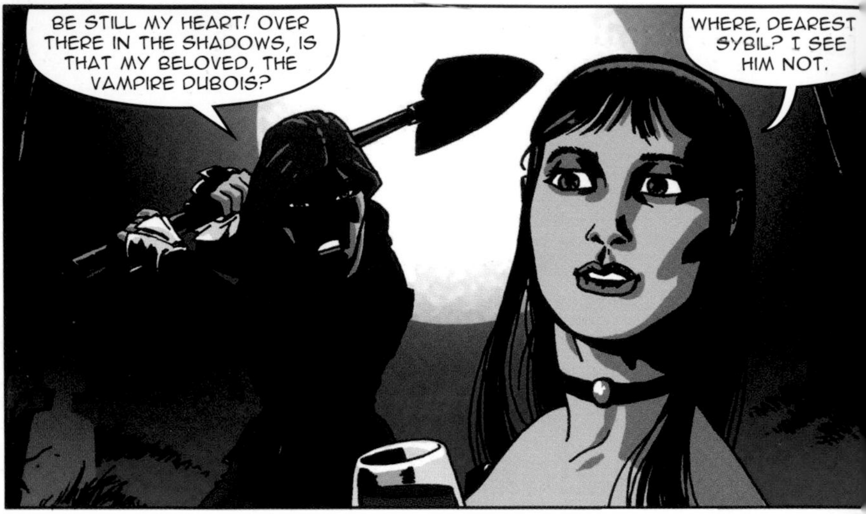
BE STILL MY HEART! OVER THERE IN THE SHADOWS, IS THAT MY BELOVED, THE VAMPIRE DUBOIS?
WHERE, DEAREST SYBIL? I SEE HIM NOT.

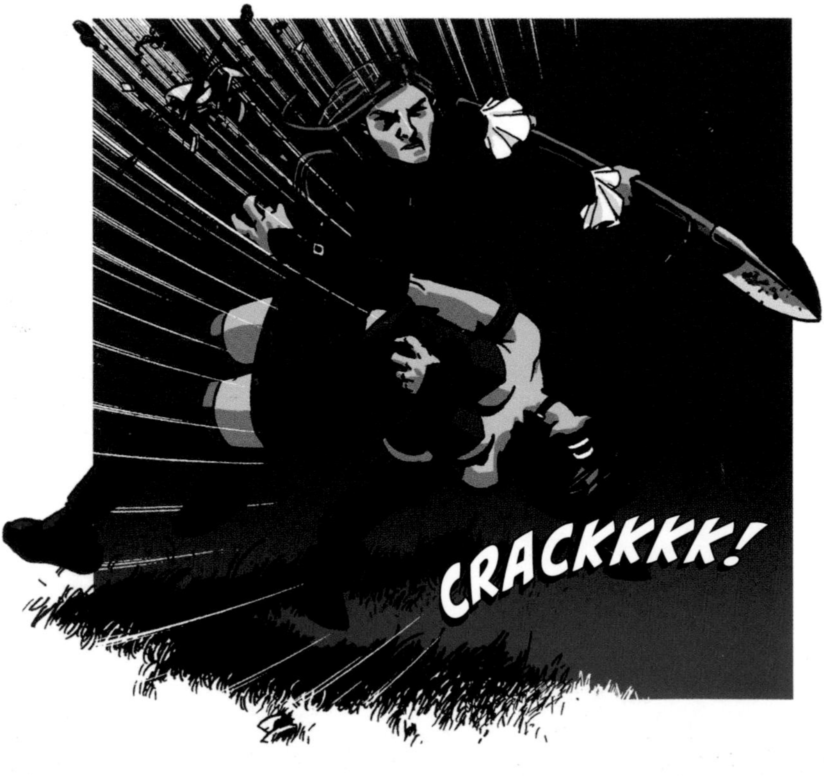
CRACKKKK!

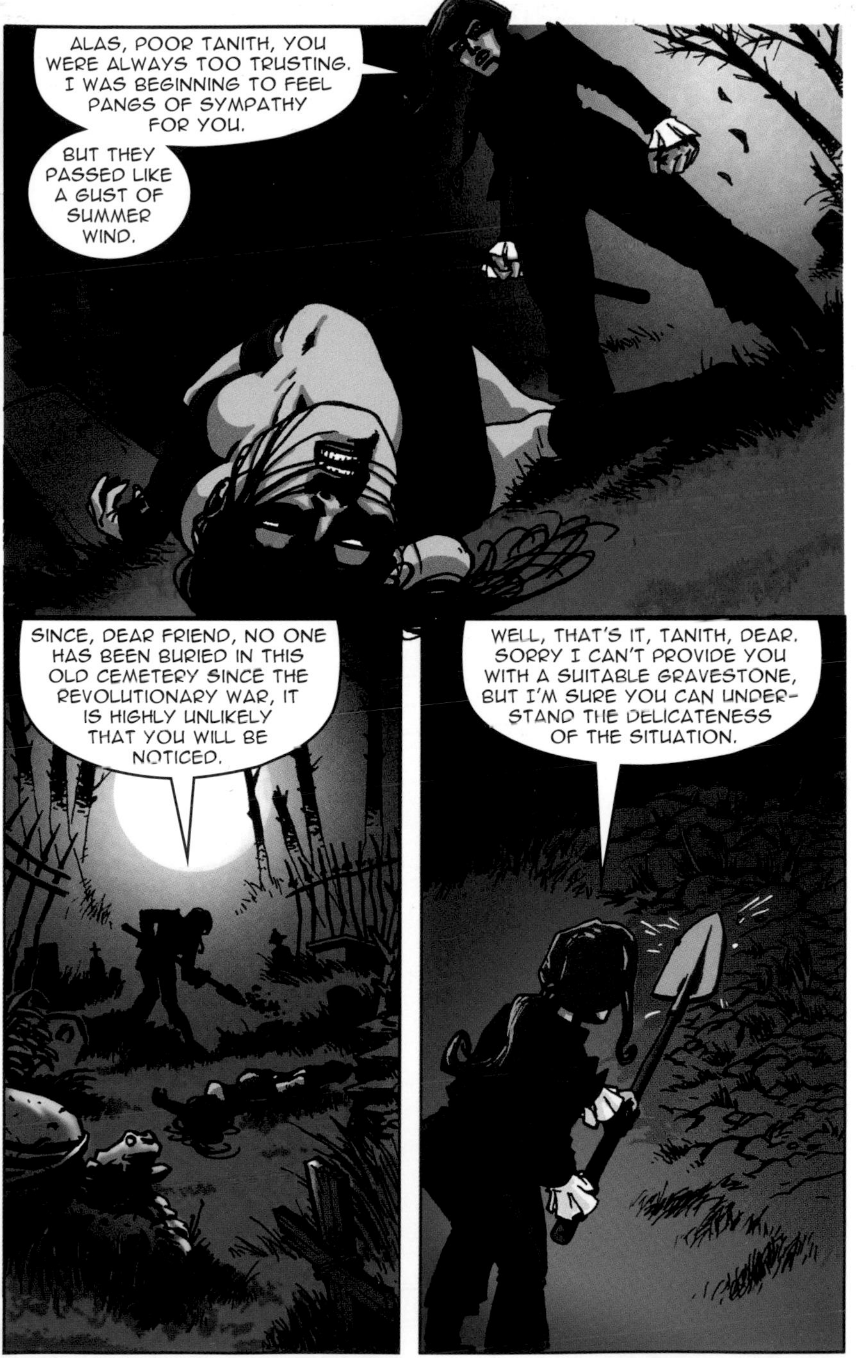
ALAS, POOR TANITH, YOU WERE ALWAYS TOO TRUSTING. I WAS BEGINNING TO FEEL PANGS OF SYMPATHY FOR YOU.
BUT THEY PASSED LIKE A GUST OF SUMMER WIND.
SINCE, DEAR FRIEND, NO ONE HAS BEEN BURIED IN THIS OLD CEMETERY SINCE THE REVOLUTIONARY WAR, IT IS HIGHLY UNLIKELY THAT YOU WILL BE NOTICED.
WELL, THAT'S IT, TANITH, DEAR. SORRY I CAN'T PROVIDE YOU WITH A SUITABLE GRAVESTONE, BUT I'M SURE YOU CAN UNDERSTAND THE DELICATENESS OF THE SITUATION.

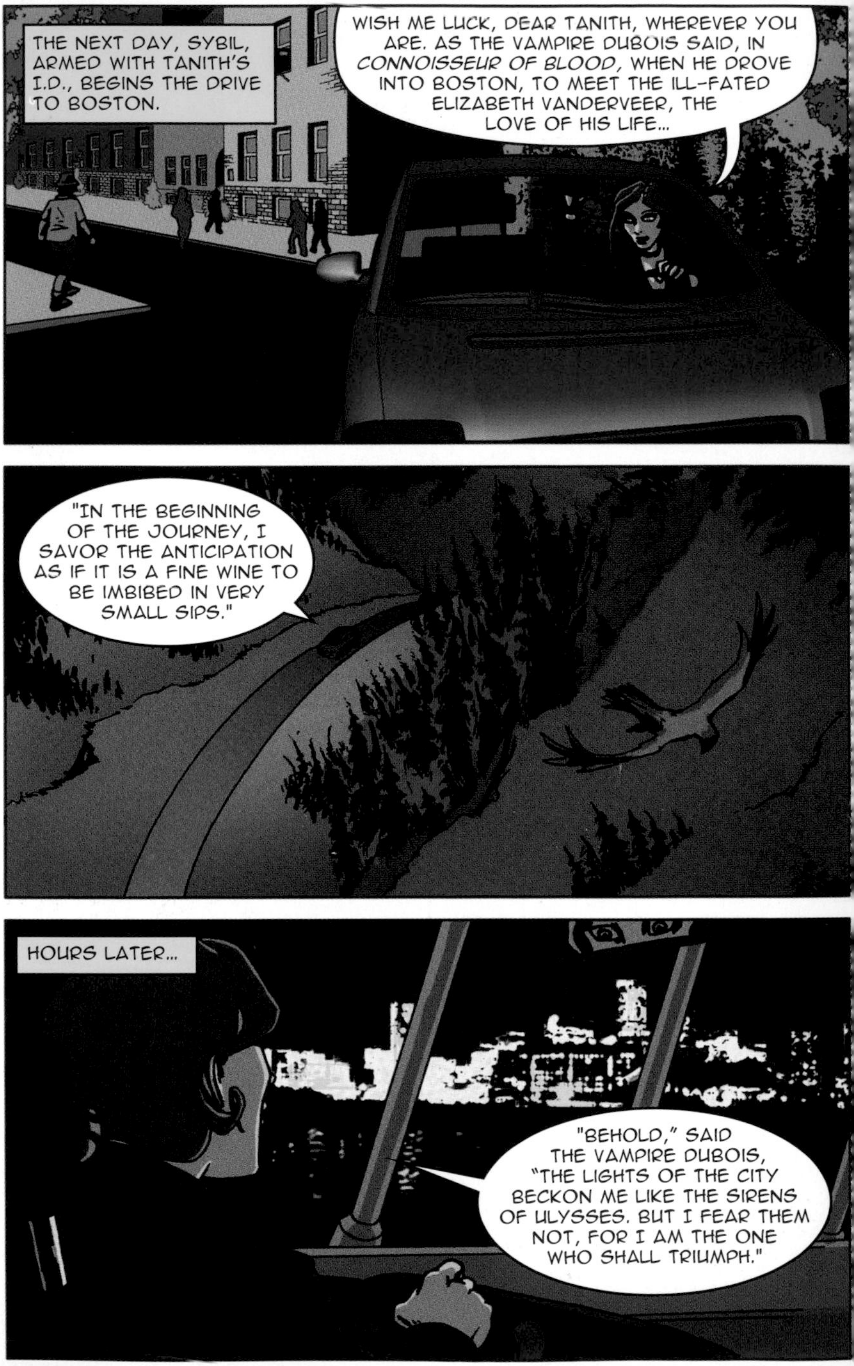
THE NEXT DAY, SYBIL, ARMED WITH TANITH'S I.D., BEGINS THE DRIVE TO BOSTON.
WISH ME LUCK, DEAR TANITH, WHEREVER YOU ARE. AS THE VAMPIRE DUBOIS SAID, IN *CONNOISSEUR OF BLOOD*, WHEN HE DROVE INTO BOSTON, TO MEET THE ILL-FATED ELIZABETH VANDERVEER, THE LOVE OF HIS LIFE...
"IN THE BEGINNING OF THE JOURNEY, I SAVOR THE ANTICIPATION AS IF IT IS A FINE WINE TO BE IMBIBED IN VERY SMALL SIPS."
HOURS LATER...
"BEHOLD," SAID THE VAMPIRE DUBOIS, "THE LIGHTS OF THE CITY BECKON ME LIKE THE SIRENS OF ULYSSES. BUT I FEAR THEM NOT, FOR I AM THE ONE WHO SHALL TRIUMPH."

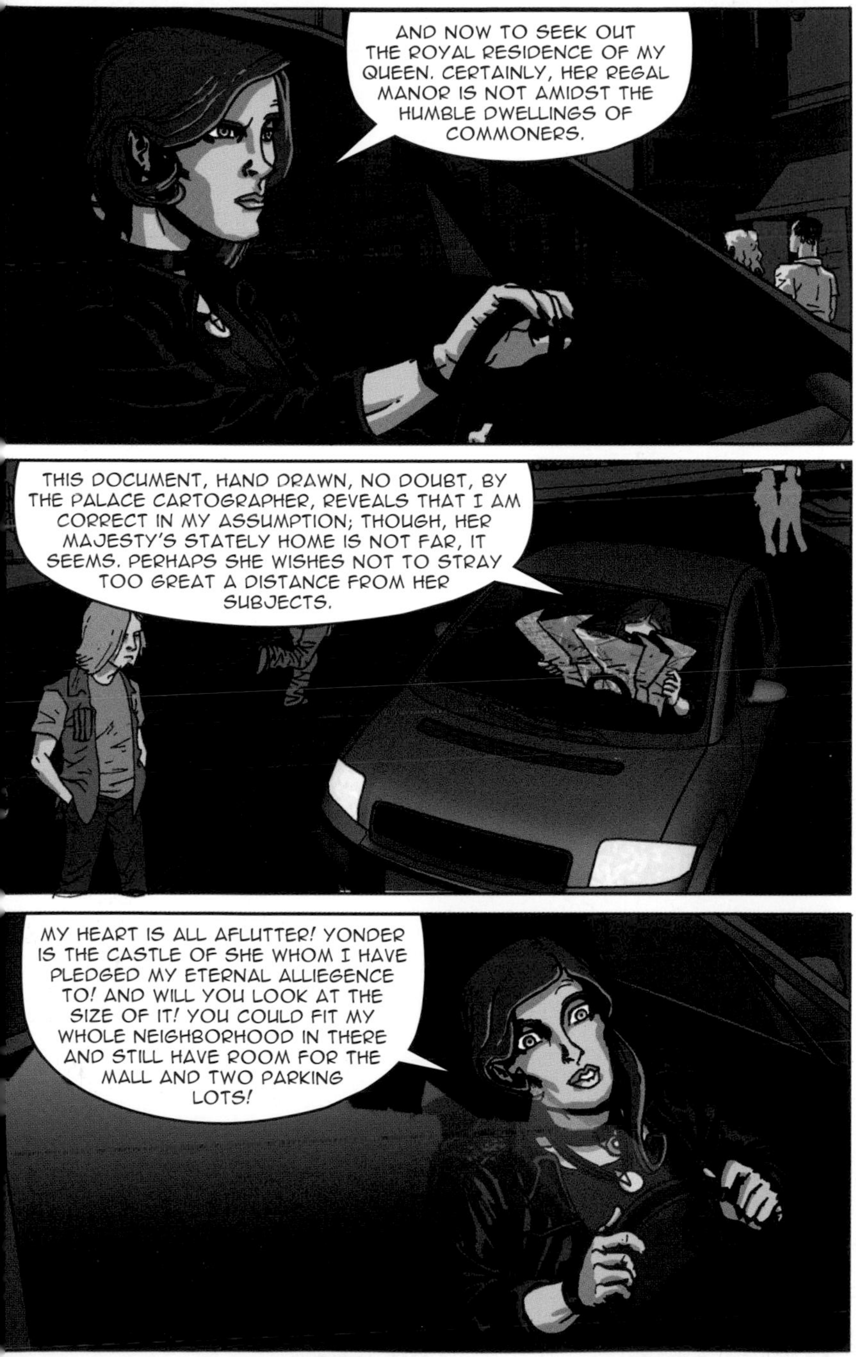
AND NOW TO SEEK OUT THE ROYAL RESIDENCE OF MY QUEEN. CERTAINLY, HER REGAL MANOR IS NOT AMIDST THE HUMBLE DWELLINGS OF COMMONERS.
THIS DOCUMENT, HAND DRAWN, NO DOUBT, BY THE PALACE CARTOGRAPHER, REVEALS THAT I AM CORRECT IN MY ASSUMPTION; THOUGH, HER MAJESTY'S STATELY HOME IS NOT FAR, IT SEEMS. PERHAPS SHE WISHES NOT TO STRAY TOO GREAT A DISTANCE FROM HER SUBJECTS.
MY HEART IS ALL AFLUTTER! YONDER IS THE CASTLE OF SHE WHOM I HAVE PLEDGED MY ETERNAL ALLIEGENCE TO! AND WILL YOU LOOK AT THE SIZE OF IT! YOU COULD FIT MY WHOLE NEIGHBORHOOD IN THERE AND STILL HAVE ROOM FOR THE MALL AND TWO PARKING LOTS!

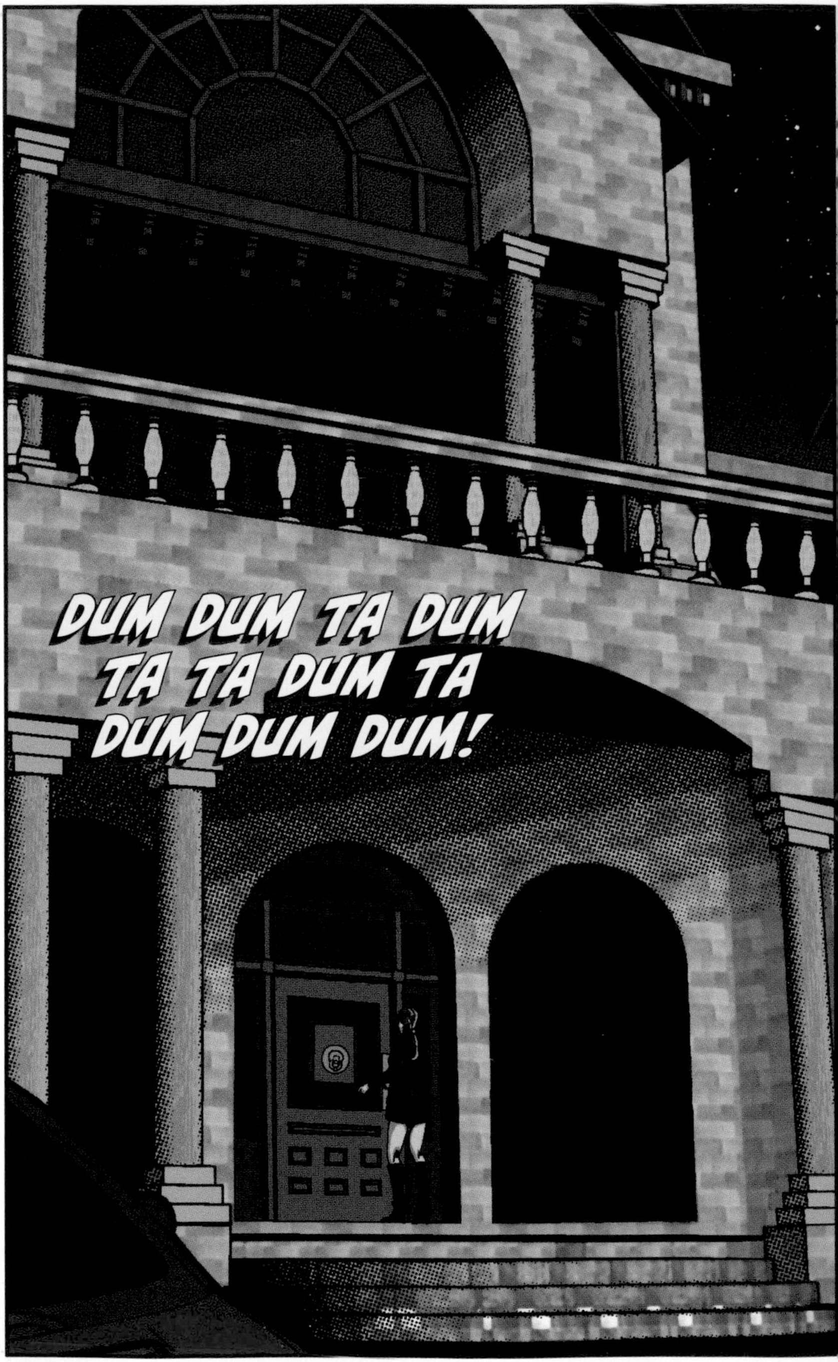
DUM DUM TA DUM
TA TA DUM TA
DUM DUM DUM!

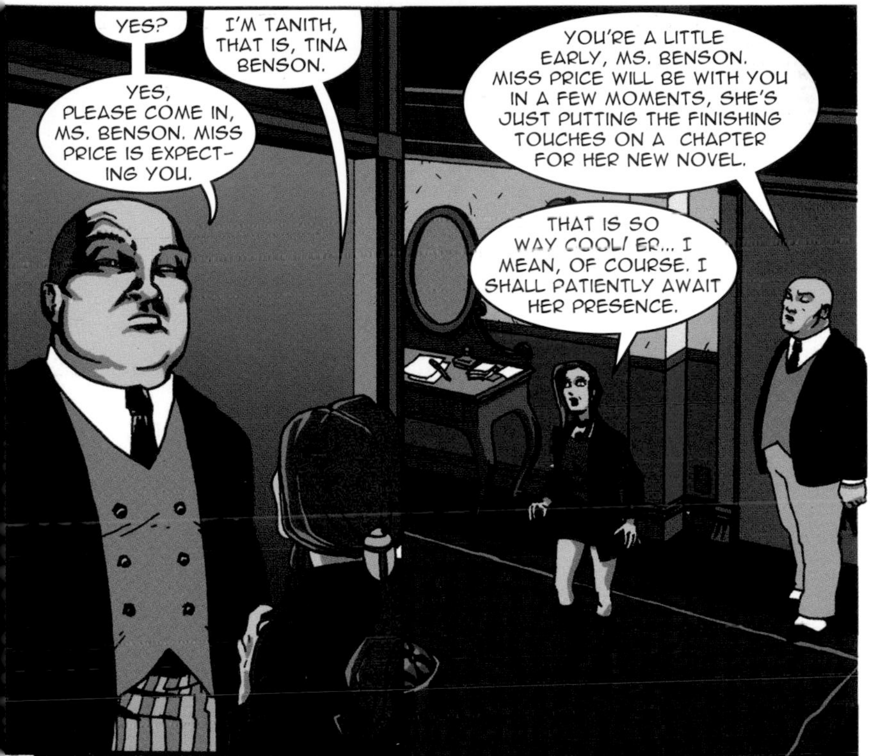
YES?
I'M TANITH, THAT IS, TINA BENSON.
YES, PLEASE COME IN, MS. BENSON. MISS PRICE IS EXPECTING YOU.
YOU'RE A LITTLE EARLY, MS. BENSON. MISS PRICE WILL BE WITH YOU IN A FEW MOMENTS, SHE'S JUST PUTTING THE FINISHING TOUCHES ON A CHAPTER FOR HER NEW NOVEL.
THAT IS SO WAY COOL! ER... I MEAN, OF COURSE. I SHALL PATIENTLY AWAIT HER PRESENCE.

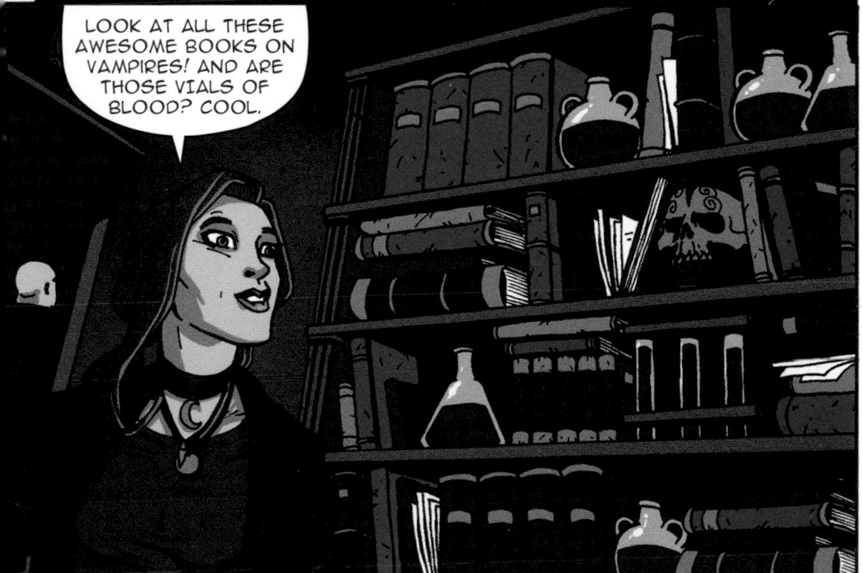
LOOK AT ALL THESE AWESOME BOOKS ON VAMPIRES! AND ARE THOSE VIALS OF BLOOD? COOL.

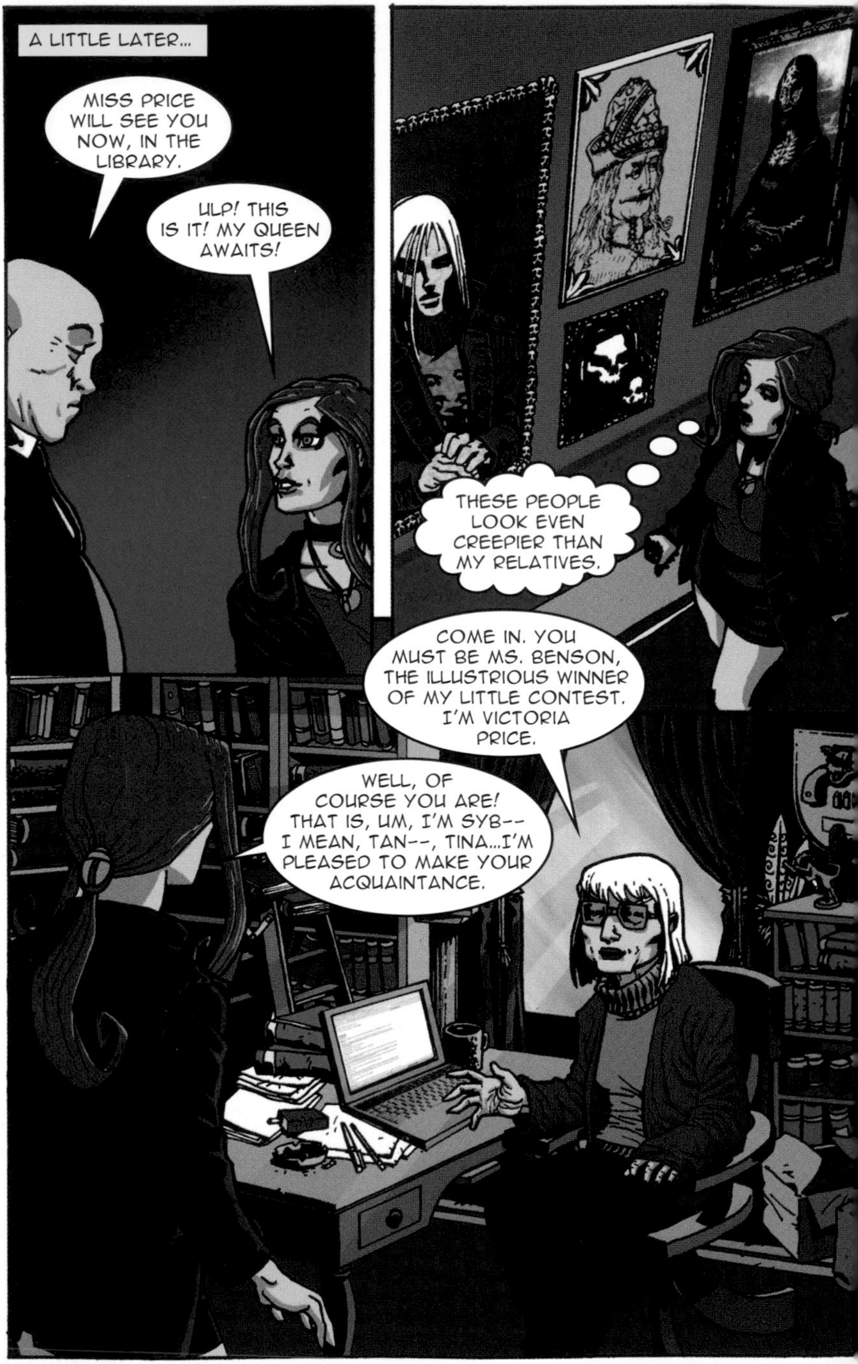
A LITTLE LATER...
MISS PRICE WILL SEE YOU NOW, IN THE LIBRARY.
ULP! THIS IS IT! MY QUEEN AWAITS!
THESE PEOPLE LOOK EVEN CREEPIER THAN MY RELATIVES.
COME IN. YOU MUST BE MS. BENSON, THE ILLUSTRIOUS WINNER OF MY LITTLE CONTEST. I'M VICTORIA PRICE.
WELL, OF COURSE YOU ARE! THAT IS, UM, I'M SYB-- I MEAN, TAN--, TINA...I'M PLEASED TO MAKE YOUR ACQUAINTANCE.

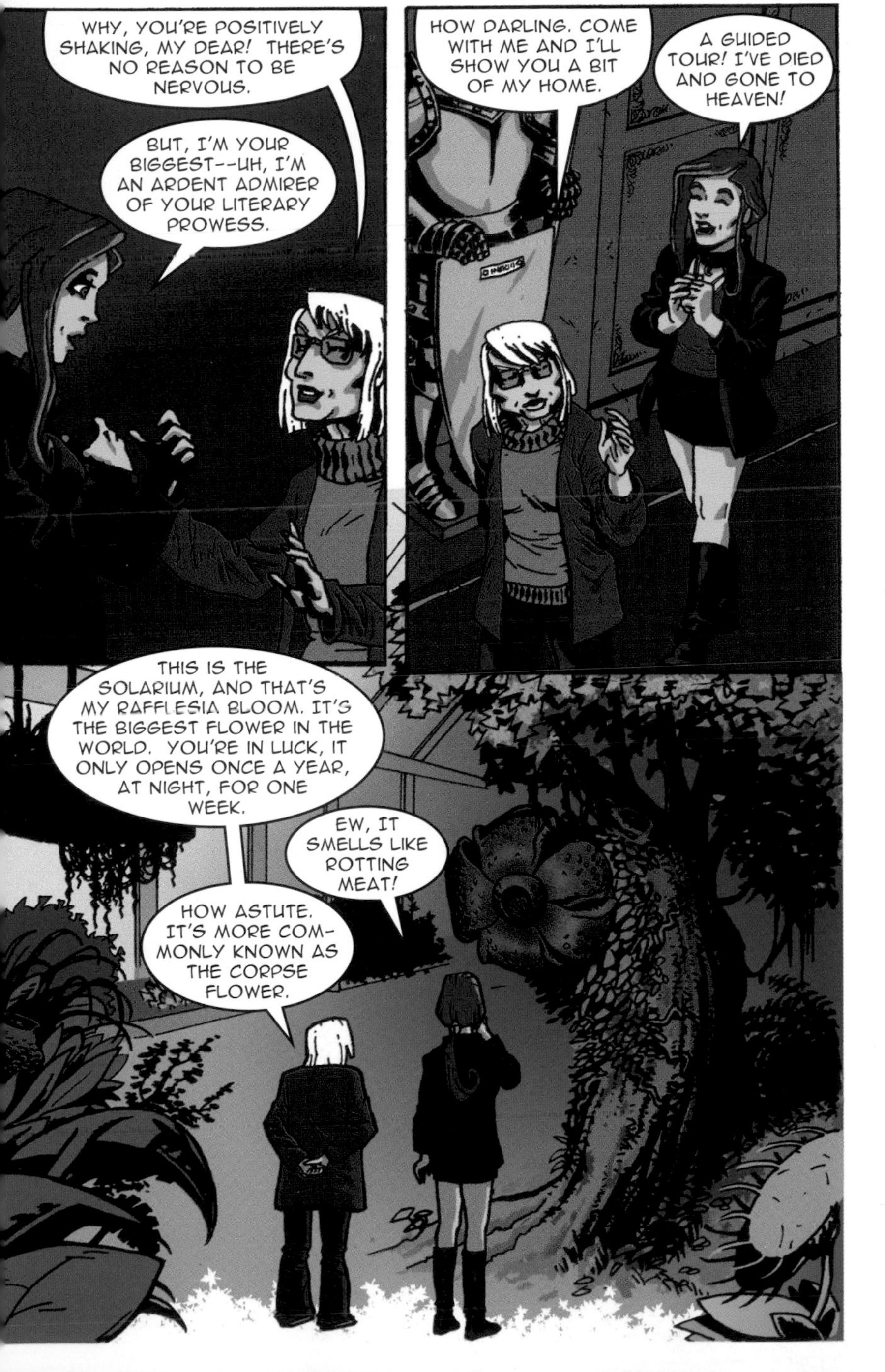
WHY, YOU'RE POSITIVELY SHAKING, MY DEAR! THERE'S NO REASON TO BE NERVOUS.
BUT, I'M YOUR BIGGEST--UH, I'M AN ARDENT ADMIRER OF YOUR LITERARY PROWESS.
HOW DARLING. COME WITH ME AND I'LL SHOW YOU A BIT OF MY HOME.
A GUIDED TOUR! I'VE DIED AND GONE TO HEAVEN!
THIS IS THE SOLARIUM, AND THAT'S MY RAFFLESIA BLOOM. IT'S THE BIGGEST FLOWER IN THE WORLD. YOU'RE IN LUCK, IT ONLY OPENS ONCE A YEAR, AT NIGHT, FOR ONE WEEK.
EW, IT SMELLS LIKE ROTTING MEAT!
HOW ASTUTE. IT'S MORE COM-MONLY KNOWN AS THE CORPSE FLOWER.

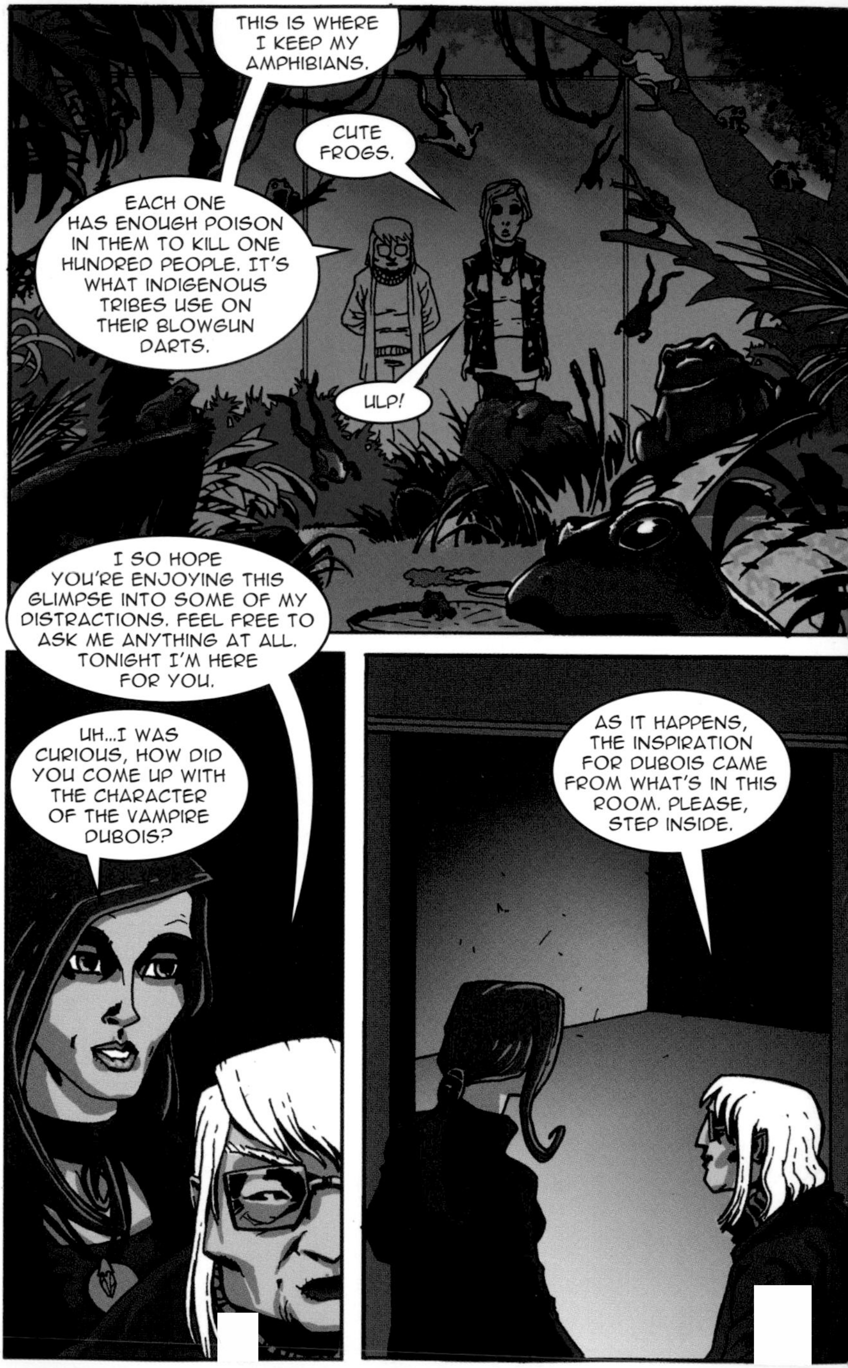
THIS IS WHERE I KEEP MY AMPHIBIANS.
CUTE FROGS.
EACH ONE HAS ENOUGH POISON IN THEM TO KILL ONE HUNDRED PEOPLE. IT'S WHAT INDIGENOUS TRIBES USE ON THEIR BLOWGUN DARTS.
ULP!
I SO HOPE YOU'RE ENJOYING THIS GLIMPSE INTO SOME OF MY DISTRACTIONS. FEEL FREE TO ASK ME ANYTHING AT ALL. TONIGHT I'M HERE FOR YOU.
UH...I WAS CURIOUS, HOW DID YOU COME UP WITH THE CHARACTER OF THE VAMPIRE DUBOIS?
AS IT HAPPENS, THE INSPIRATION FOR DUBOIS CAME FROM WHAT'S IN THIS ROOM. PLEASE, STEP INSIDE.

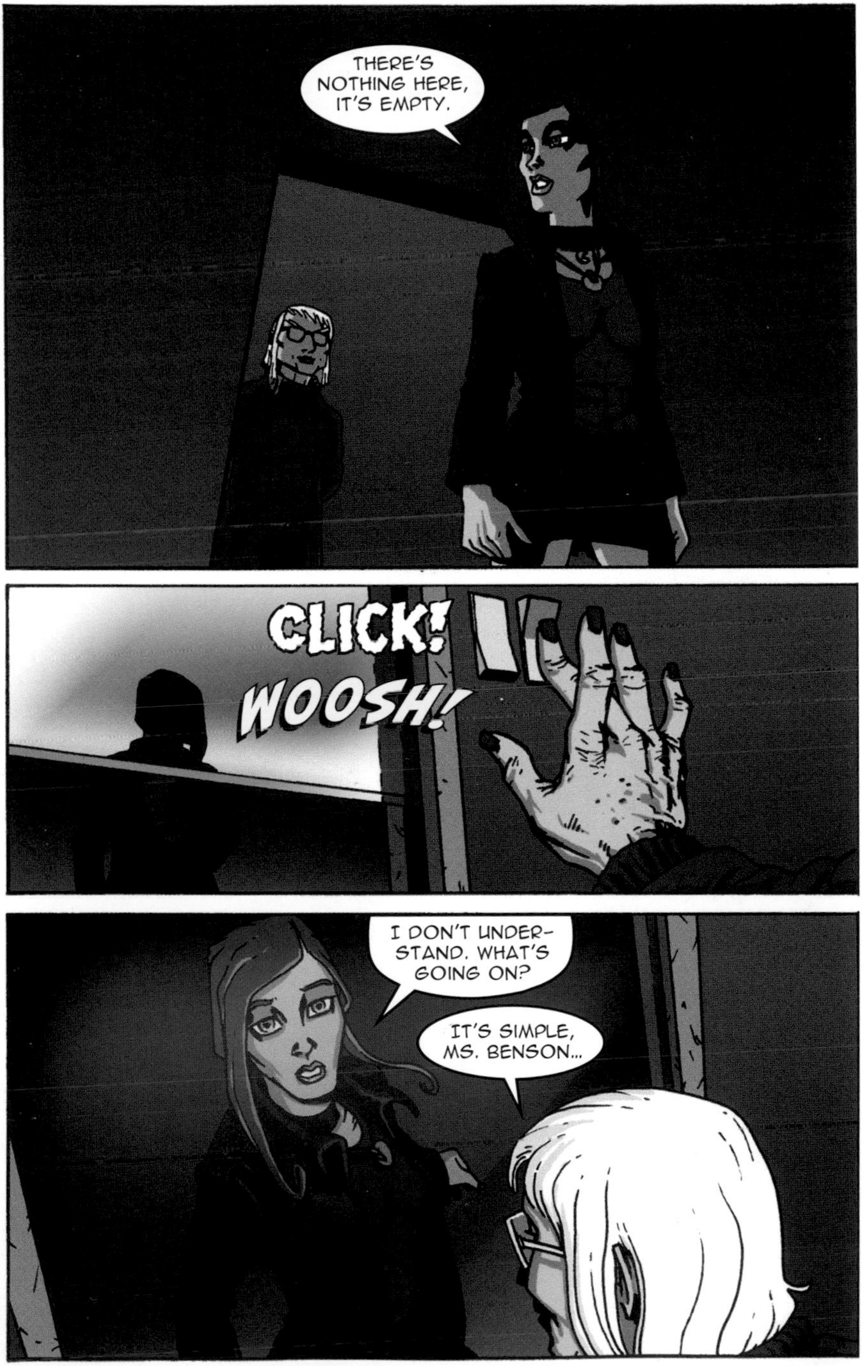
THERE'S NOTHING HERE, IT'S EMPTY.
CLICK!
WOOSH!
I DON'T UNDER-STAND. WHAT'S GOING ON?
IT'S SIMPLE, MS. BENSON...

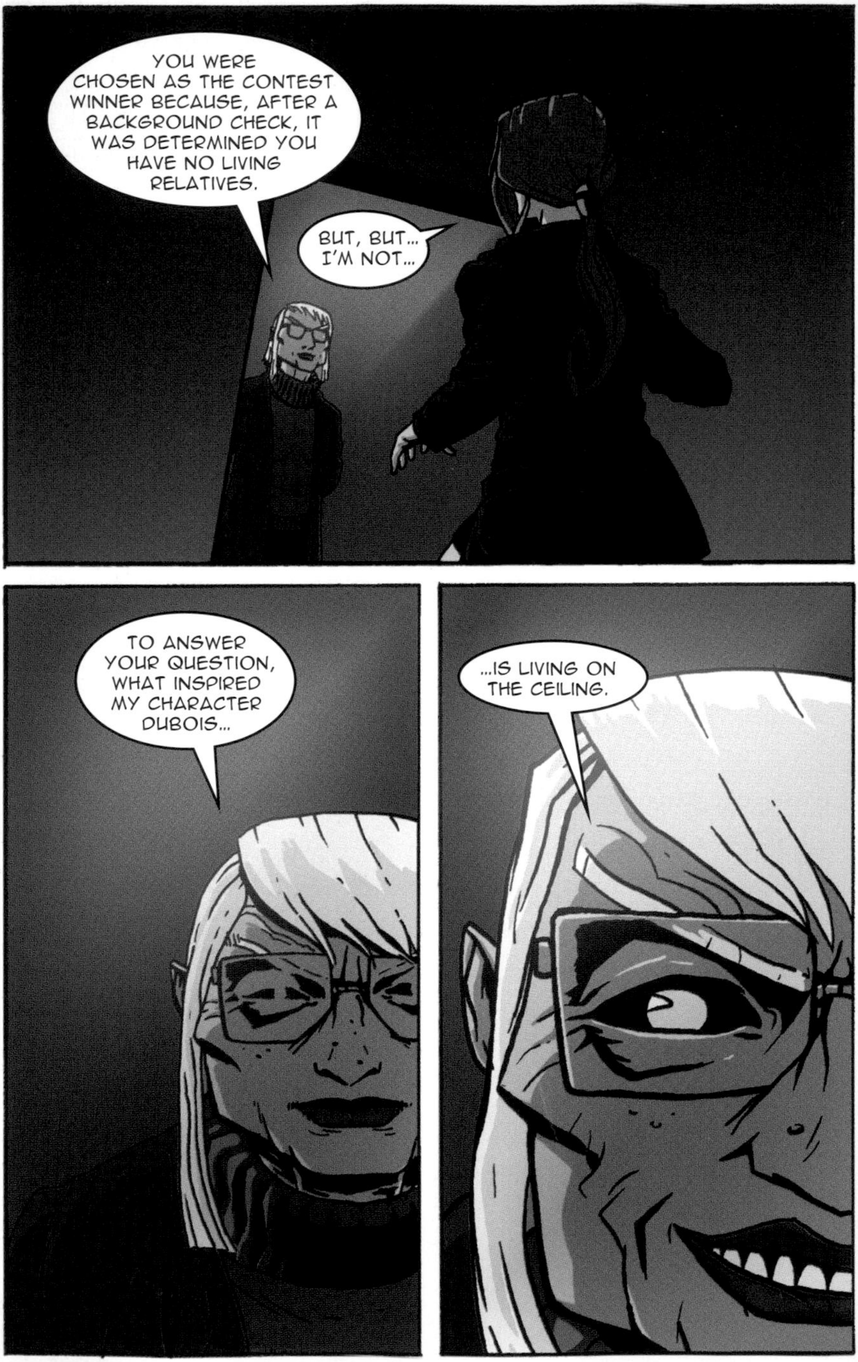
YOU WERE CHOSEN AS THE CONTEST WINNER BECAUSE, AFTER A BACKGROUND CHECK, IT WAS DETERMINED YOU HAVE NO LIVING RELATIVES.
BUT, BUT... I'M NOT...
TO ANSWER YOUR QUESTION, WHAT INSPIRED MY CHARACTER DUBOIS...
...IS LIVING ON THE CEILING.

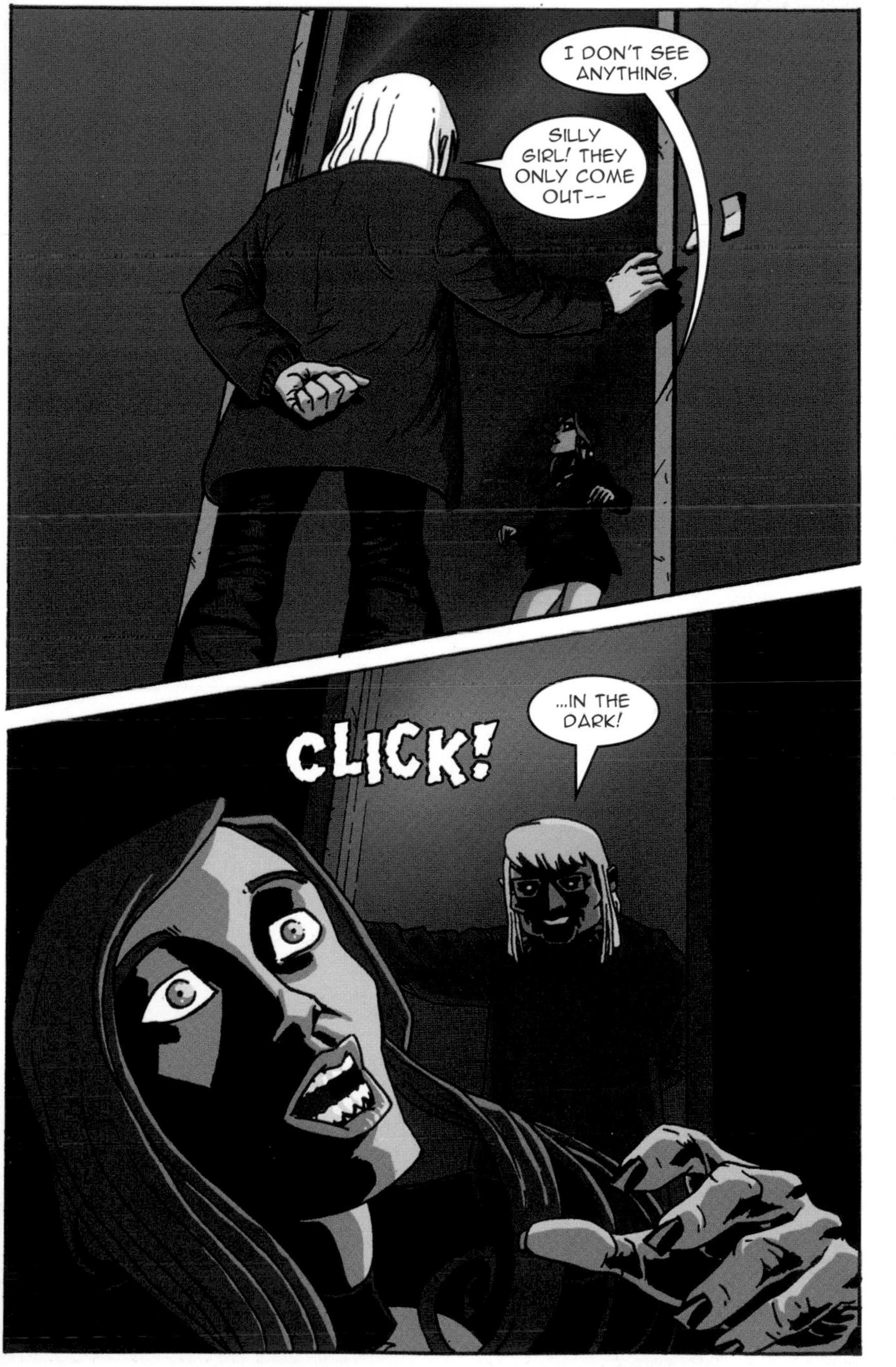
I DON'T SEE ANYTHING.
SILLY GIRL! THEY ONLY COME OUT--
CLICK!
...IN THE DARK!

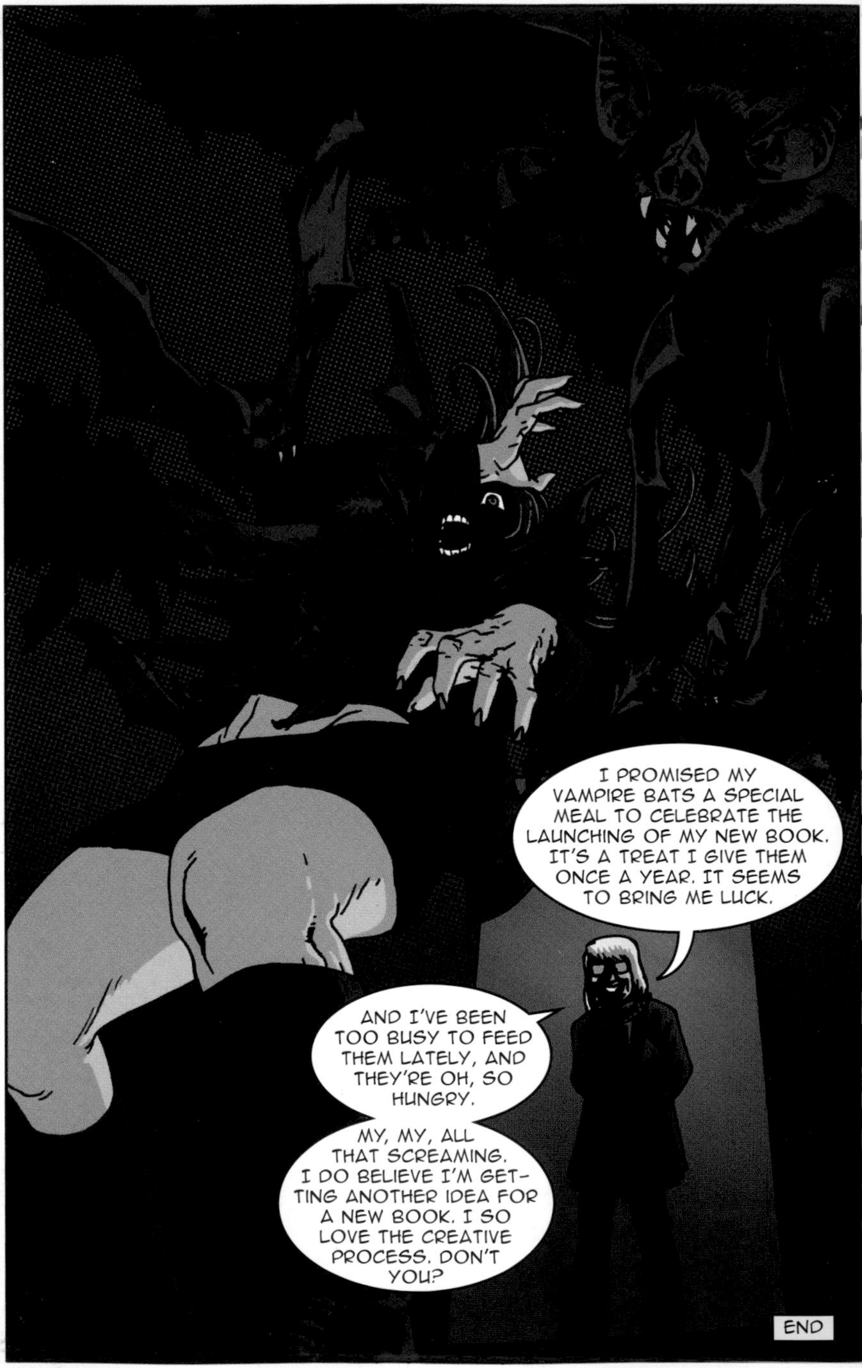
I PROMISED MY VAMPIRE BATS A SPECIAL MEAL TO CELEBRATE THE LAUNCHING OF MY NEW BOOK. IT'S A TREAT I GIVE THEM ONCE A YEAR. IT SEEMS TO BRING ME LUCK.
AND I'VE BEEN TOO BUSY TO FEED THEM LATELY, AND THEY'RE OH, SO HUNGRY.
MY, MY, ALL THAT SCREAMING. I DO BELIEVE I'M GET-TING ANOTHER IDEA FOR A NEW BOOK. I SO LOVE THE CREATIVE PROCESS. DON'T YOU?
END

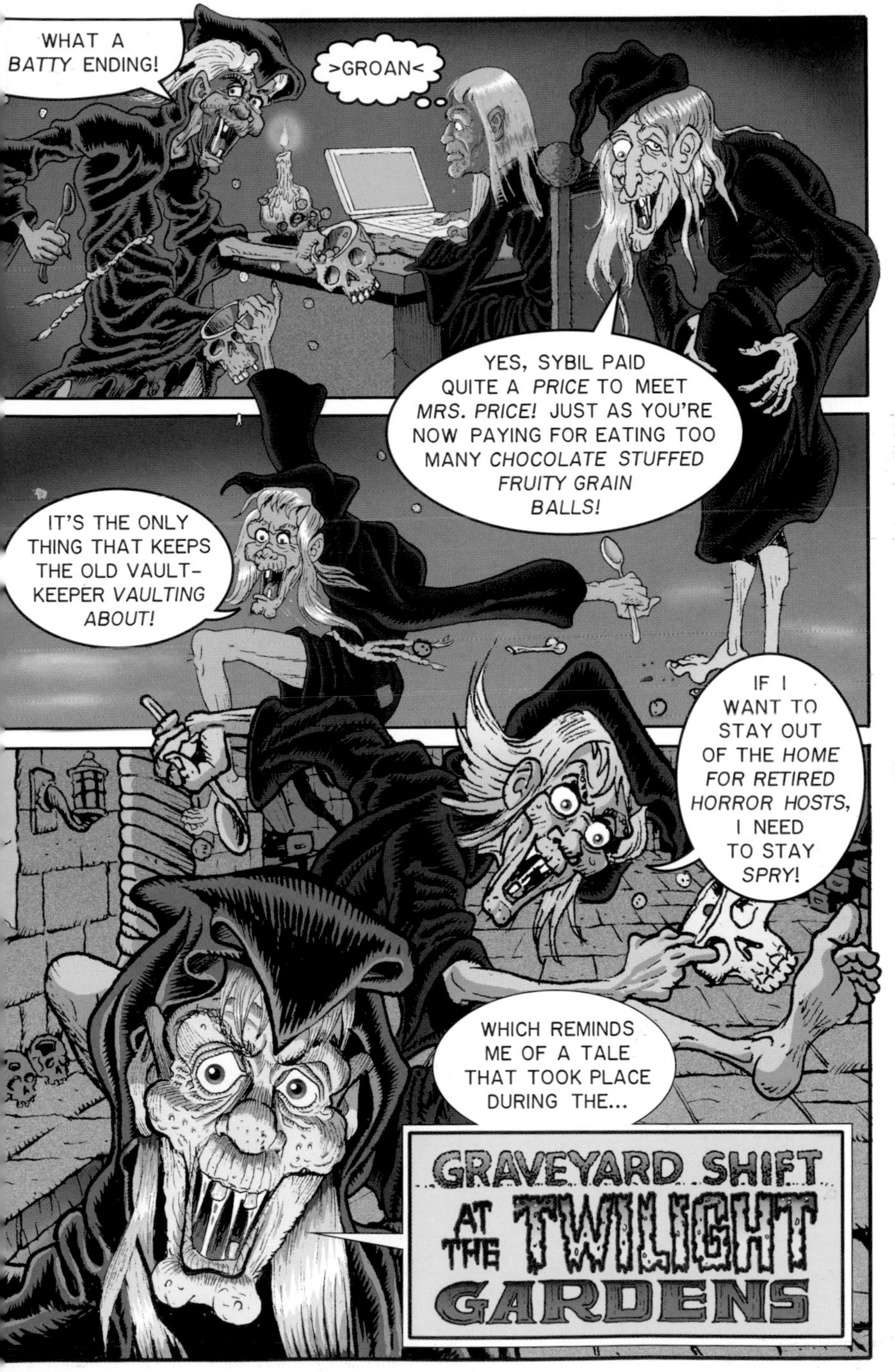
WHAT A BATTY ENDING!
>GROAN<
YES, SYBIL PAID QUITE A PRICE TO MEET MRS. PRICE! JUST AS YOU'RE NOW PAYING FOR EATING TOO MANY CHOCOLATE STUFFED FRUITY GRAIN BALLS!
IT'S THE ONLY THING THAT KEEPS THE OLD VAULT-KEEPER VAULTING ABOUT!
IF I WANT TO STAY OUT OF THE HOME FOR RETIRED HORROR HOSTS, I NEED TO STAY SPRY!
WHICH REMINDS ME OF A TALE THAT TOOK PLACE DURING THE...
GRAVEYARD SHIFT AT THE TWILIGHT GARDENS

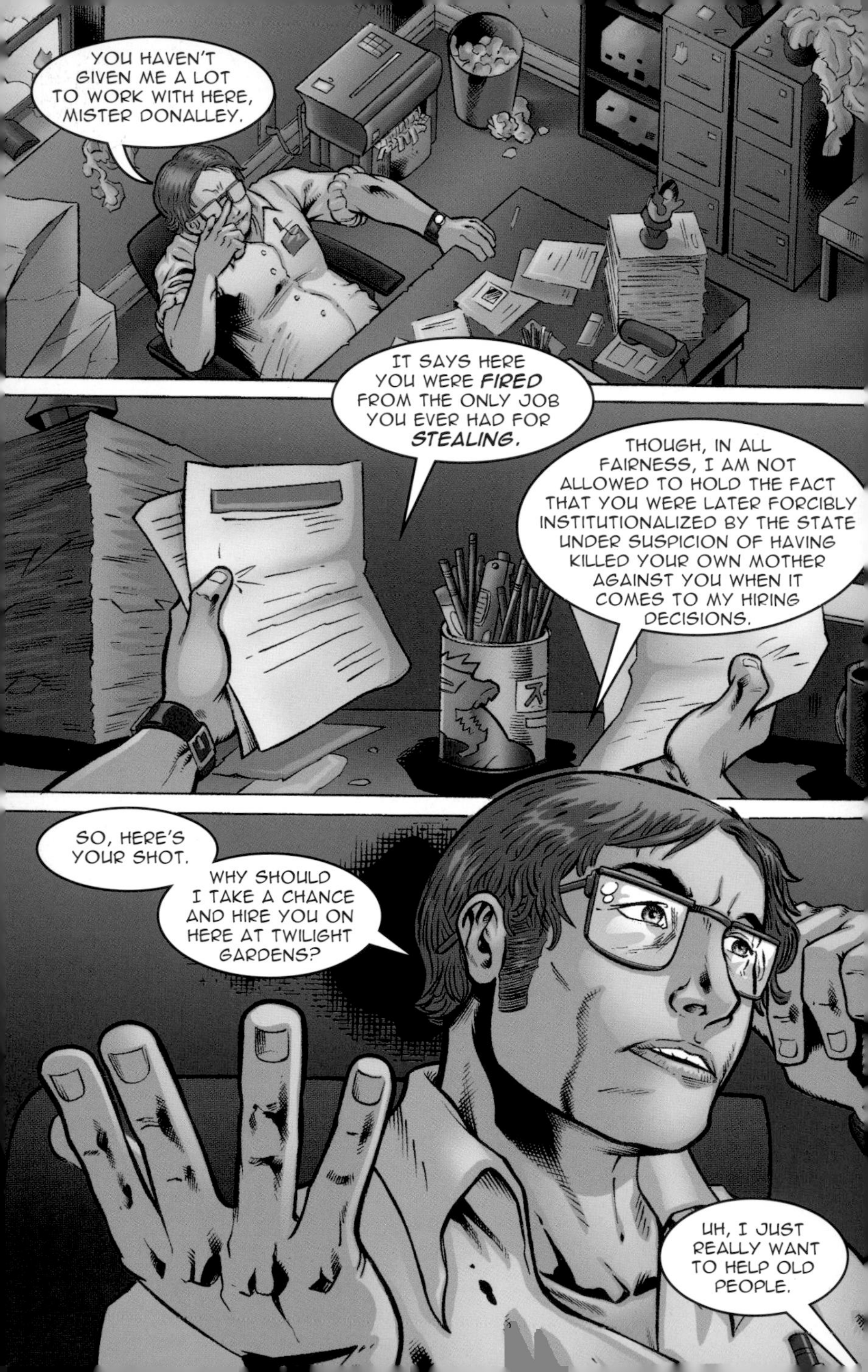
YOU HAVEN'T GIVEN ME A LOT TO WORK WITH HERE, MISTER DONALLEY.
IT SAYS HERE YOU WERE *FIRED* FROM THE ONLY JOB YOU EVER HAD FOR *STEALING.*
THOUGH, IN ALL FAIRNESS, I AM NOT ALLOWED TO HOLD THE FACT THAT YOU WERE LATER FORCIBLY INSTITUTIONALIZED BY THE STATE UNDER SUSPICION OF HAVING KILLED YOUR OWN MOTHER AGAINST YOU WHEN IT COMES TO MY HIRING DECISIONS.
SO, HERE'S YOUR SHOT.
WHY SHOULD I TAKE A CHANCE AND HIRE YOU ON HERE AT TWILIGHT GARDENS?
UH, I JUST REALLY WANT TO HELP OLD PEOPLE.

AND, YOU KNOW... GET PAID FOR IT.

TO ANOTHER MAN, PERHAPS ALSO FRESHLY RELEASED FROM THE STATE PSYCHIATRIC WARD, TWILIGHT GARDENS MIGHT HAVE LOOKED LIKE A PLACE TO BEGIN REBUILDING HIS FUTURE.

YOU EVER USE A MOP BEFORE, THOMAS?

DUH, LIKE A MILLION TIMES.

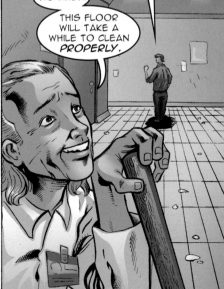

BUT FOR THOMAS DONALLEY, FORMER GROCERY SACKER, FORMER MOMMA'S BOY, FORMER *MADMAN*...

START HERE AND ROSE'LL BE ALONG SHORTLY TO DIRECT YOU.

NO RUSH.

THIS FLOOR WILL TAKE A WHILE TO CLEAN *PROPERLY*.

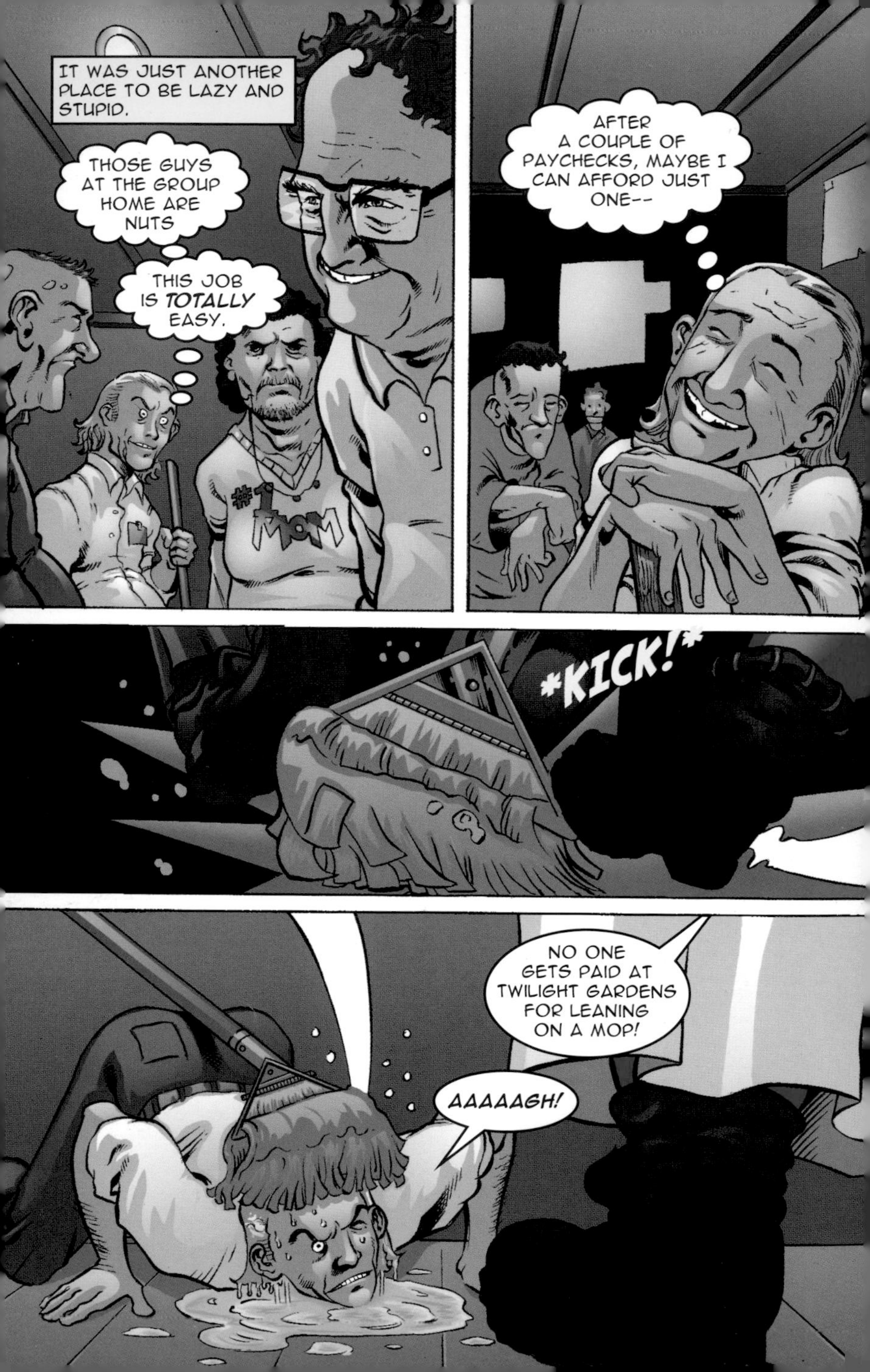
IT WAS JUST ANOTHER PLACE TO BE LAZY AND STUPID.
THOSE GUYS AT THE GROUP HOME ARE NUTS
THIS JOB IS *TOTALLY* EASY.
#1 MOM
AFTER A COUPLE OF PAYCHECKS, MAYBE I CAN AFFORD JUST ONE--
KICK!
NO ONE GETS PAID AT TWILIGHT GARDENS FOR LEANING ON A MOP!
AAAAAGH!

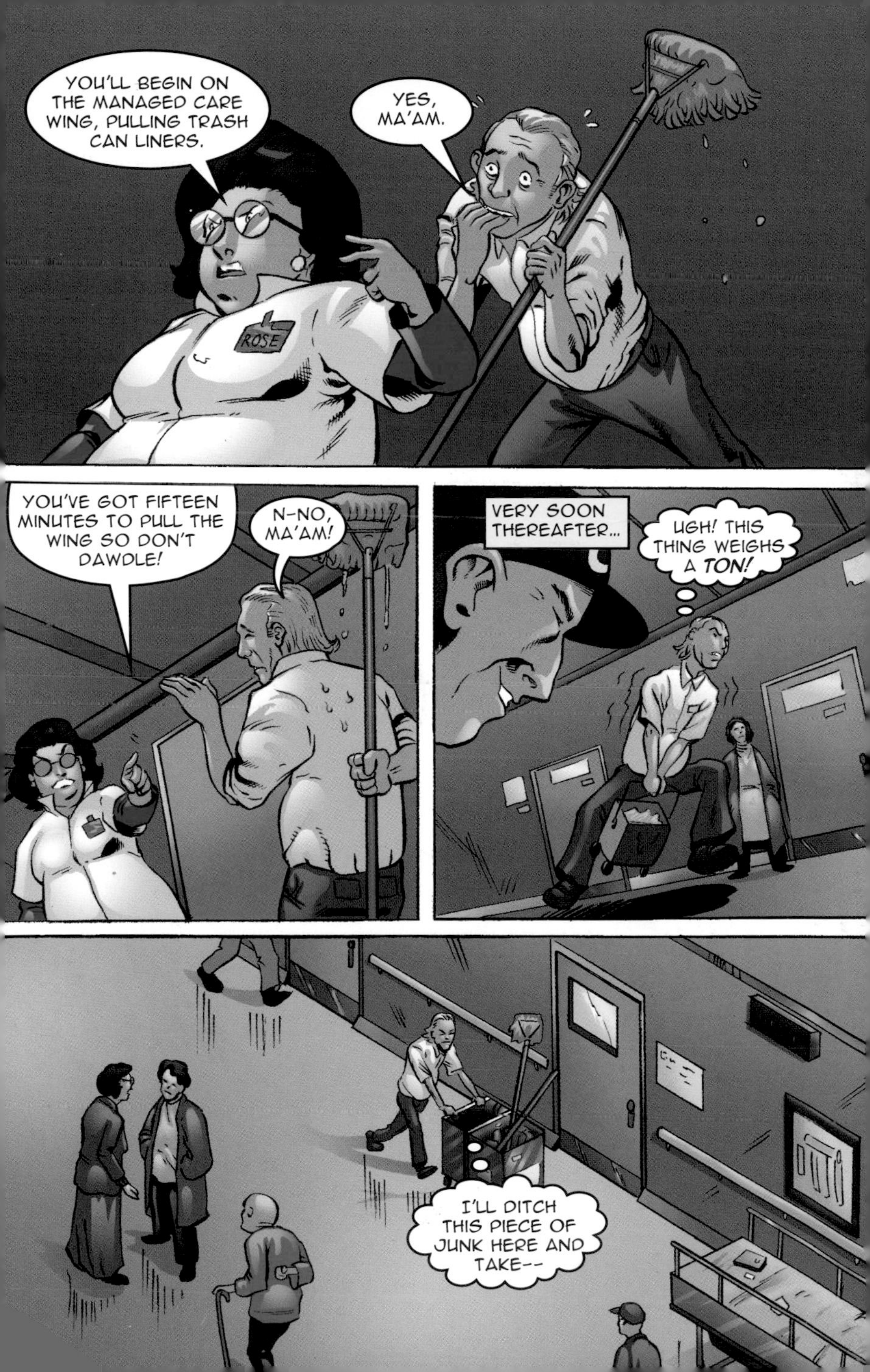
YOU'LL BEGIN ON THE MANAGED CARE WING, PULLING TRASH CAN LINERS.
YES, MA'AM.
ROSE
YOU'VE GOT FIFTEEN MINUTES TO PULL THE WING SO DON'T DAWDLE!
N-NO, MA'AM!
VERY SOON THEREAFTER...
UGH! THIS THING WEIGHS A **TON!**
I'LL DITCH THIS PIECE OF JUNK HERE AND TAKE--

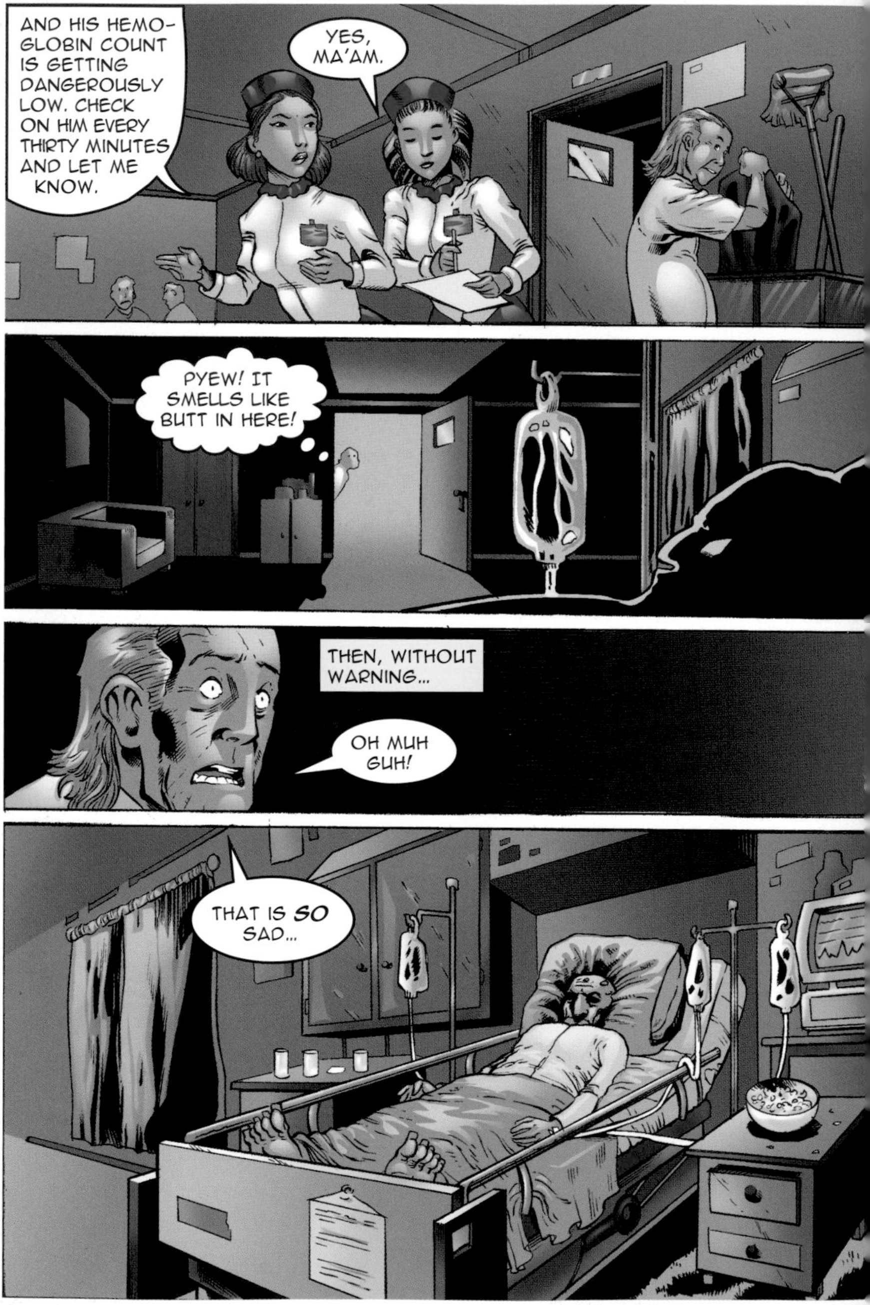
AND HIS HEMO-GLOBIN COUNT IS GETTING DANGEROUSLY LOW. CHECK ON HIM EVERY THIRTY MINUTES AND LET ME KNOW.
YES, MA'AM.
PYEW! IT SMELLS LIKE BUTT IN HERE!
THEN, WITHOUT WARNING...
OH MUH GUH!
THAT IS *SO* SAD...

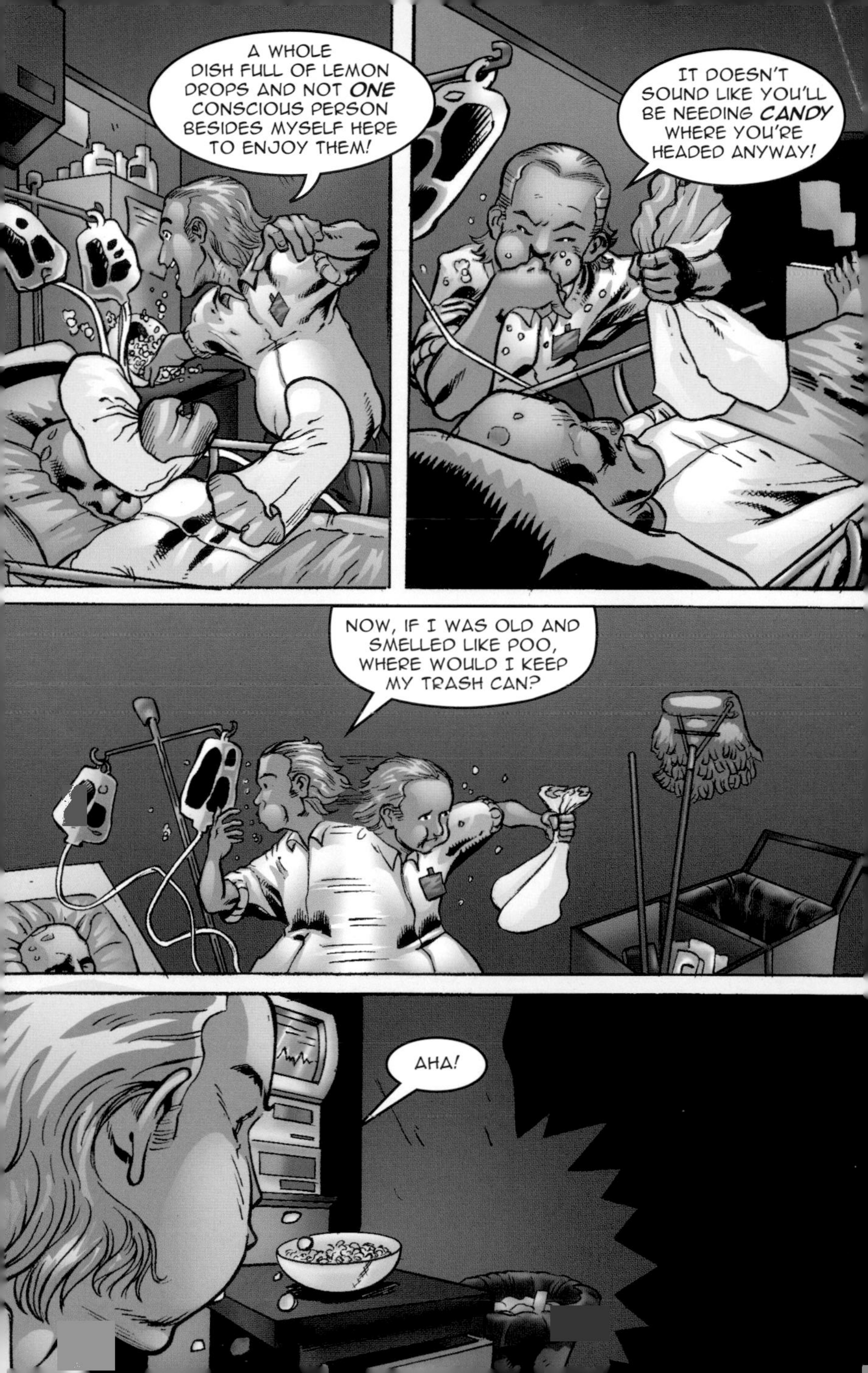
A WHOLE DISH FULL OF LEMON DROPS AND NOT ONE CONSCIOUS PERSON BESIDES MYSELF HERE TO ENJOY THEM!
IT DOESN'T SOUND LIKE YOU'LL BE NEEDING CANDY WHERE YOU'RE HEADED ANYWAY!
NOW, IF I WAS OLD AND SMELLED LIKE POO, WHERE WOULD I KEEP MY TRASH CAN?
AHA!

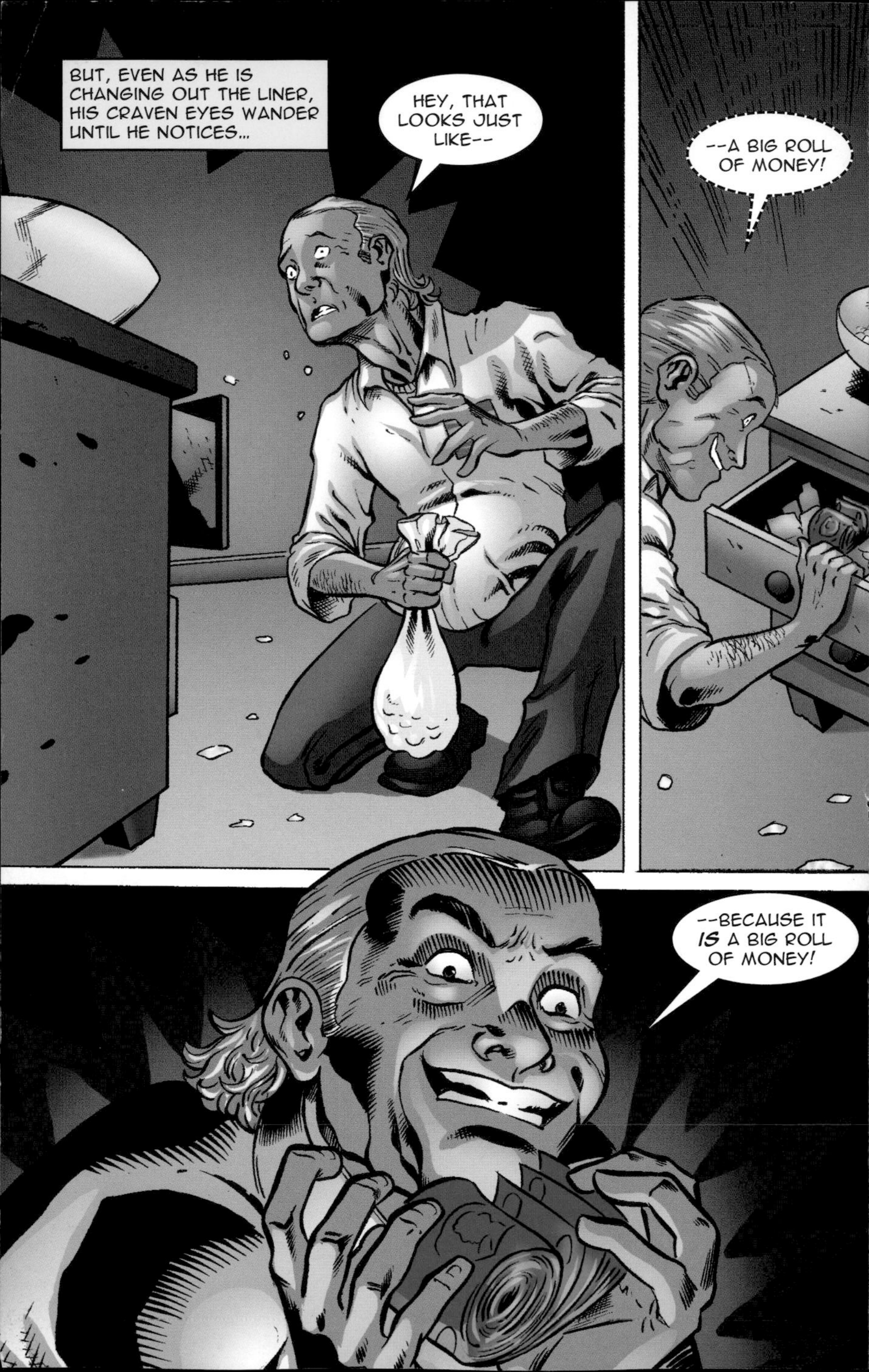
BUT, EVEN AS HE IS CHANGING OUT THE LINER, HIS CRAVEN EYES WANDER UNTIL HE NOTICES...
HEY, THAT LOOKS JUST LIKE--
--A BIG ROLL OF MONEY!
--BECAUSE IT IS A BIG ROLL OF MONEY!

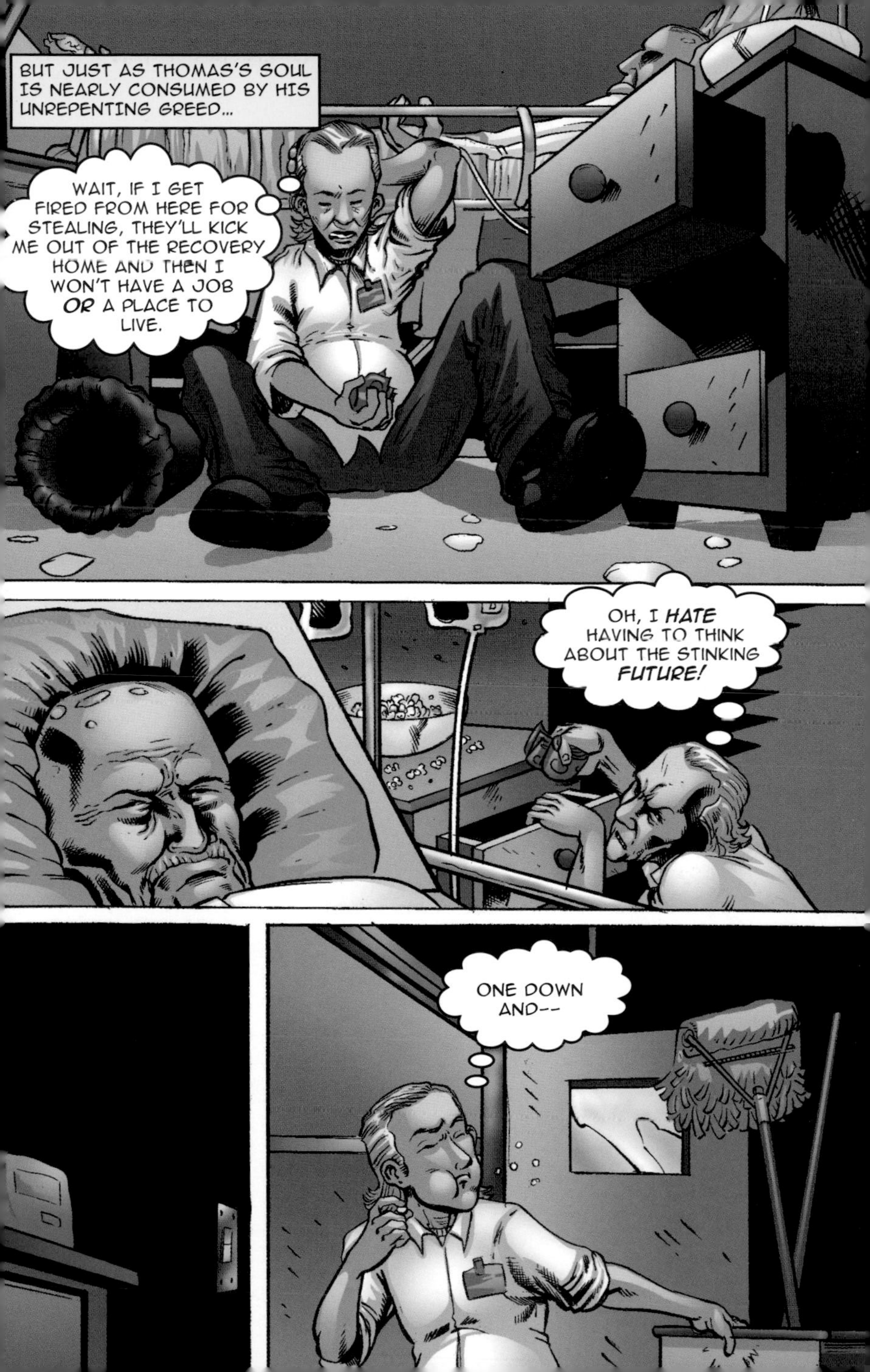

BUT JUST AS THOMAS'S SOUL IS NEARLY CONSUMED BY HIS UNREPENTING GREED...
WAIT, IF I GET FIRED FROM HERE FOR STEALING, THEY'LL KICK ME OUT OF THE RECOVERY HOME AND THEN I WON'T HAVE A JOB **OR** A PLACE TO LIVE.
OH, I **HATE** HAVING TO THINK ABOUT THE STINKING **FUTURE!**
ONE DOWN AND--

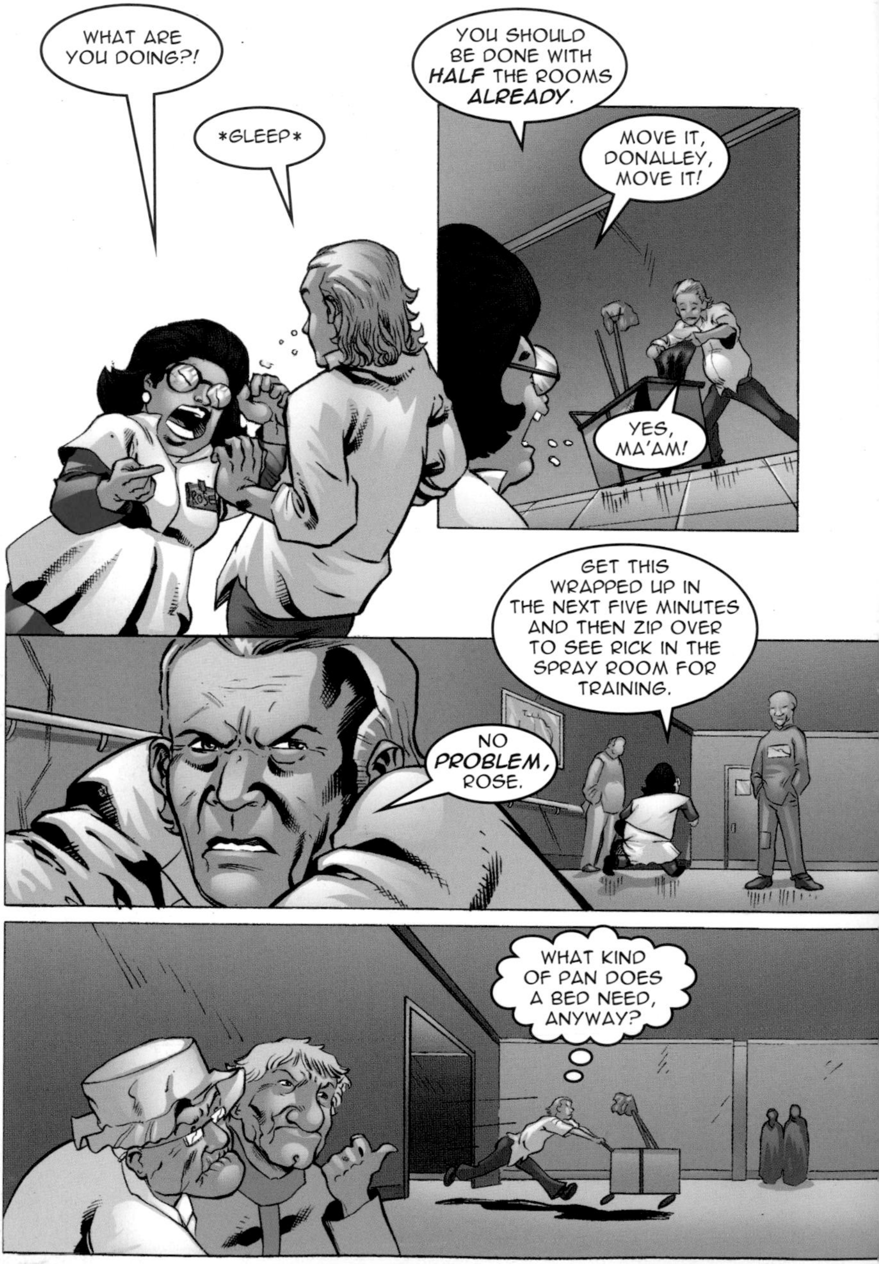
WHAT ARE YOU DOING?!
GLEEP
YOU SHOULD BE DONE WITH HALF THE ROOMS ALREADY.
MOVE IT, DONALLEY, MOVE IT!
YES, MA'AM!
GET THIS WRAPPED UP IN THE NEXT FIVE MINUTES AND THEN ZIP OVER TO SEE RICK IN THE SPRAY ROOM FOR TRAINING.
NO PROBLEM, ROSE.
WHAT KIND OF PAN DOES A BED NEED, ANYWAY?

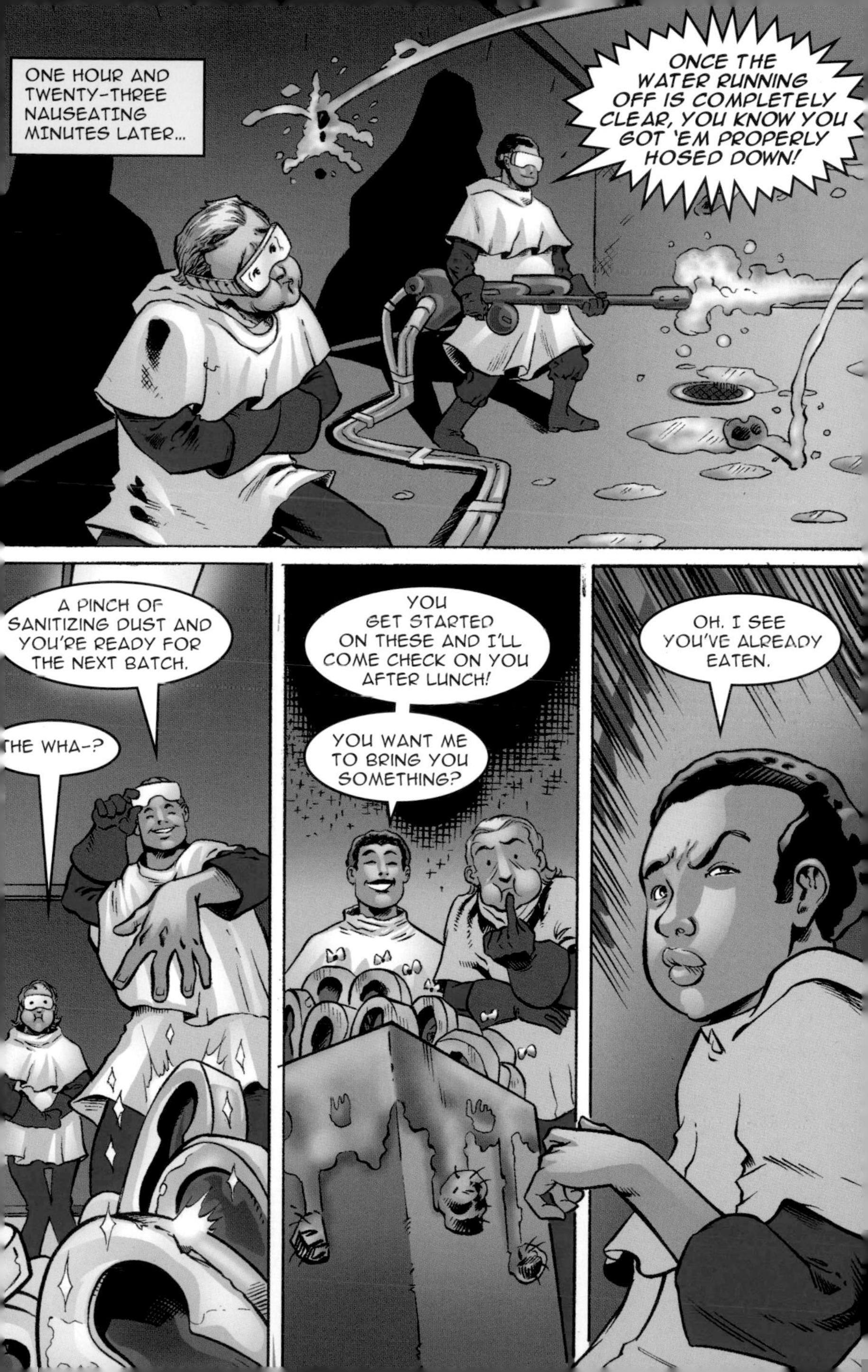
ONE HOUR AND TWENTY-THREE NAUSEATING MINUTES LATER...
ONCE THE WATER RUNNING OFF IS COMPLETELY CLEAR, YOU KNOW YOU GOT 'EM PROPERLY HOSED DOWN!
A PINCH OF SANITIZING DUST AND YOU'RE READY FOR THE NEXT BATCH.
THE WHA-?
YOU GET STARTED ON THESE AND I'LL COME CHECK ON YOU AFTER LUNCH!
YOU WANT ME TO BRING YOU SOMETHING?
OH. I SEE YOU'VE ALREADY EATEN.

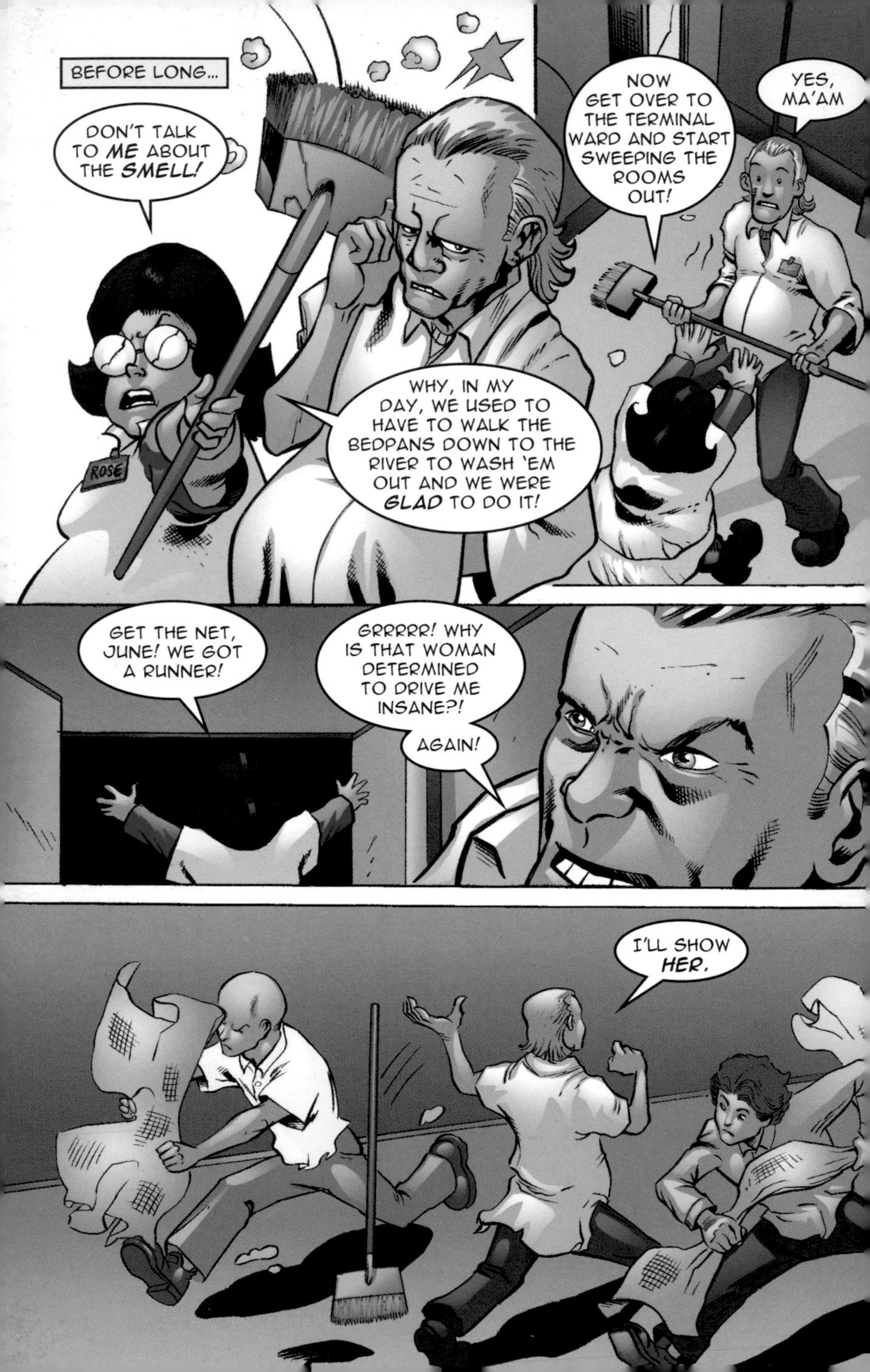
BEFORE LONG...
DON'T TALK TO ME ABOUT THE SMELL!
WHY, IN MY DAY, WE USED TO HAVE TO WALK THE BEDPANS DOWN TO THE RIVER TO WASH 'EM OUT AND WE WERE GLAD TO DO IT!
NOW GET OVER TO THE TERMINAL WARD AND START SWEEPING THE ROOMS OUT!
YES, MA'AM
GET THE NET, JUNE! WE GOT A RUNNER!
GRRRRR! WHY IS THAT WOMAN DETERMINED TO DRIVE ME INSANE?!
AGAIN!
I'LL SHOW HER.

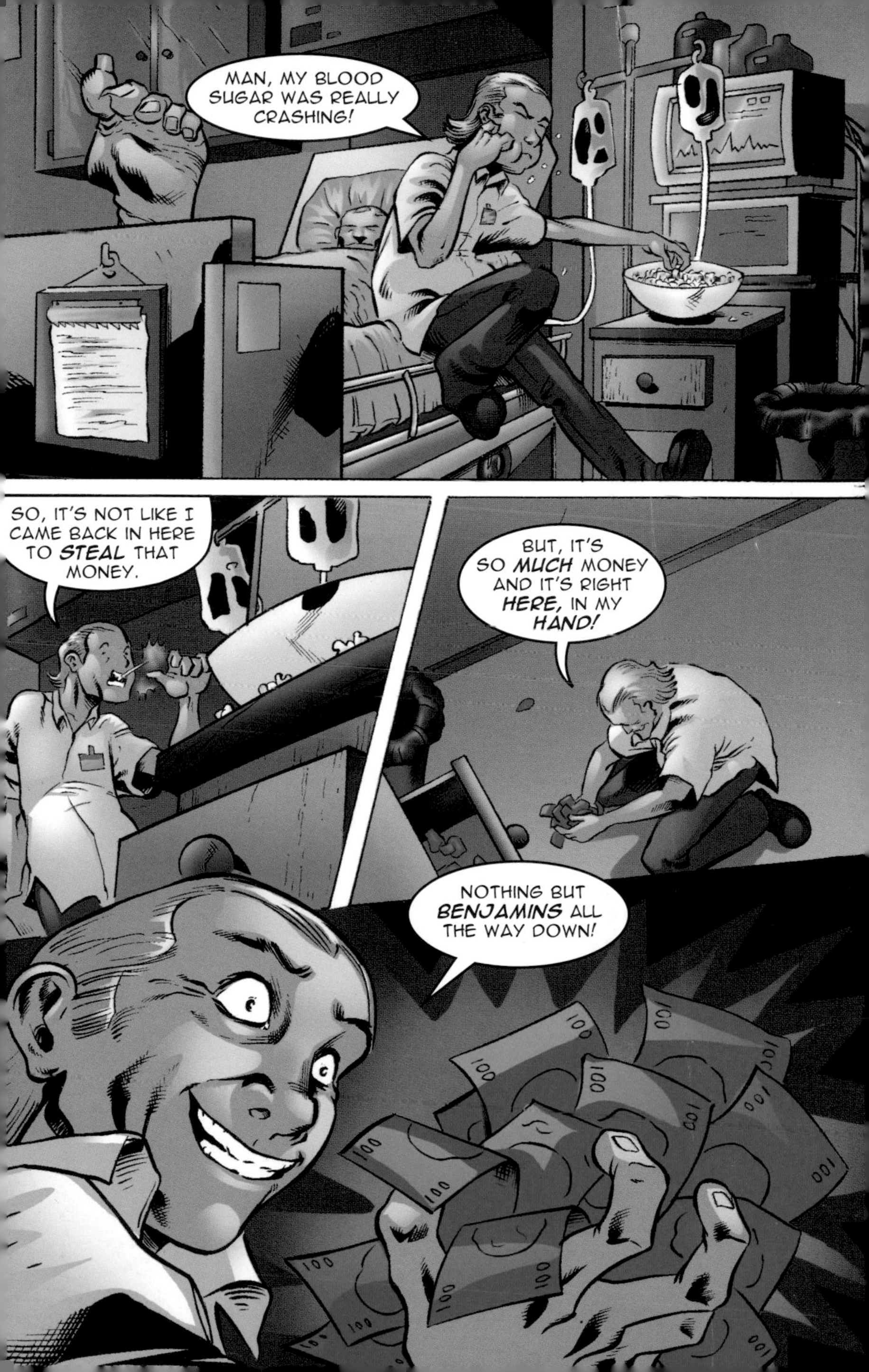
MAN, MY BLOOD SUGAR WAS REALLY CRASHING!
SO, IT'S NOT LIKE I CAME BACK IN HERE TO STEAL THAT MONEY.
BUT, IT'S SO MUCH MONEY AND IT'S RIGHT HERE, IN MY HAND!
NOTHING BUT BENJAMINS ALL THE WAY DOWN!
100

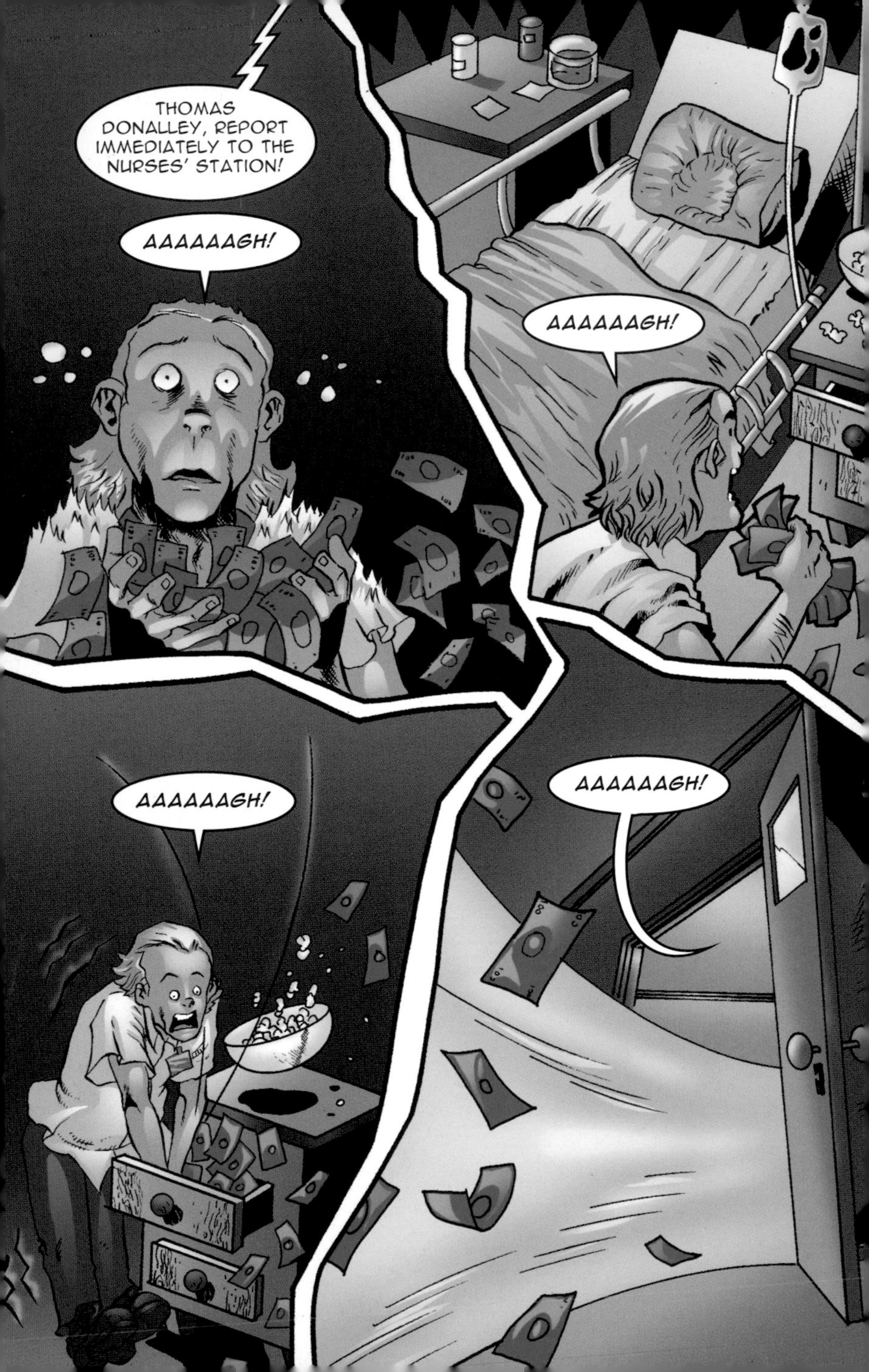
THOMAS DONALLEY, REPORT IMMEDIATELY TO THE NURSES' STATION!
AAAAAAGH!
AAAAAAGH!
AAAAAAGH!
AAAAAAGH!

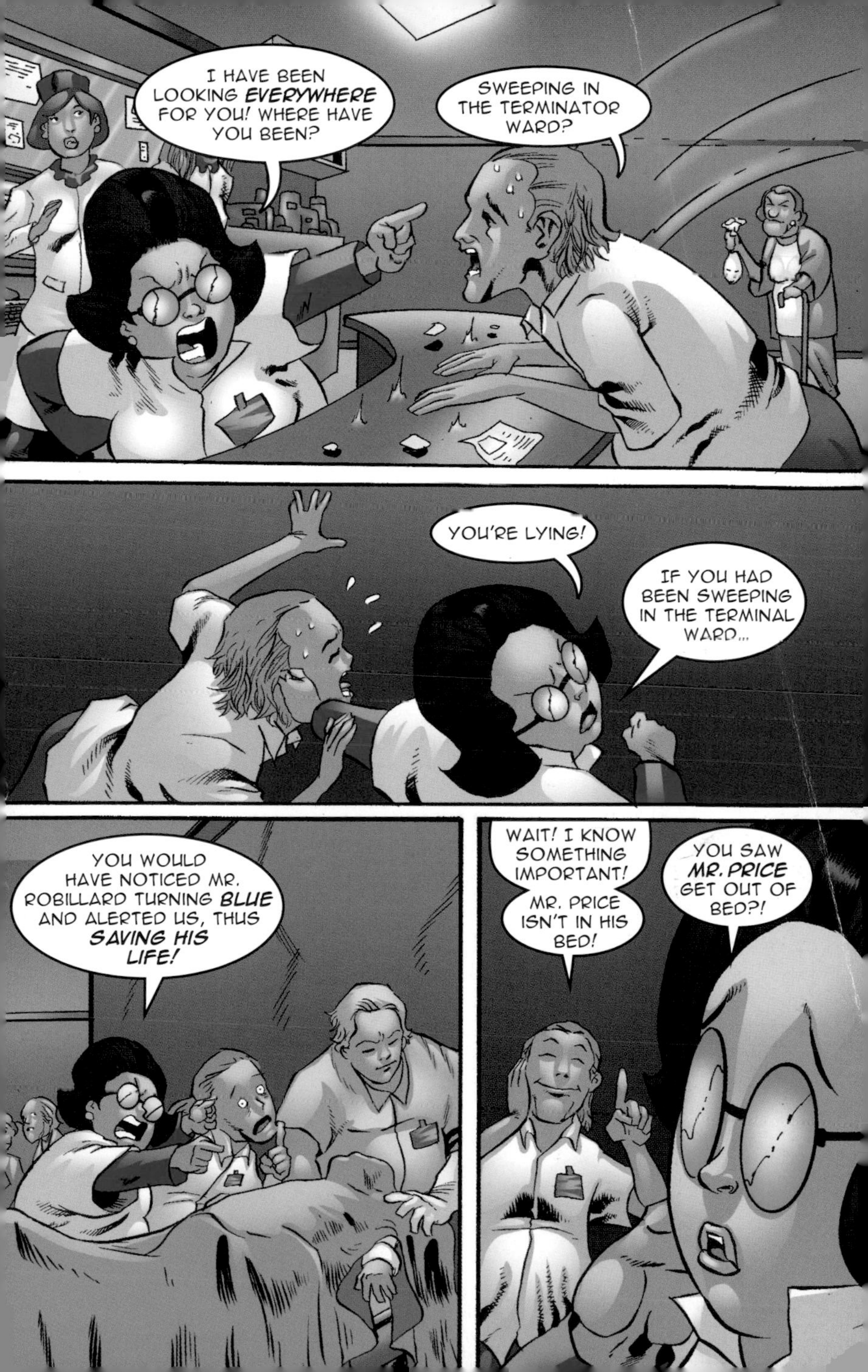
I HAVE BEEN LOOKING EVERYWHERE FOR YOU! WHERE HAVE YOU BEEN?
SWEEPING IN THE TERMINATOR WARD?
YOU'RE LYING!
IF YOU HAD BEEN SWEEPING IN THE TERMINAL WARD...
YOU WOULD HAVE NOTICED MR. ROBILLARD TURNING BLUE AND ALERTED US, THUS SAVING HIS LIFE!
WAIT! I KNOW SOMETHING IMPORTANT!
MR. PRICE ISN'T IN HIS BED!
YOU SAW MR. PRICE GET OUT OF BED?!

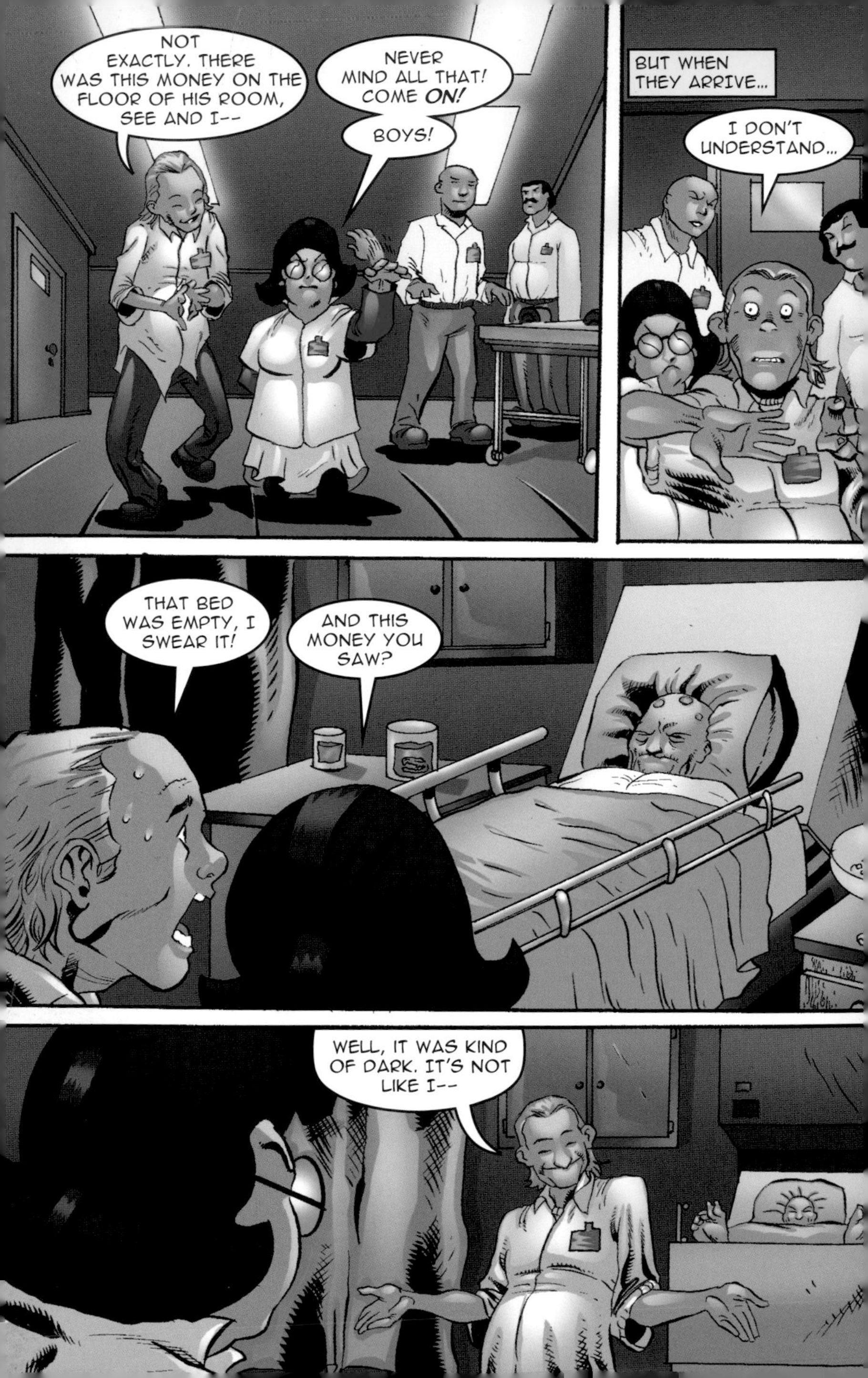
NOT EXACTLY. THERE WAS THIS MONEY ON THE FLOOR OF HIS ROOM, SEE AND I--
NEVER MIND ALL THAT! COME ON!
BOYS!
BUT WHEN THEY ARRIVE...
I DON'T UNDERSTAND...
THAT BED WAS EMPTY, I SWEAR IT!
AND THIS MONEY YOU SAW?
WELL, IT WAS KIND OF DARK. IT'S NOT LIKE I--

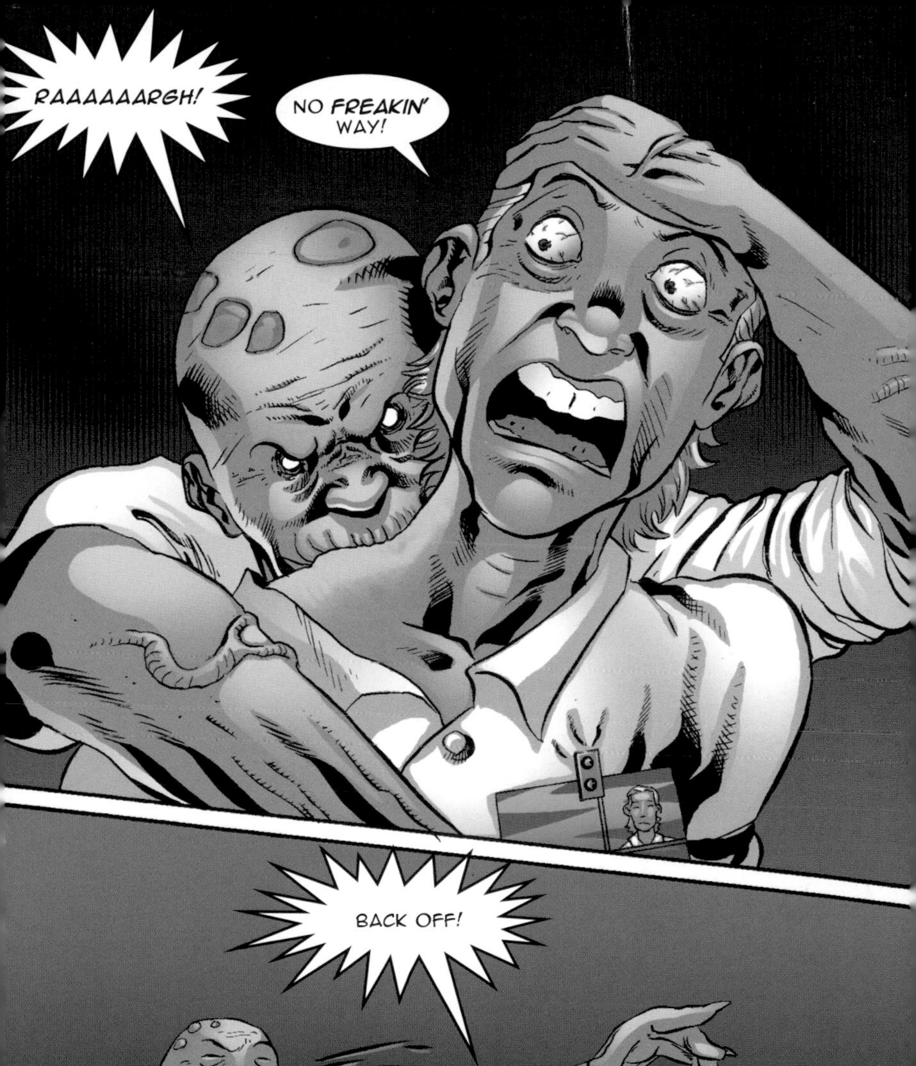
RAAAAAAARGH!
NO FREAKIN' WAY!

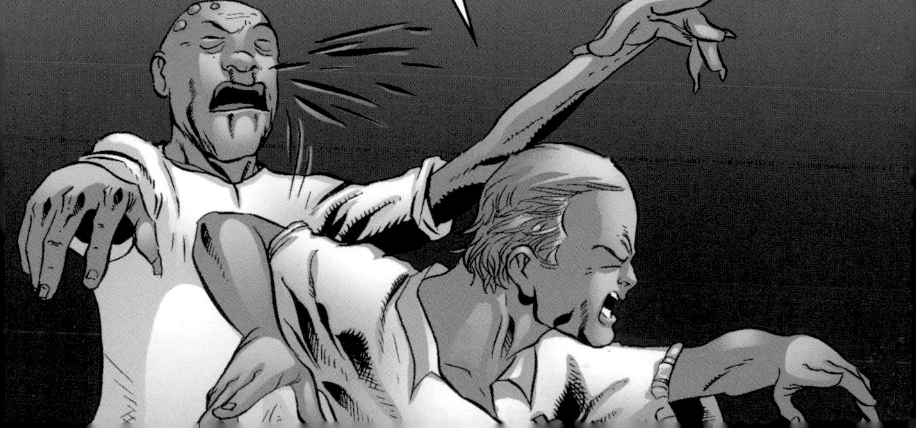
BACK OFF!

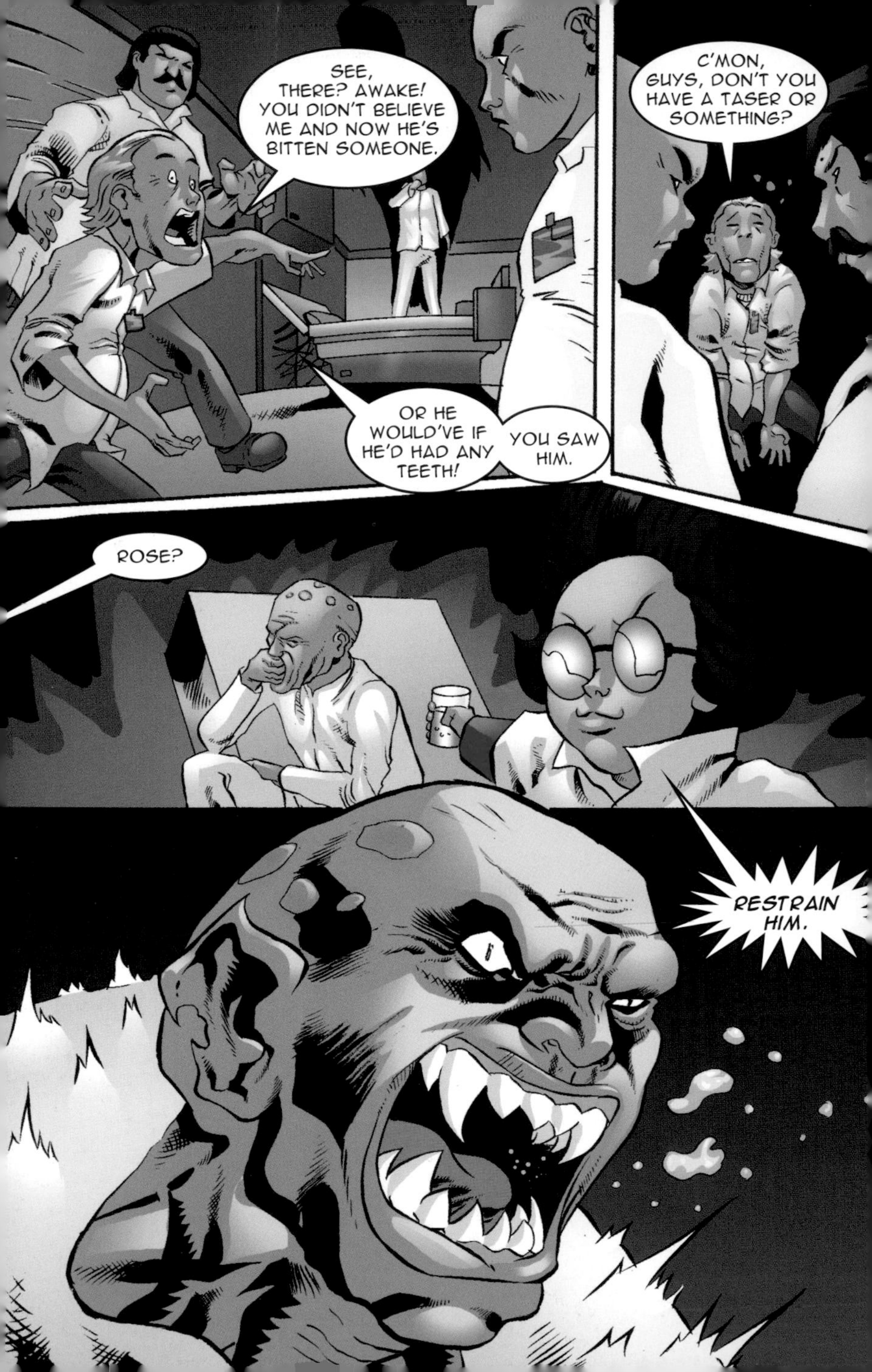
SEE, THERE? AWAKE! YOU DIDN'T BELIEVE ME AND NOW HE'S BITTEN SOMEONE.
OR HE WOULD'VE IF HE'D HAD ANY TEETH!
YOU SAW HIM.
C'MON, GUYS, DON'T YOU HAVE A TASER OR SOMETHING?
ROSE?
RESTRAIN HIM.

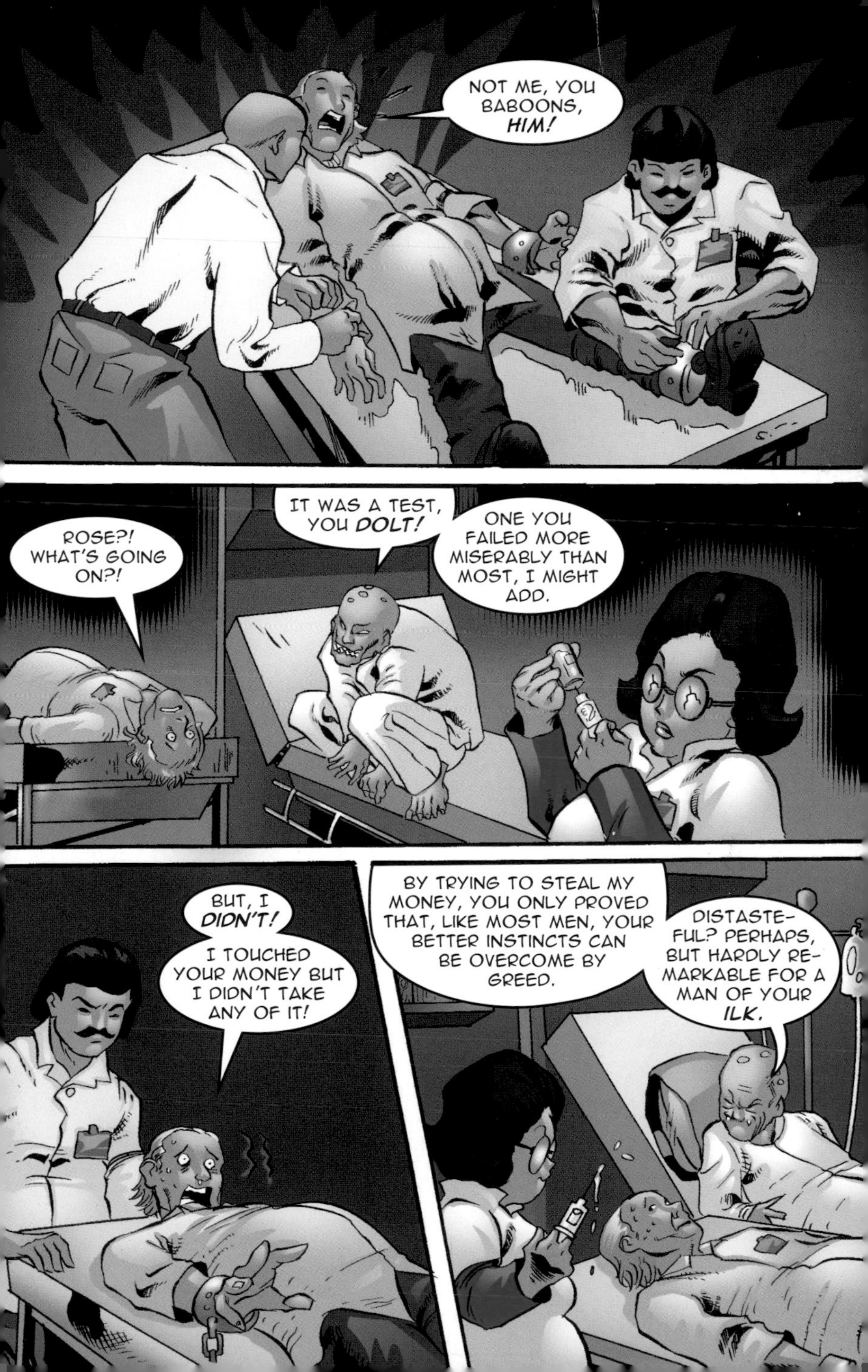
NOT ME, YOU BABOONS, HIM!
ROSE?! WHAT'S GOING ON?!
IT WAS A TEST, YOU DOLT!
ONE YOU FAILED MORE MISERABLY THAN MOST, I MIGHT ADD.
BUT, I DIDN'T!
I TOUCHED YOUR MONEY BUT I DIDN'T TAKE ANY OF IT!
BY TRYING TO STEAL MY MONEY, YOU ONLY PROVED THAT, LIKE MOST MEN, YOUR BETTER INSTINCTS CAN BE OVERCOME BY GREED.
DISTASTE-FUL? PERHAPS, BUT HARDLY RE-MARKABLE FOR A MAN OF YOUR ILK.

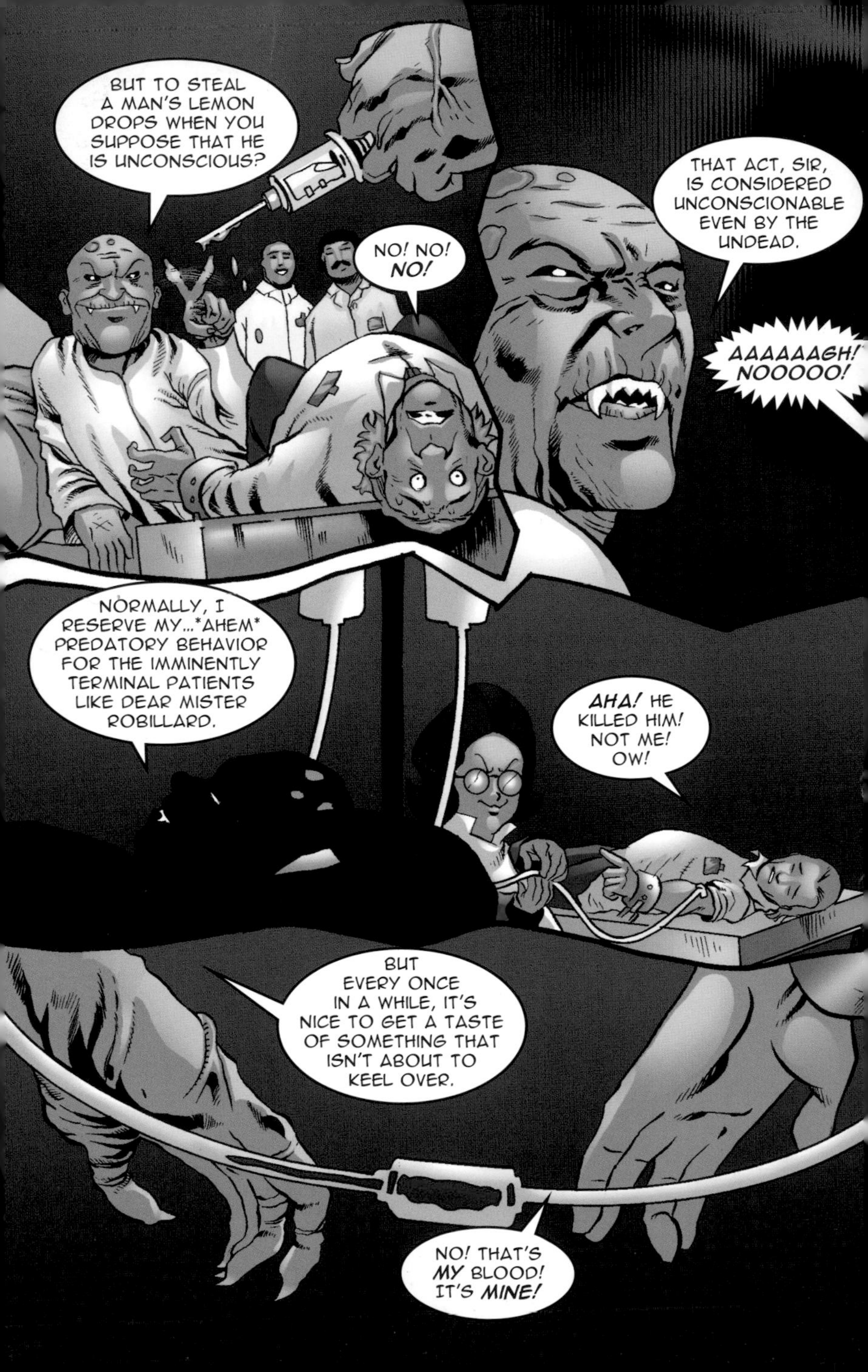
BUT TO STEAL A MAN'S LEMON DROPS WHEN YOU SUPPOSE THAT HE IS UNCONSCIOUS?
NO! NO! NO!
THAT ACT, SIR, IS CONSIDERED UNCONSCIONABLE EVEN BY THE UNDEAD.
AAAAAAGH! NOOOOO!
NORMALLY, I RESERVE MY...*AHEM* PREDATORY BEHAVIOR FOR THE IMMINENTLY TERMINAL PATIENTS LIKE DEAR MISTER ROBILLARD.
AHA! HE KILLED HIM! NOT ME! OW!
BUT EVERY ONCE IN A WHILE, IT'S NICE TO GET A TASTE OF SOMETHING THAT ISN'T ABOUT TO KEEL OVER.
NO! THAT'S MY BLOOD! IT'S MINE!

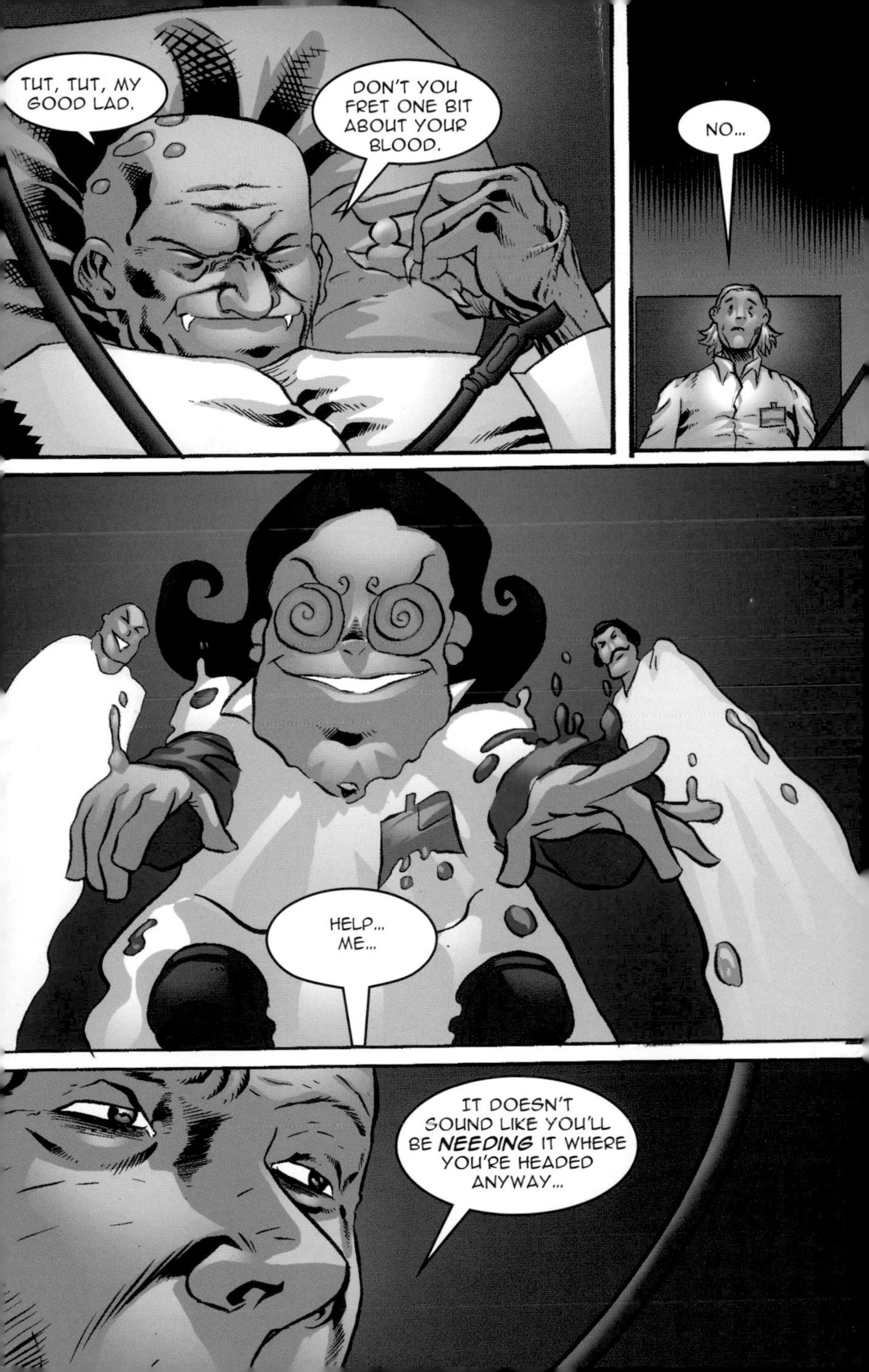
TUT, TUT, MY GOOD LAD.
DON'T YOU FRET ONE BIT ABOUT YOUR BLOOD.
NO...
HELP... ME...
IT DOESN'T SOUND LIKE YOU'LL BE NEEDING IT WHERE YOU'RE HEADED ANYWAY...

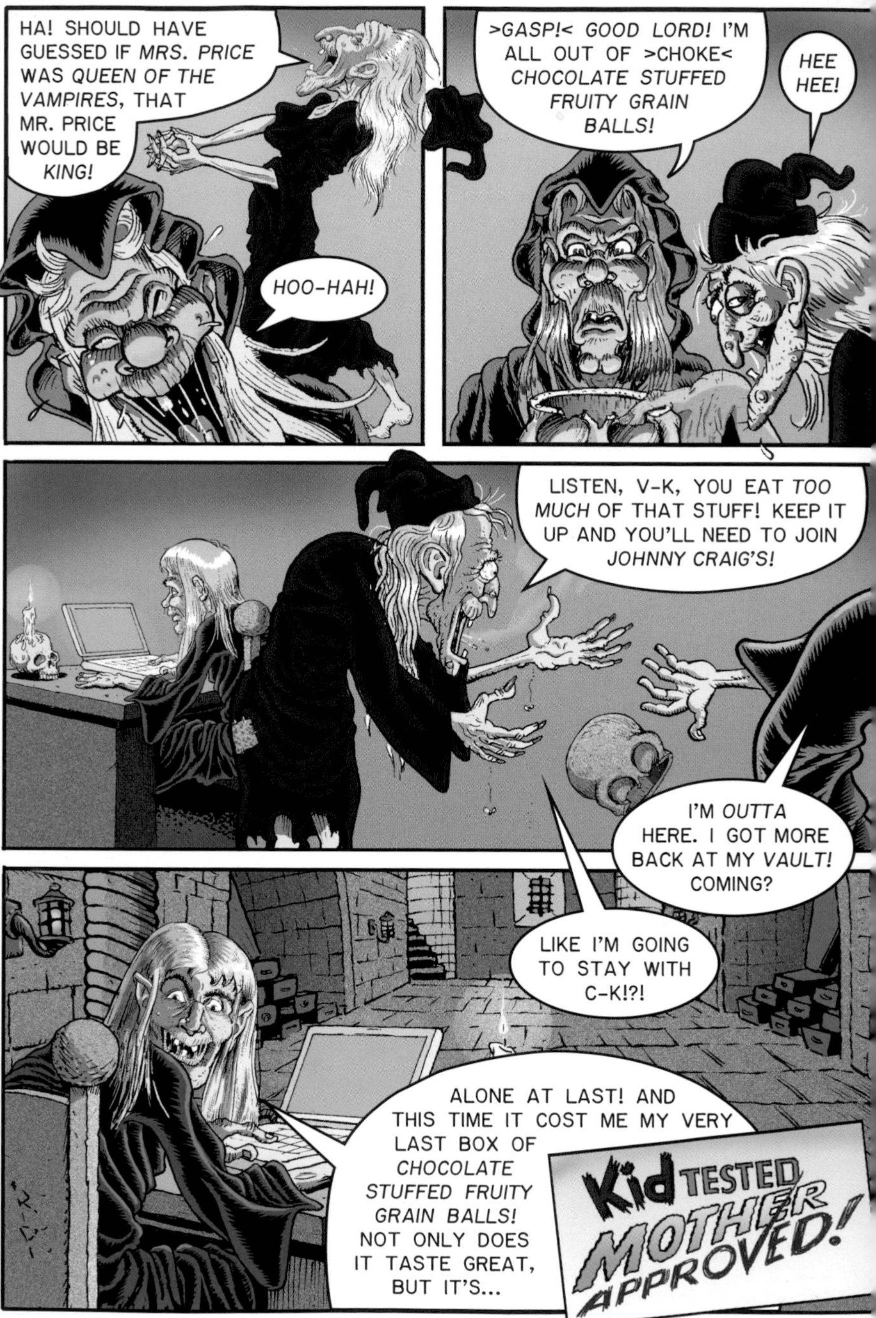
HA! SHOULD HAVE GUESSED IF MRS. PRICE WAS QUEEN OF THE VAMPIRES, THAT MR. PRICE WOULD BE KING!
HOO-HAH!
>GASP!< GOOD LORD! I'M ALL OUT OF >CHOKE< CHOCOLATE STUFFED FRUITY GRAIN BALLS!
HEE HEE!
LISTEN, V-K, YOU EAT TOO MUCH OF THAT STUFF! KEEP IT UP AND YOU'LL NEED TO JOIN JOHNNY CRAIG'S!
I'M OUTTA HERE. I GOT MORE BACK AT MY VAULT! COMING?
LIKE I'M GOING TO STAY WITH C-K!?!
ALONE AT LAST! AND THIS TIME IT COST ME MY VERY LAST BOX OF CHOCOLATE STUFFED FRUITY GRAIN BALLS! NOT ONLY DOES IT TASTE GREAT, BUT IT'S...
Kid TESTED MOTHER APPROVED!

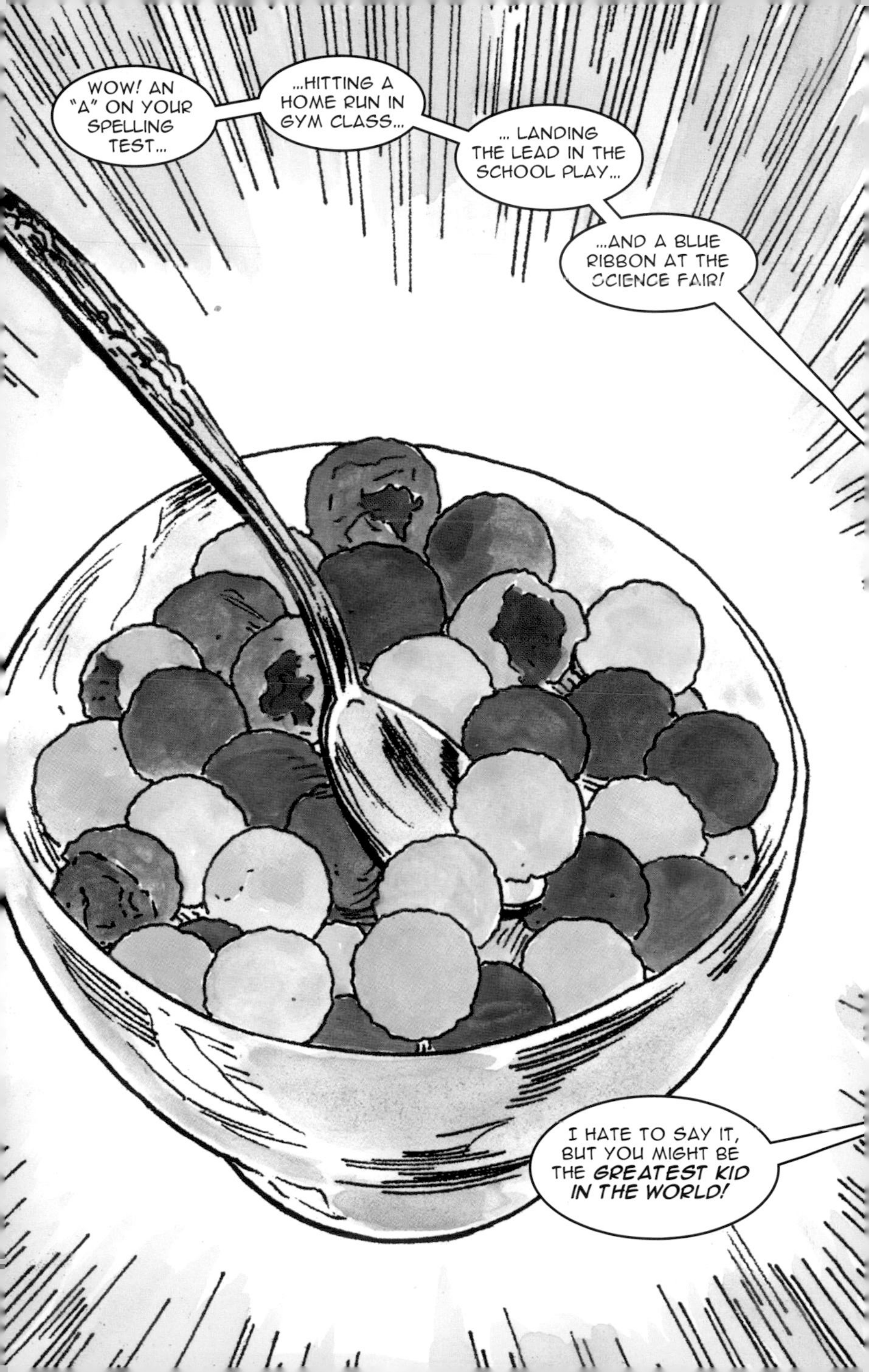

WOW! AN "A" ON YOUR SPELLING TEST...
...HITTING A HOME RUN IN GYM CLASS...
... LANDING THE LEAD IN THE SCHOOL PLAY...
...AND A BLUE RIBBON AT THE SCIENCE FAIR!
I HATE TO SAY IT, BUT YOU MIGHT BE THE *GREATEST KID IN THE WORLD!*

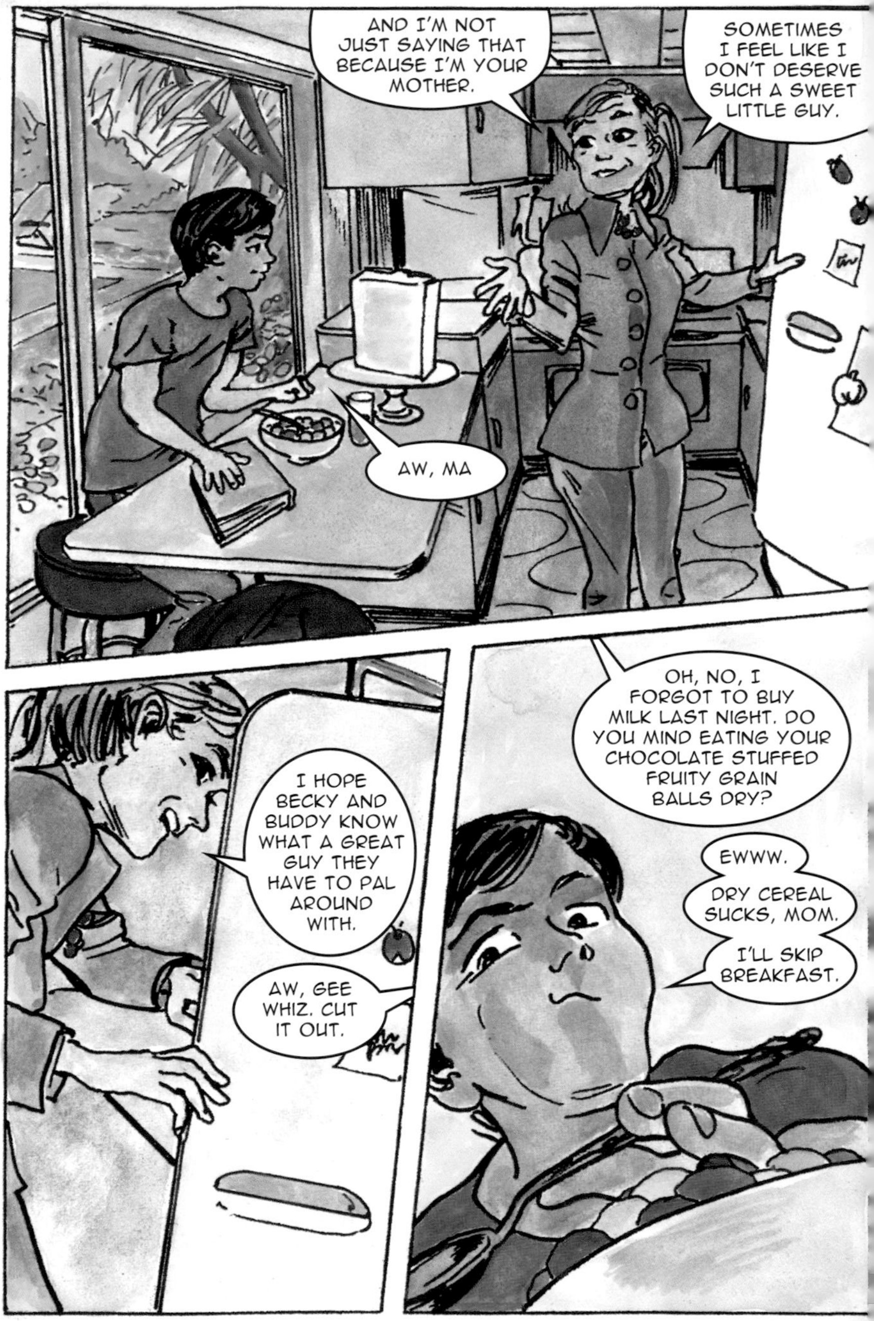
AND I'M NOT JUST SAYING THAT BECAUSE I'M YOUR MOTHER.
SOMETIMES I FEEL LIKE I DON'T DESERVE SUCH A SWEET LITTLE GUY.
AW, MA
I HOPE BECKY AND BUDDY KNOW WHAT A GREAT GUY THEY HAVE TO PAL AROUND WITH.
AW, GEE WHIZ. CUT IT OUT.
OH, NO, I FORGOT TO BUY MILK LAST NIGHT. DO YOU MIND EATING YOUR CHOCOLATE STUFFED FRUITY GRAIN BALLS DRY?
EWWW.
DRY CEREAL SUCKS, MOM.
I'LL SKIP BREAKFAST.

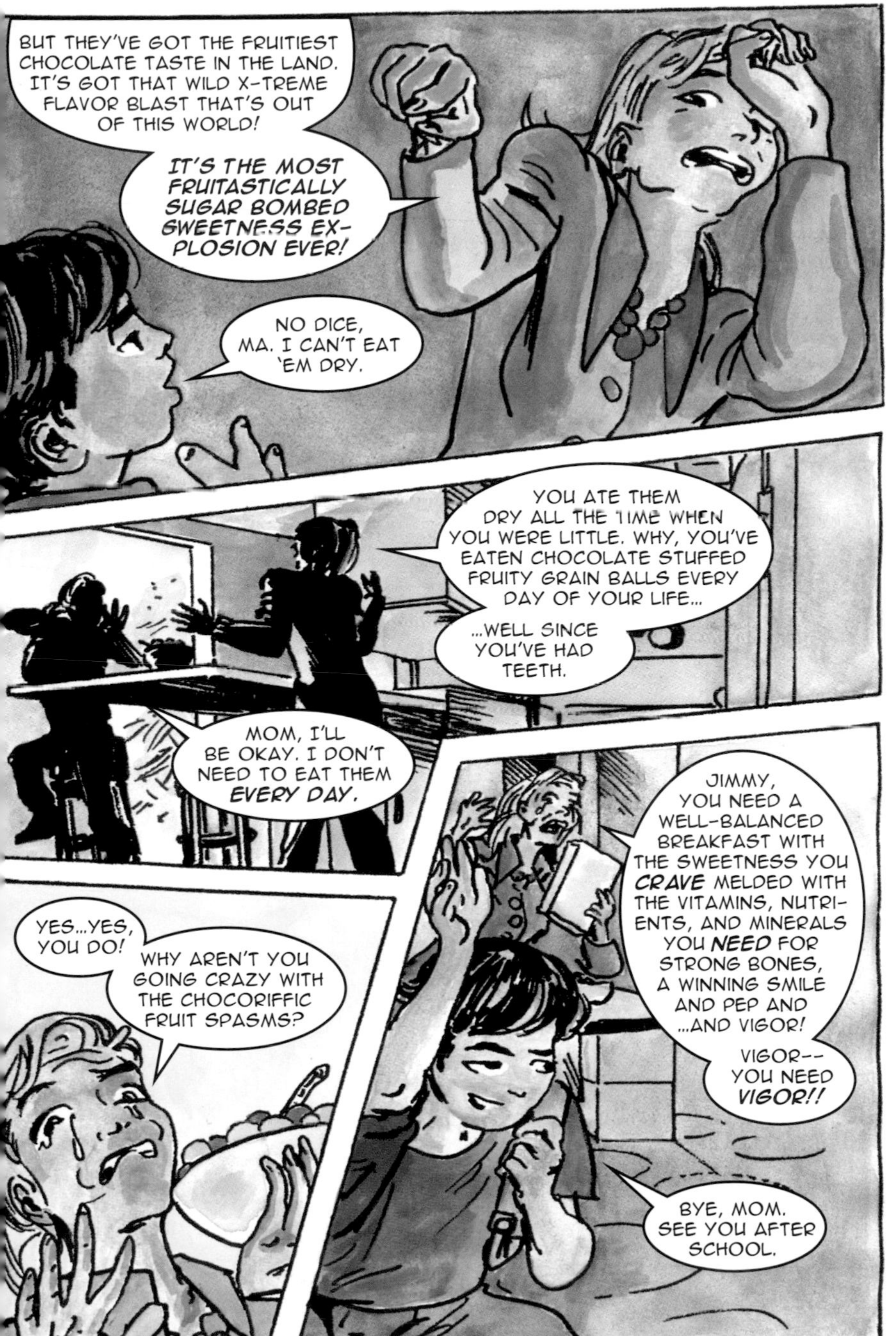
BUT THEY'VE GOT THE FRUITIEST CHOCOLATE TASTE IN THE LAND. IT'S GOT THAT WILD X-TREME FLAVOR BLAST THAT'S OUT OF THIS WORLD!
IT'S THE MOST FRUITASTICALLY SUGAR BOMBED SWEETNESS EXPLOSION EVER!
NO DICE, MA. I CAN'T EAT 'EM DRY.
YOU ATE THEM DRY ALL THE TIME WHEN YOU WERE LITTLE. WHY, YOU'VE EATEN CHOCOLATE STUFFED FRUITY GRAIN BALLS EVERY DAY OF YOUR LIFE...
...WELL SINCE YOU'VE HAD TEETH.
MOM, I'LL BE OKAY. I DON'T NEED TO EAT THEM EVERY DAY.
YES...YES, YOU DO!
WHY AREN'T YOU GOING CRAZY WITH THE CHOCORIFFIC FRUIT SPASMS?
JIMMY, YOU NEED A WELL-BALANCED BREAKFAST WITH THE SWEETNESS YOU CRAVE MELDED WITH THE VITAMINS, NUTRIENTS, AND MINERALS YOU NEED FOR STRONG BONES, A WINNING SMILE AND PEP AND ...AND VIGOR!
VIGOR-- YOU NEED VIGOR!!
BYE, MOM. SEE YOU AFTER SCHOOL.

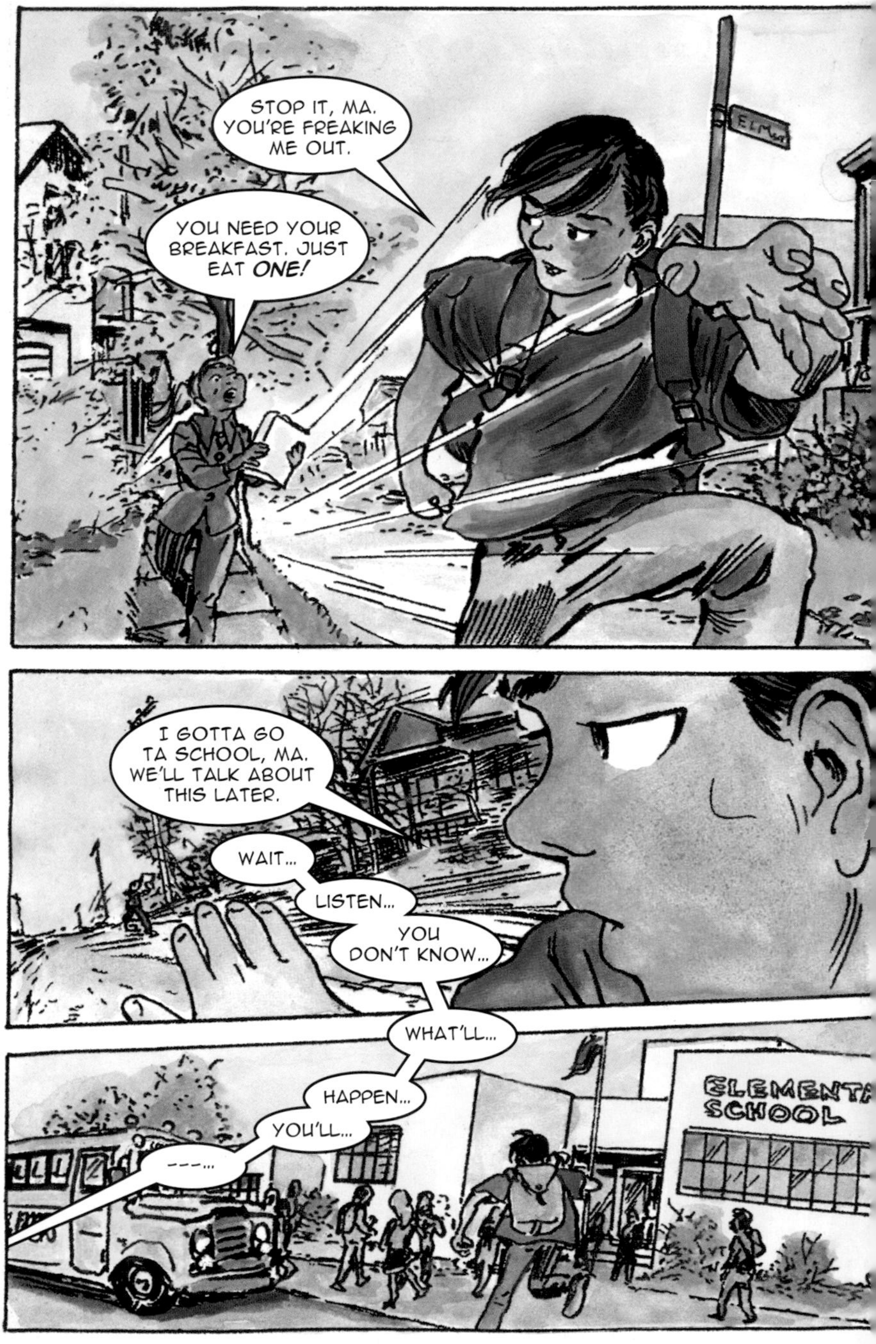
STOP IT, MA. YOU'RE FREAKING ME OUT.
YOU NEED YOUR BREAKFAST. JUST EAT *ONE!*
I GOTTA GO TA SCHOOL, MA. WE'LL TALK ABOUT THIS LATER.
WAIT...
LISTEN...
YOU DON'T KNOW...
WHAT'LL...
HAPPEN...
YOU'LL...
---...
ELEMENT
SCHOOL

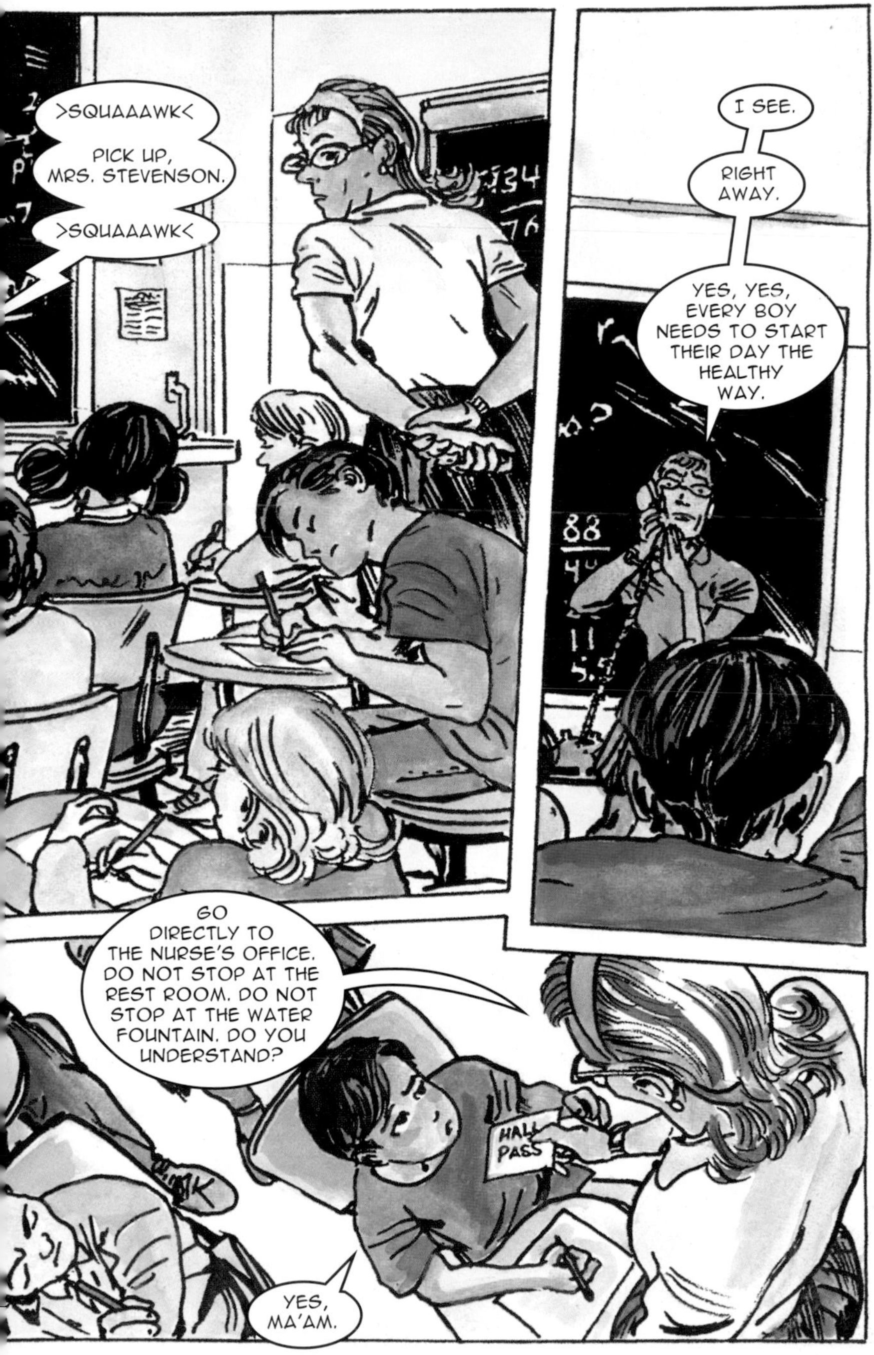
>SQUAAAWK<
PICK UP, MRS. STEVENSON.
>SQUAAAWK<
I SEE.
RIGHT AWAY.
YES, YES, EVERY BOY NEEDS TO START THEIR DAY THE HEALTHY WAY.
GO DIRECTLY TO THE NURSE'S OFFICE. DO NOT STOP AT THE REST ROOM. DO NOT STOP AT THE WATER FOUNTAIN. DO YOU UNDERSTAND?
HALL PASS
YES, MA'AM.

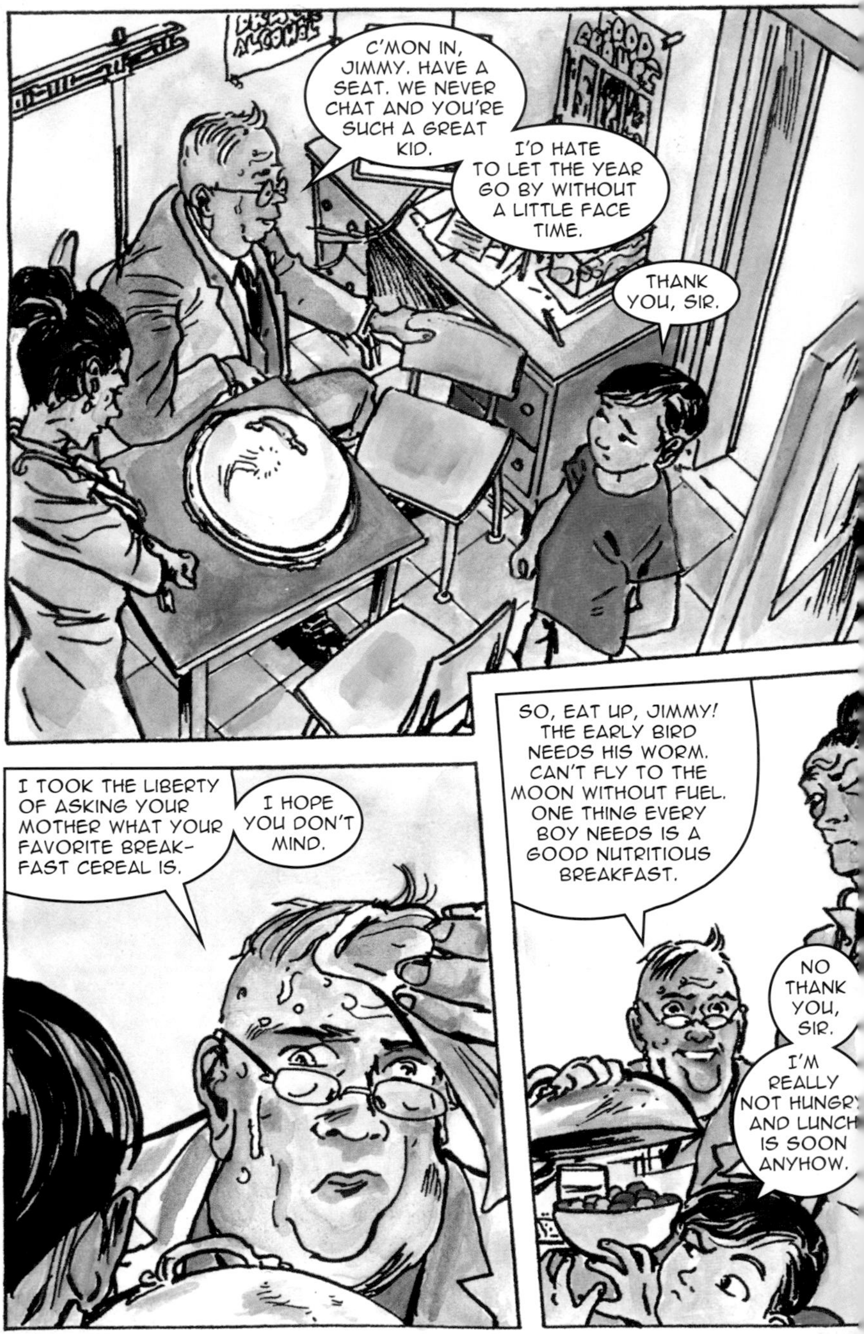
C'MON IN, JIMMY. HAVE A SEAT. WE NEVER CHAT AND YOU'RE SUCH A GREAT KID.
I'D HATE TO LET THE YEAR GO BY WITHOUT A LITTLE FACE TIME.
THANK YOU, SIR.
I TOOK THE LIBERTY OF ASKING YOUR MOTHER WHAT YOUR FAVORITE BREAK-FAST CEREAL IS.
I HOPE YOU DON'T MIND.
SO, EAT UP, JIMMY! THE EARLY BIRD NEEDS HIS WORM. CAN'T FLY TO THE MOON WITHOUT FUEL. ONE THING EVERY BOY NEEDS IS A GOOD NUTRITIOUS BREAKFAST.
NO THANK YOU, SIR.
I'M REALLY NOT HUNGRY AND LUNCH IS SOON ANYHOW.

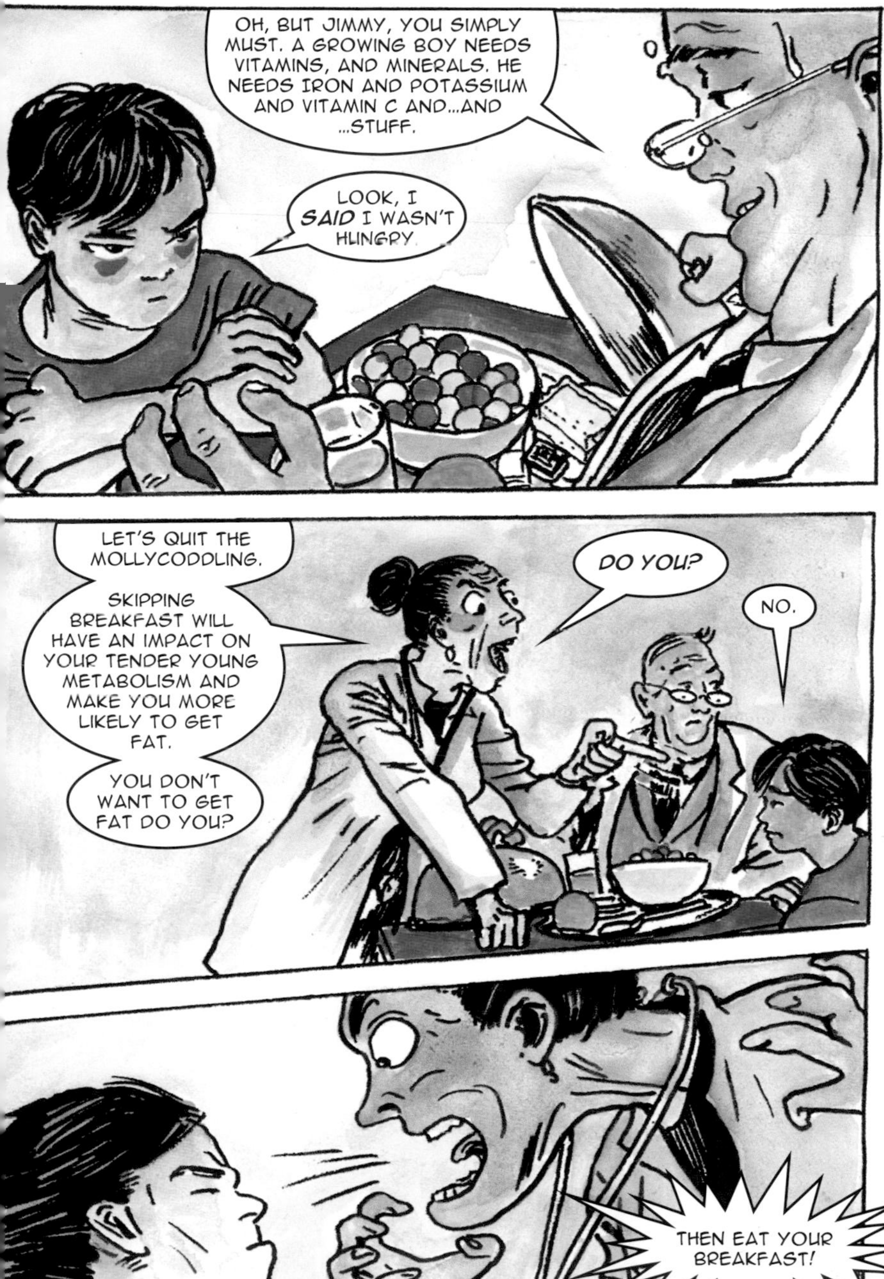
OH, BUT JIMMY, YOU SIMPLY MUST. A GROWING BOY NEEDS VITAMINS, AND MINERALS. HE NEEDS IRON AND POTASSIUM AND VITAMIN C AND...AND ...STUFF.
LOOK, I *SAID* I WASN'T HUNGRY.
LET'S QUIT THE MOLLYCODDLING.
SKIPPING BREAKFAST WILL HAVE AN IMPACT ON YOUR TENDER YOUNG METABOLISM AND MAKE YOU MORE LIKELY TO GET FAT.
YOU DON'T WANT TO GET FAT DO YOU?
DO YOU?
NO.
THEN EAT YOUR BREAKFAST!

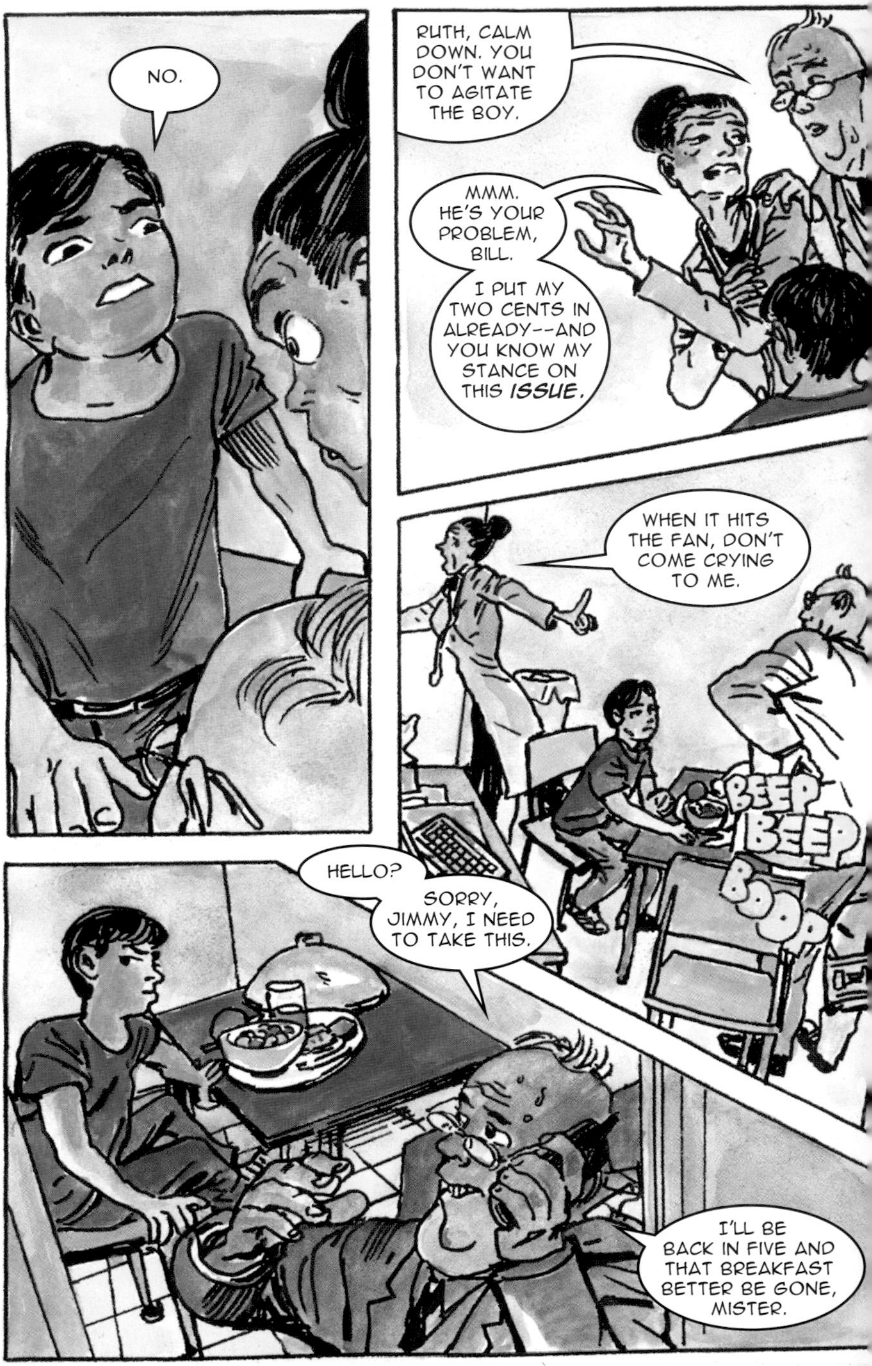
NO.
RUTH, CALM DOWN. YOU DON'T WANT TO AGITATE THE BOY.
MMM. HE'S YOUR PROBLEM, BILL.
I PUT MY TWO CENTS IN ALREADY--AND YOU KNOW MY STANCE ON THIS *ISSUE*.
WHEN IT HITS THE FAN, DON'T COME CRYING TO ME.
BEEP
BEEP
BOOP
HELLO?
SORRY, JIMMY, I NEED TO TAKE THIS.
I'LL BE BACK IN FIVE AND THAT BREAKFAST BETTER BE GONE, MISTER.

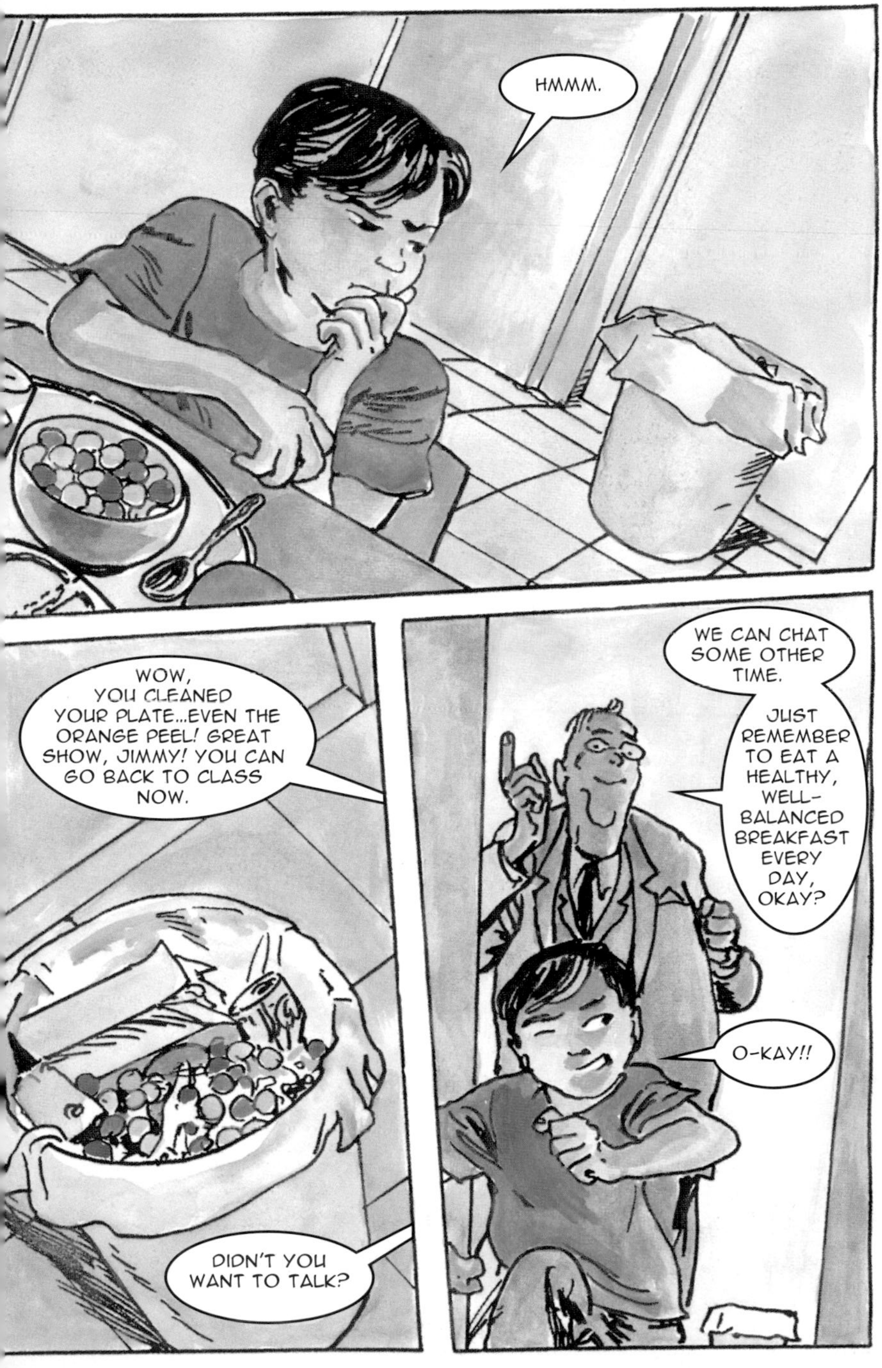
HMMM.
WOW, YOU CLEANED YOUR PLATE...EVEN THE ORANGE PEEL! GREAT SHOW, JIMMY! YOU CAN GO BACK TO CLASS NOW.
DIDN'T YOU WANT TO TALK?
WE CAN CHAT SOME OTHER TIME.
JUST REMEMBER TO EAT A HEALTHY, WELL-BALANCED BREAKFAST EVERY DAY, OKAY?
O-KAY!!

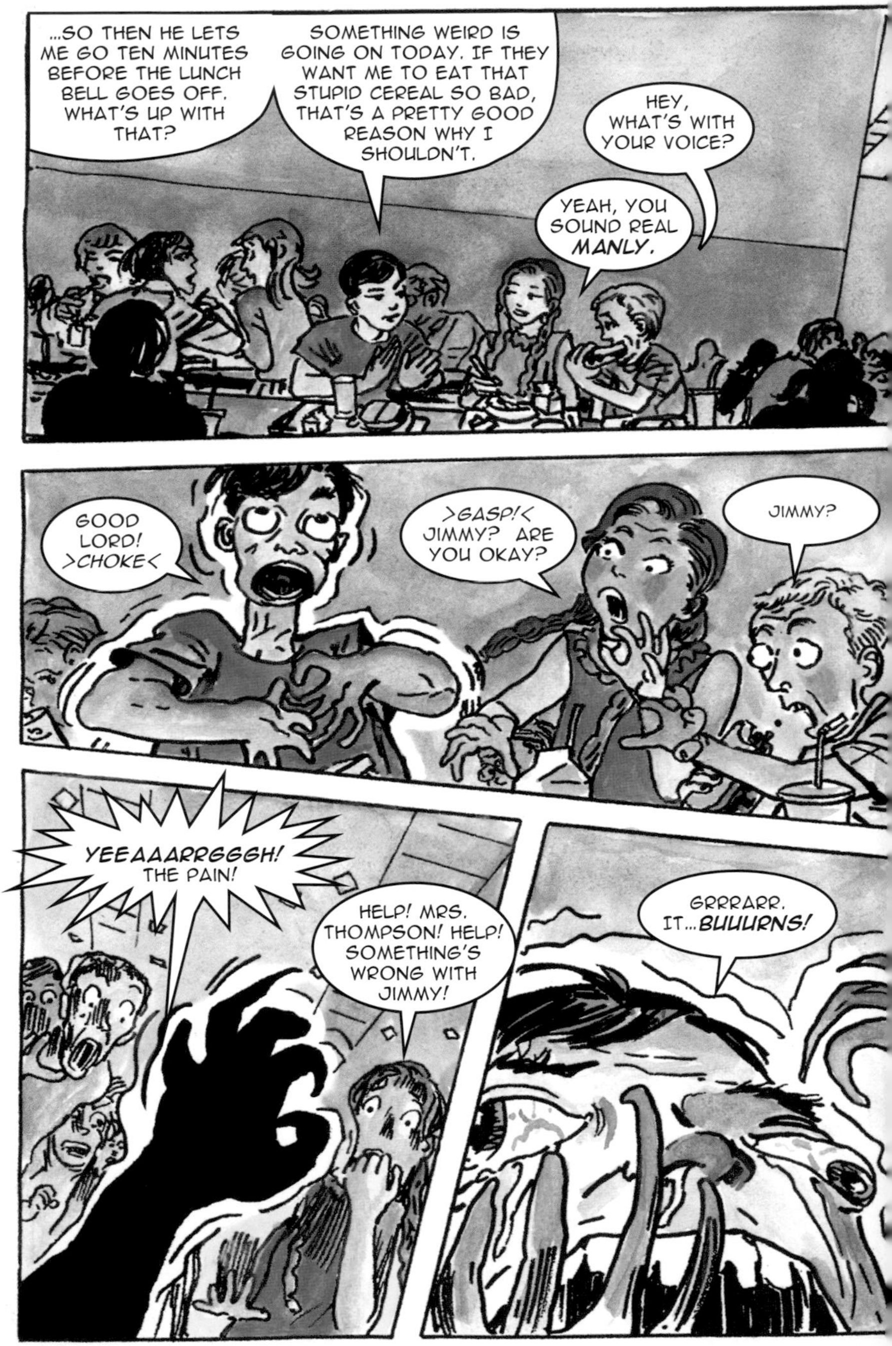
...SO THEN HE LETS ME GO TEN MINUTES BEFORE THE LUNCH BELL GOES OFF. WHAT'S UP WITH THAT?
SOMETHING WEIRD IS GOING ON TODAY. IF THEY WANT ME TO EAT THAT STUPID CEREAL SO BAD, THAT'S A PRETTY GOOD REASON WHY I SHOULDN'T.
HEY, WHAT'S WITH YOUR VOICE?
YEAH, YOU SOUND REAL MANLY.
GOOD LORD! >CHOKE<
>GASP!< JIMMY? ARE YOU OKAY?
JIMMY?
YEEAAAARRGGGH! THE PAIN!
HELP! MRS. THOMPSON! HELP! SOMETHING'S WRONG WITH JIMMY!
GRRRARR. IT...BUUURNS!

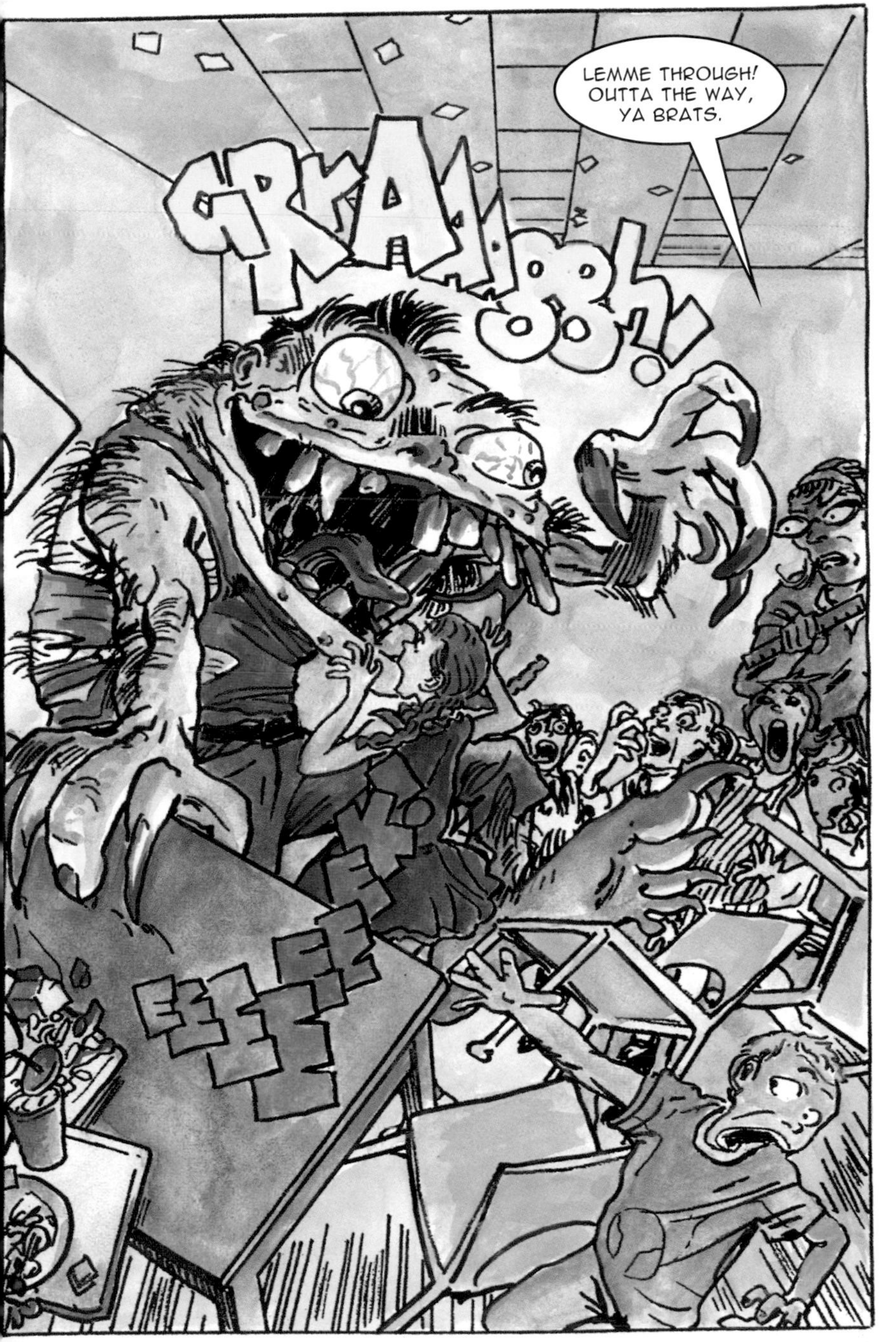
LEMME THROUGH! OUTTA THE WAY, YA BRATS.

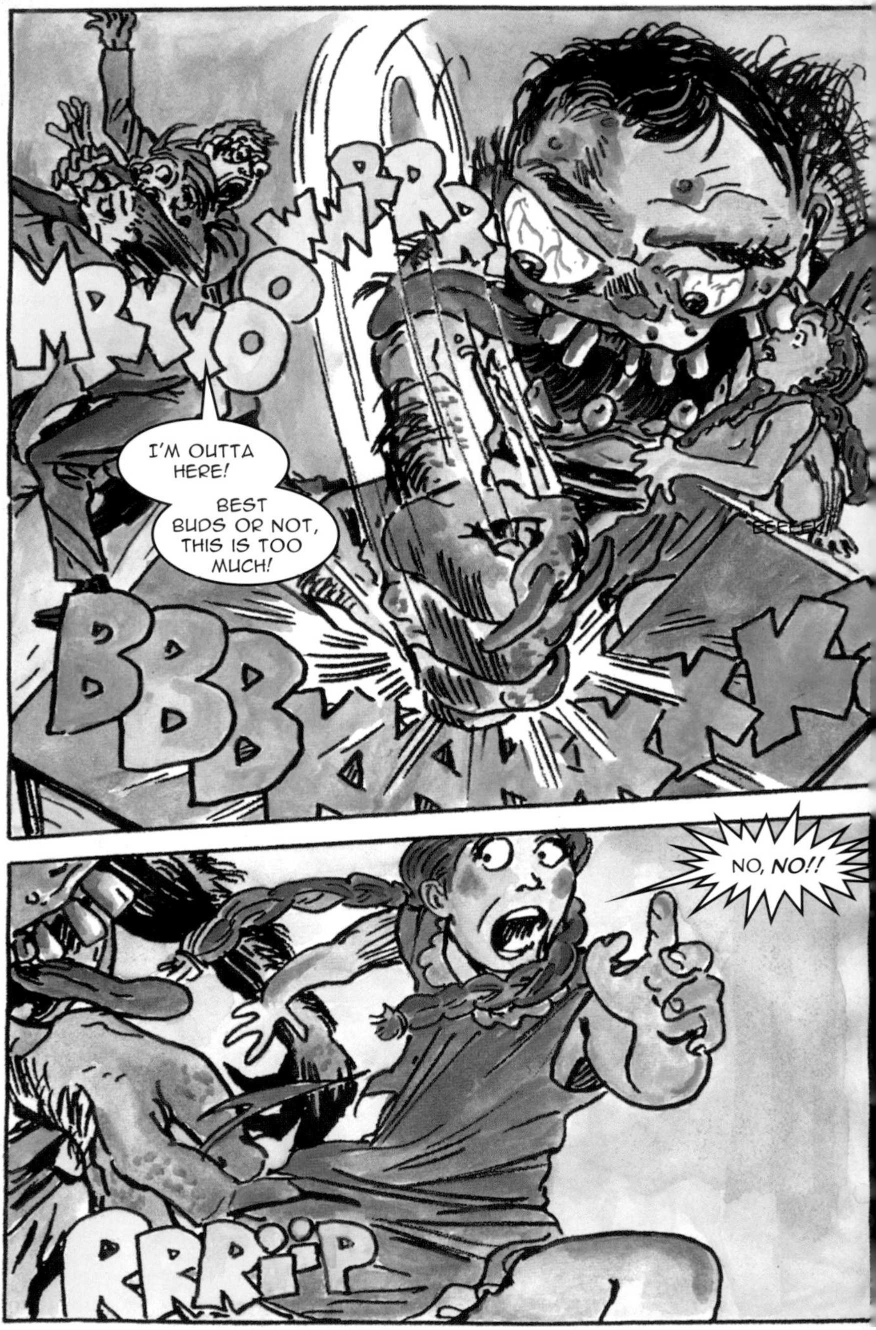
I'M OUTTA HERE!
BEST BUDS OR NOT, THIS IS TOO MUCH!
NO, NO!!
RRRIP

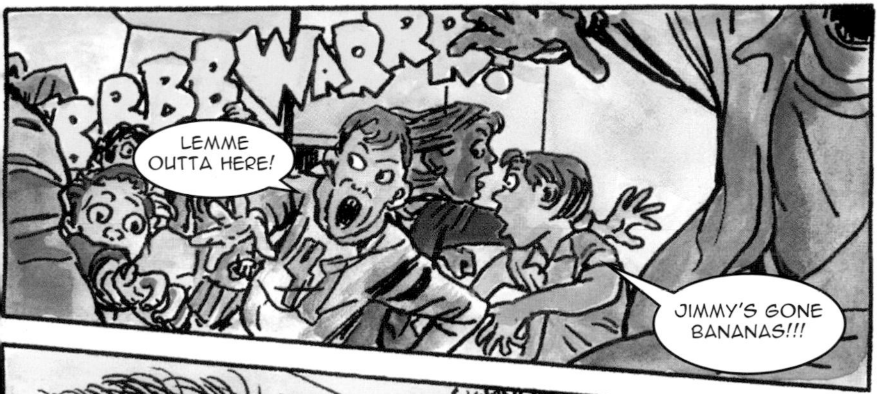
LEMME OUTTA HERE!
JIMMY'S GONE BANANAS!!!

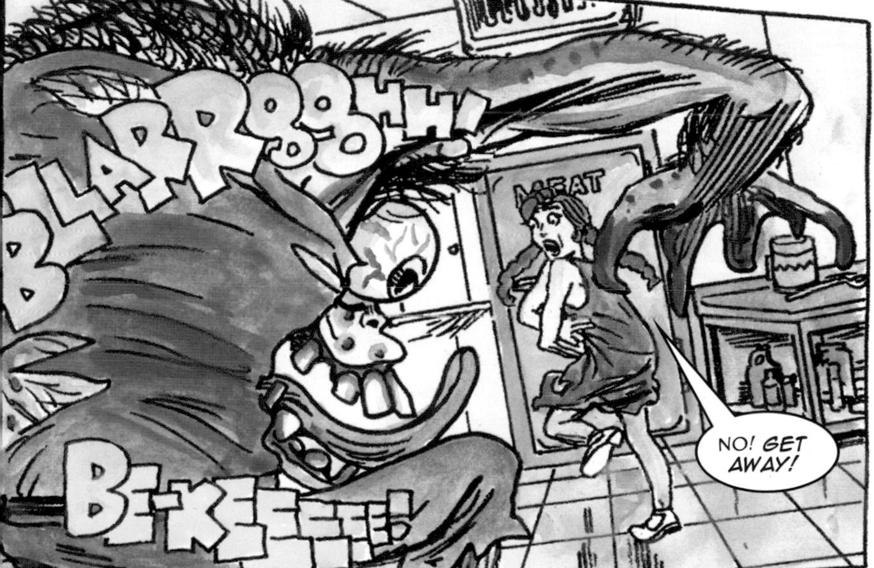
MEAT
NO! *GET AWAY!*

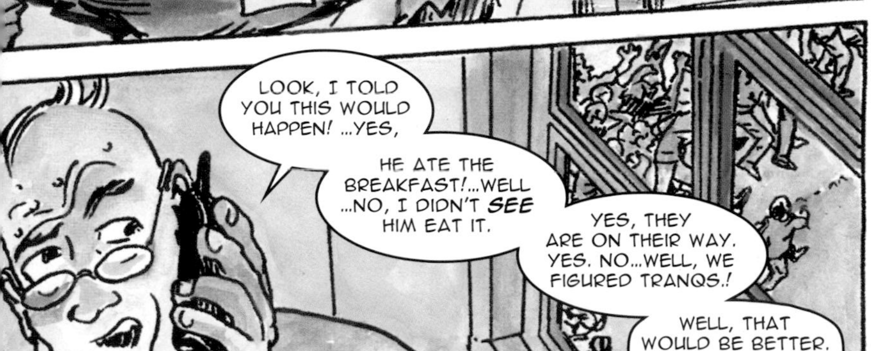
LOOK, I TOLD YOU THIS WOULD HAPPEN! ...YES,
HE ATE THE BREAKFAST!...WELL ...NO, I DIDN'T *SEE* HIM EAT IT.
YES, THEY ARE ON THEIR WAY. YES. NO...WELL, WE FIGURED TRANQS.!
WELL, THAT WOULD BE BETTER.

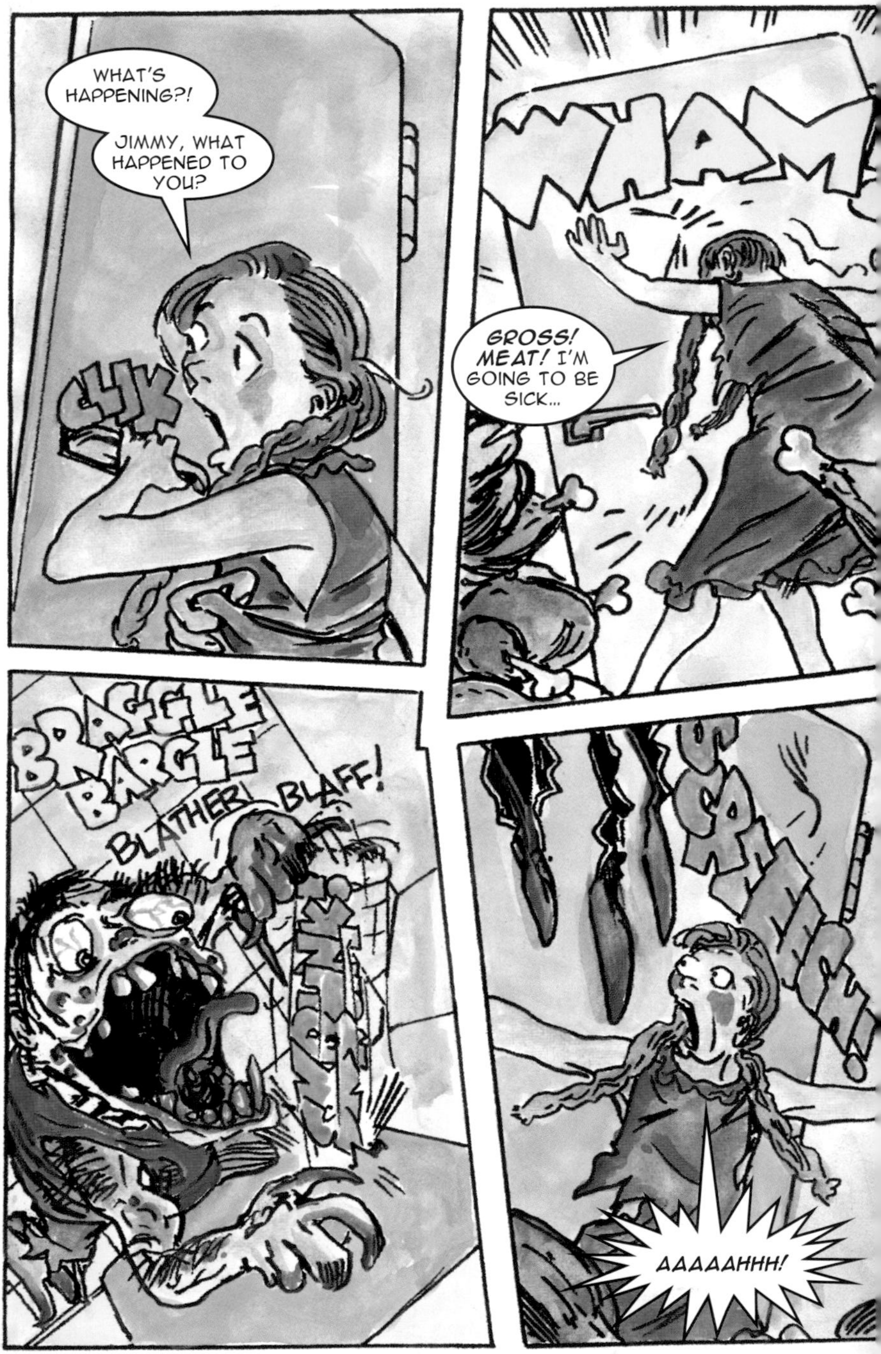

WHAT'S HAPPENING?!
JIMMY, WHAT HAPPENED TO YOU?
CLIK
WHAM
GROSS! MEAT! I'M GOING TO BE SICK...
BRAGGLE BARGLE
BLATHER BLAFF!
AAAAAHHH!

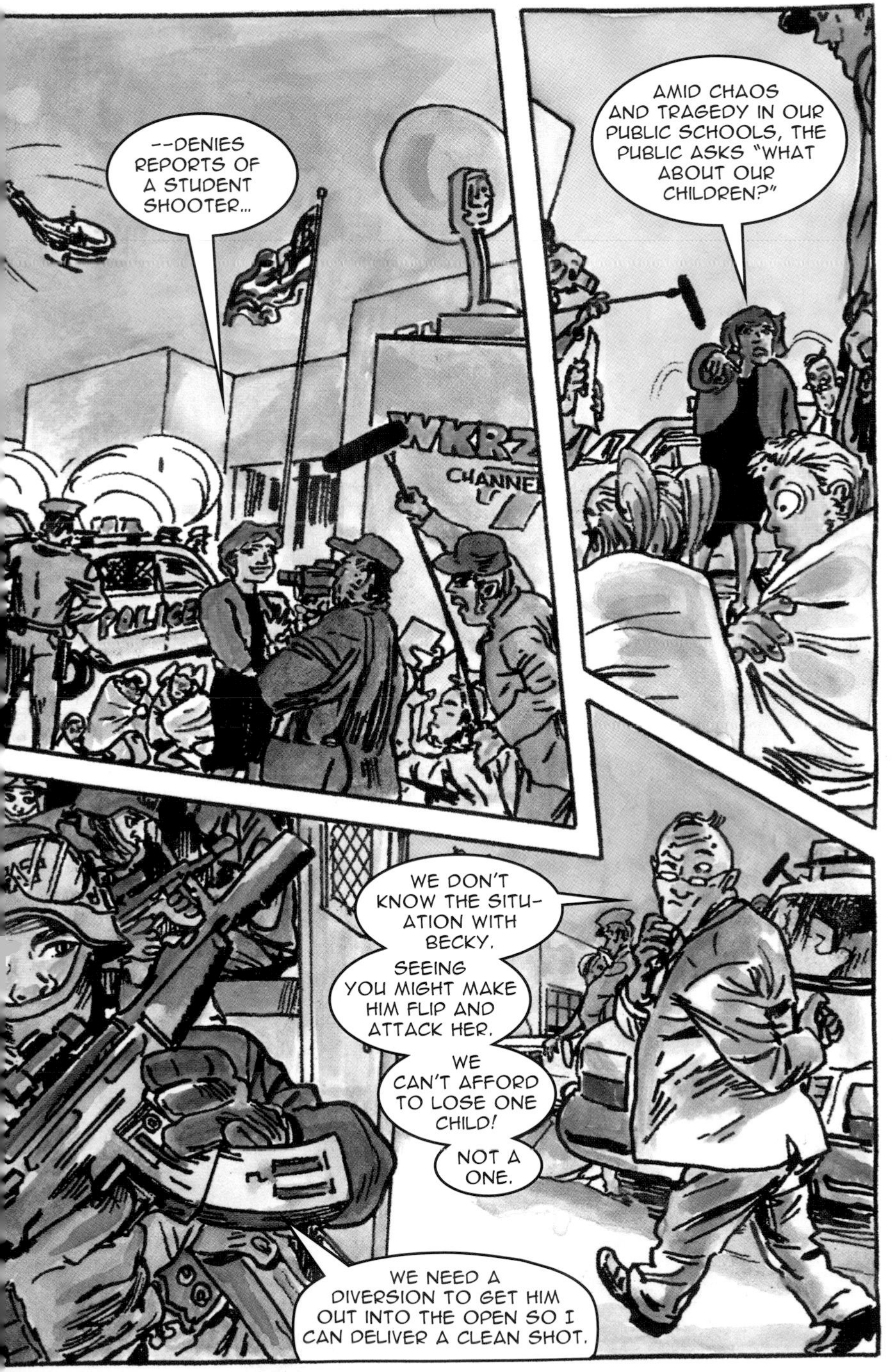
--DENIES REPORTS OF A STUDENT SHOOTER...
WKRZ
CHANNEL 7
POLICE
AMID CHAOS AND TRAGEDY IN OUR PUBLIC SCHOOLS, THE PUBLIC ASKS "WHAT ABOUT OUR CHILDREN?"
WE DON'T KNOW THE SITU-ATION WITH BECKY.
SEEING YOU MIGHT MAKE HIM FLIP AND ATTACK HER.
WE CAN'T AFFORD TO LOSE ONE CHILD!
NOT A ONE.
WE NEED A DIVERSION TO GET HIM OUT INTO THE OPEN SO I CAN DELIVER A CLEAN SHOT.

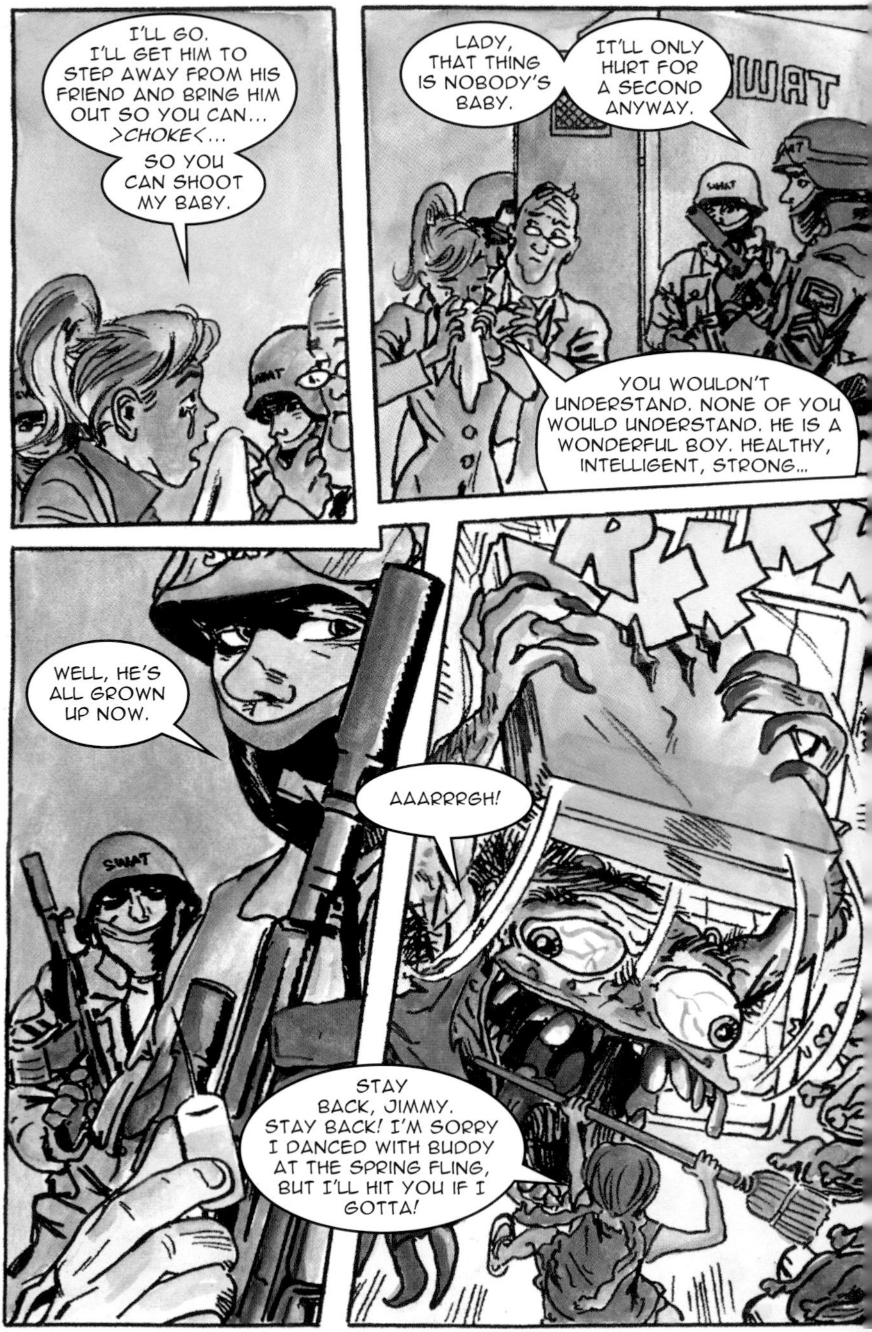
I'LL GO. I'LL GET HIM TO STEP AWAY FROM HIS FRIEND AND BRING HIM OUT SO YOU CAN... >CHOKE<...
SO YOU CAN SHOOT MY BABY.
LADY, THAT THING IS NOBODY'S BABY.
IT'LL ONLY HURT FOR A SECOND ANYWAY.
YOU WOULDN'T UNDERSTAND. NONE OF YOU WOULD UNDERSTAND. HE IS A WONDERFUL BOY. HEALTHY, INTELLIGENT, STRONG...
WELL, HE'S ALL GROWN UP NOW.
AAARRRGH!
STAY BACK, JIMMY. STAY BACK! I'M SORRY I DANCED WITH BUDDY AT THE SPRING FLING, BUT I'LL HIT YOU IF I GOTTA!

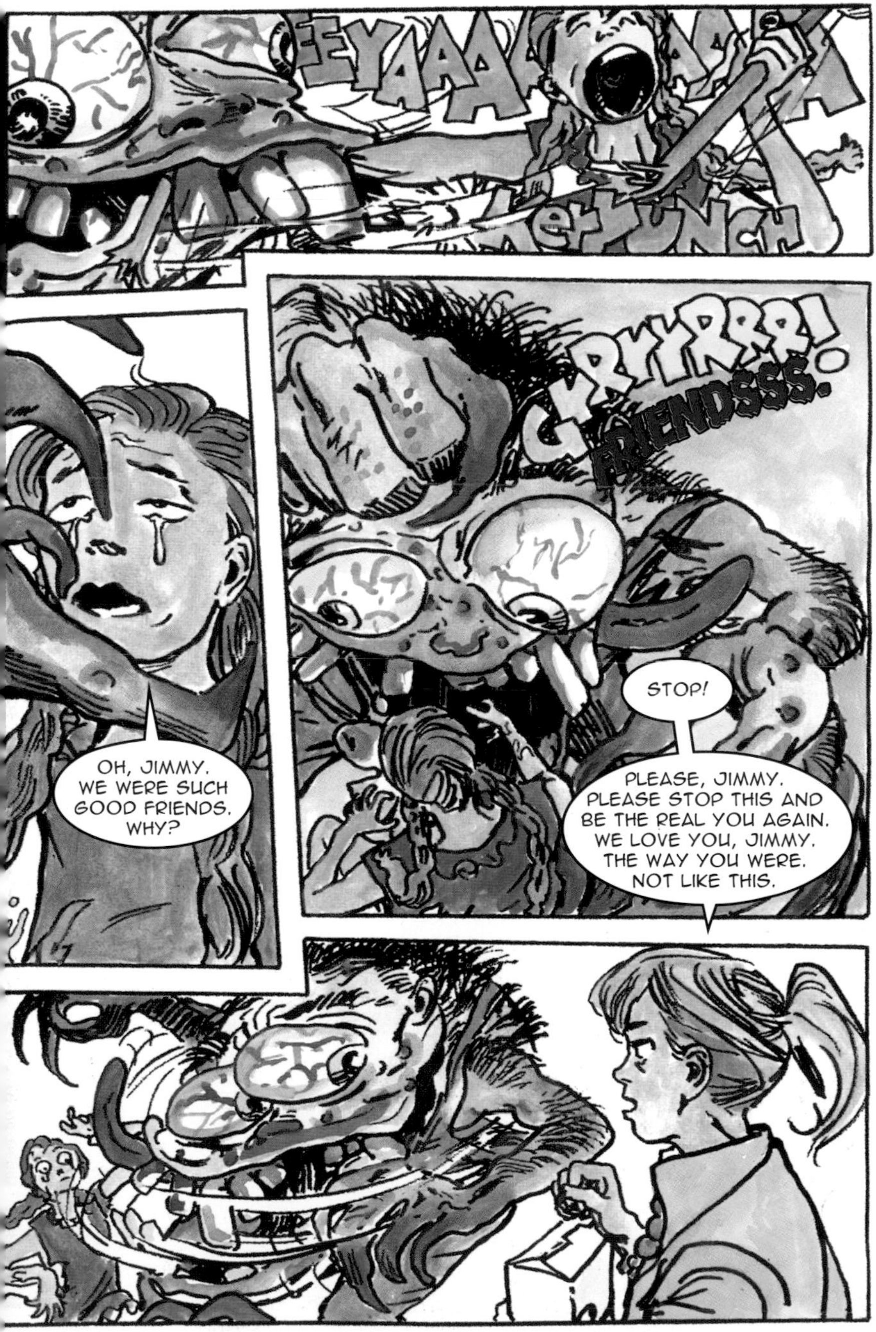
EEYAAA
OH, JIMMY. WE WERE SUCH GOOD FRIENDS. WHY?
GRRRRR! FRIENDSSS.
STOP!
PLEASE, JIMMY. PLEASE STOP THIS AND BE THE REAL YOU AGAIN. WE LOVE YOU, JIMMY. THE WAY YOU WERE. NOT LIKE THIS.

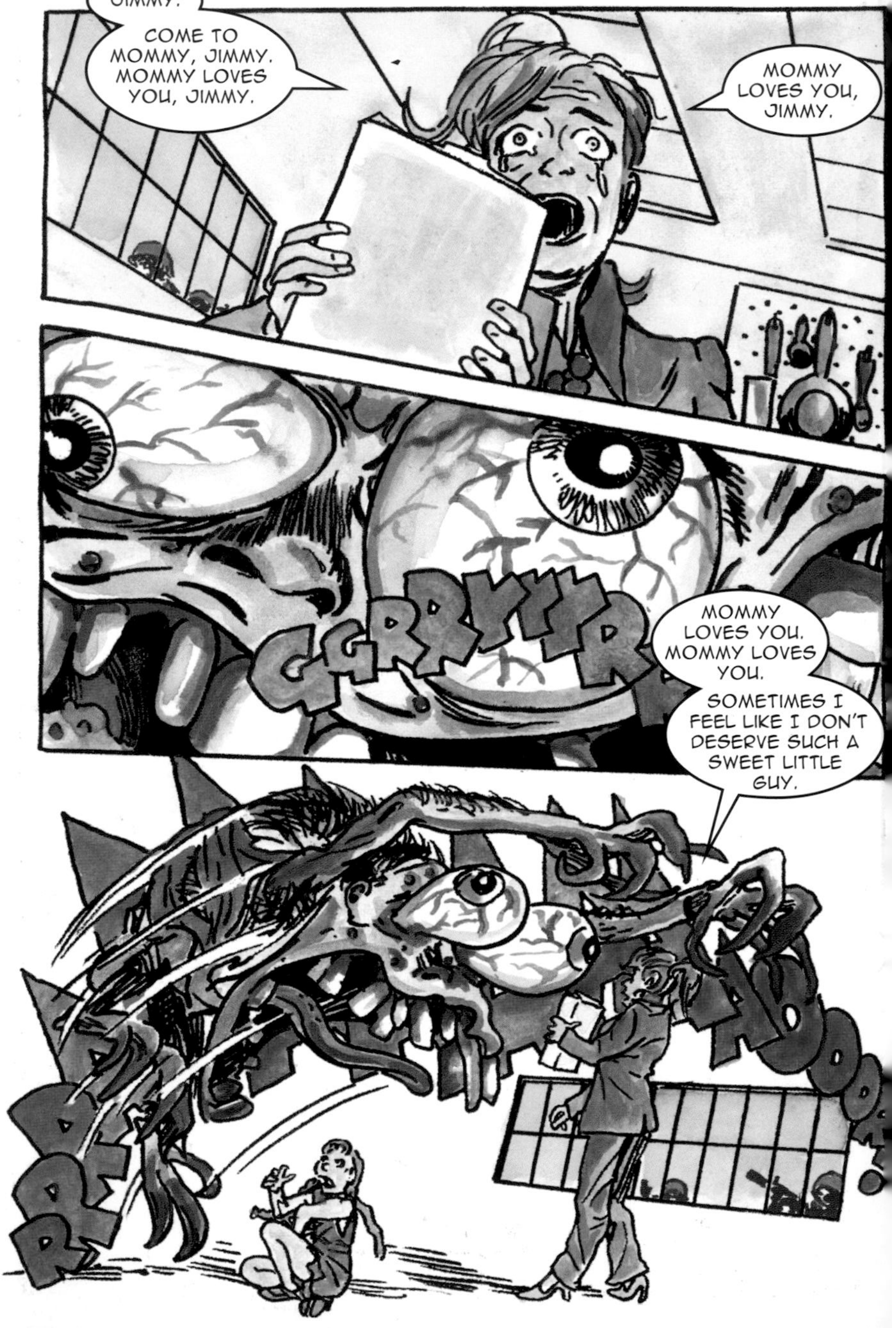
JIMMY.
COME TO MOMMY, JIMMY. MOMMY LOVES YOU, JIMMY.
MOMMY LOVES YOU, JIMMY.
MOMMY LOVES YOU. MOMMY LOVES YOU.
SOMETIMES I FEEL LIKE I DON'T DESERVE SUCH A SWEET LITTLE GUY.

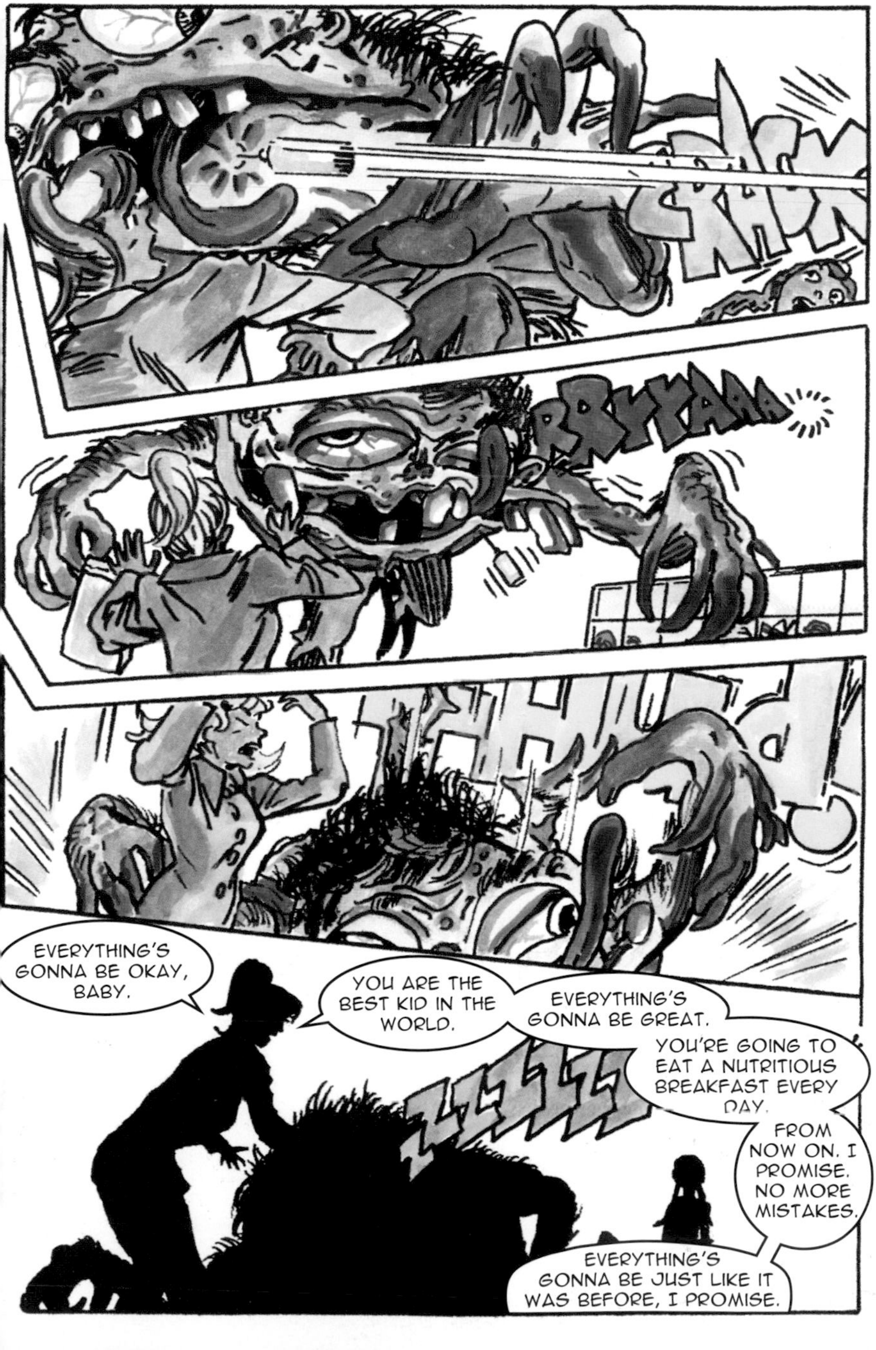

CRACK
RRYYAAA
THUD!
EVERYTHING'S GONNA BE OKAY, BABY.
YOU ARE THE BEST KID IN THE WORLD.
EVERYTHING'S GONNA BE GREAT.
YOU'RE GOING TO EAT A NUTRITIOUS BREAKFAST EVERY DAY.
FROM NOW ON. I PROMISE. NO MORE MISTAKES.
EVERYTHING'S GONNA BE JUST LIKE IT WAS BEFORE, I PROMISE.
ZZZZZ

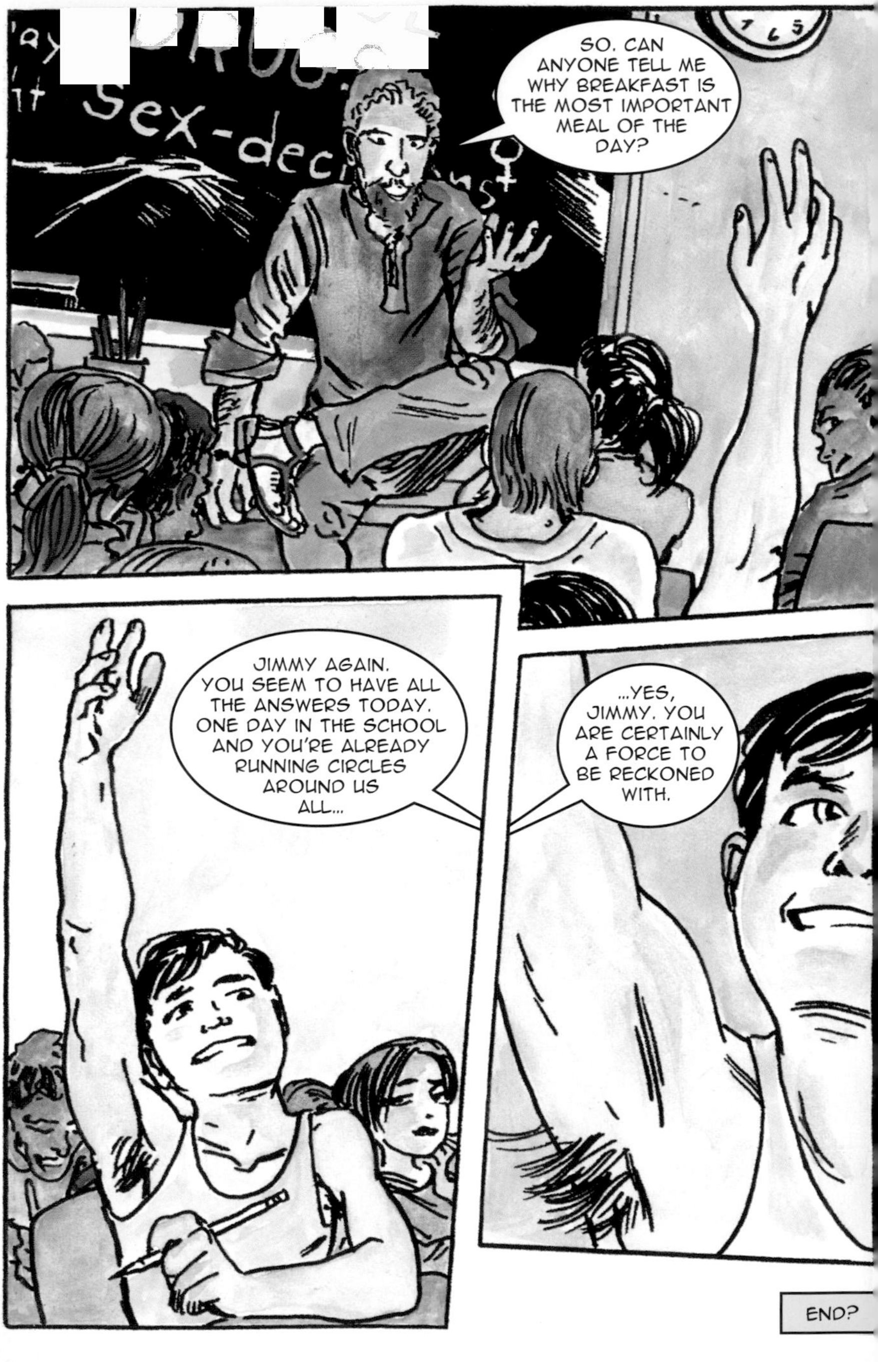
SO. CAN ANYONE TELL ME WHY BREAKFAST IS THE MOST IMPORTANT MEAL OF THE DAY?
JIMMY AGAIN. YOU SEEM TO HAVE ALL THE ANSWERS TODAY. ONE DAY IN THE SCHOOL AND YOU'RE ALREADY RUNNING CIRCLES AROUND US ALL...
...YES, JIMMY. YOU ARE CERTAINLY A FORCE TO BE RECKONED WITH.
END?

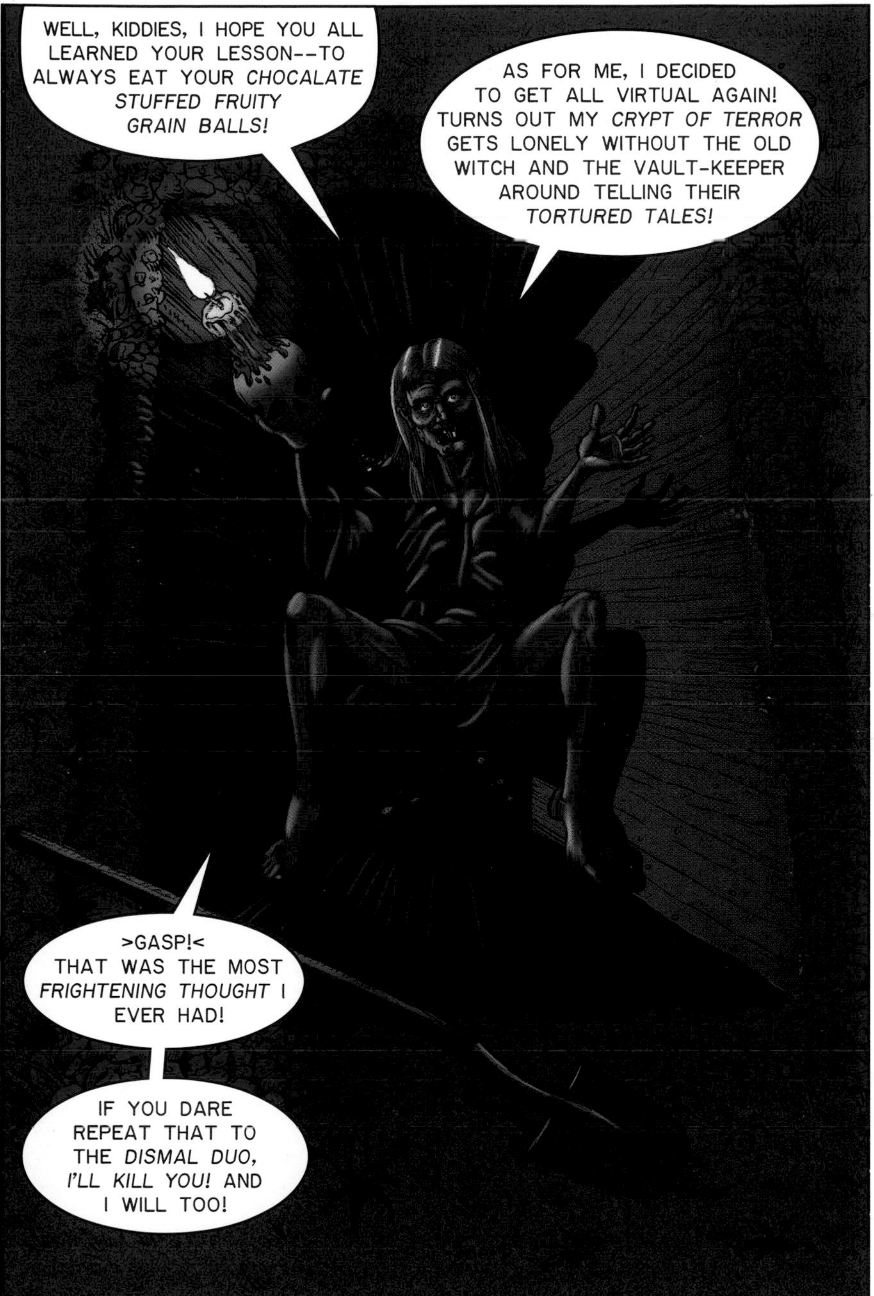
WELL, KIDDIES, I HOPE YOU ALL LEARNED YOUR LESSON--TO ALWAYS EAT YOUR *CHOCALATE STUFFED FRUITY GRAIN BALLS!*
AS FOR ME, I DECIDED TO GET ALL VIRTUAL AGAIN! TURNS OUT MY *CRYPT OF TERROR* GETS LONELY WITHOUT THE OLD WITCH AND THE VAULT-KEEPER AROUND TELLING THEIR *TORTURED TALES!*
>GASP!< THAT WAS THE MOST *FRIGHTENING THOUGHT* I EVER HAD!
IF YOU DARE REPEAT THAT TO THE *DISMAL DUO, I'LL KILL YOU!* AND I WILL TOO!

HERE'S A SNEAK PEAK AT TALES FROM THE CRYPT NO. 4 --"CRYPT-KEEPING IT REAL"

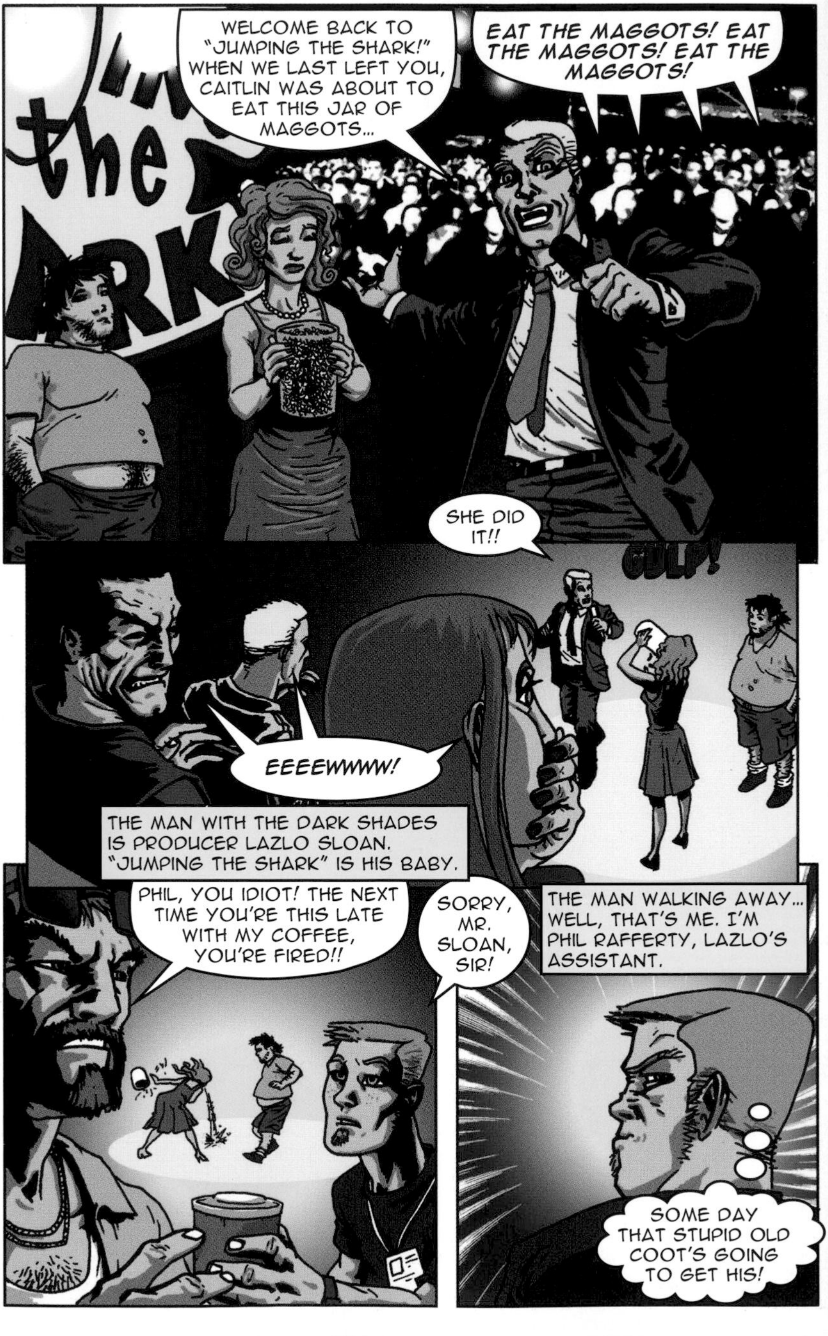

WELCOME BACK TO "JUMPING THE SHARK!" WHEN WE LAST LEFT YOU, CAITLIN WAS ABOUT TO EAT THIS JAR OF MAGGOTS...
EAT THE MAGGOTS! EAT THE MAGGOTS! EAT THE MAGGOTS!
SHE DID IT!!
GULP!
EEEEWWWW!
THE MAN WITH THE DARK SHADES IS PRODUCER LAZLO SLOAN. "JUMPING THE SHARK" IS HIS BABY.
PHIL, YOU IDIOT! THE NEXT TIME YOU'RE THIS LATE WITH MY COFFEE, YOU'RE FIRED!!
SORRY, MR. SLOAN, SIR!
THE MAN WALKING AWAY... WELL, THAT'S ME. I'M PHIL RAFFERTY, LAZLO'S ASSISTANT.
SOME DAY THAT STUPID OLD COOT'S GOING TO GET HIS!

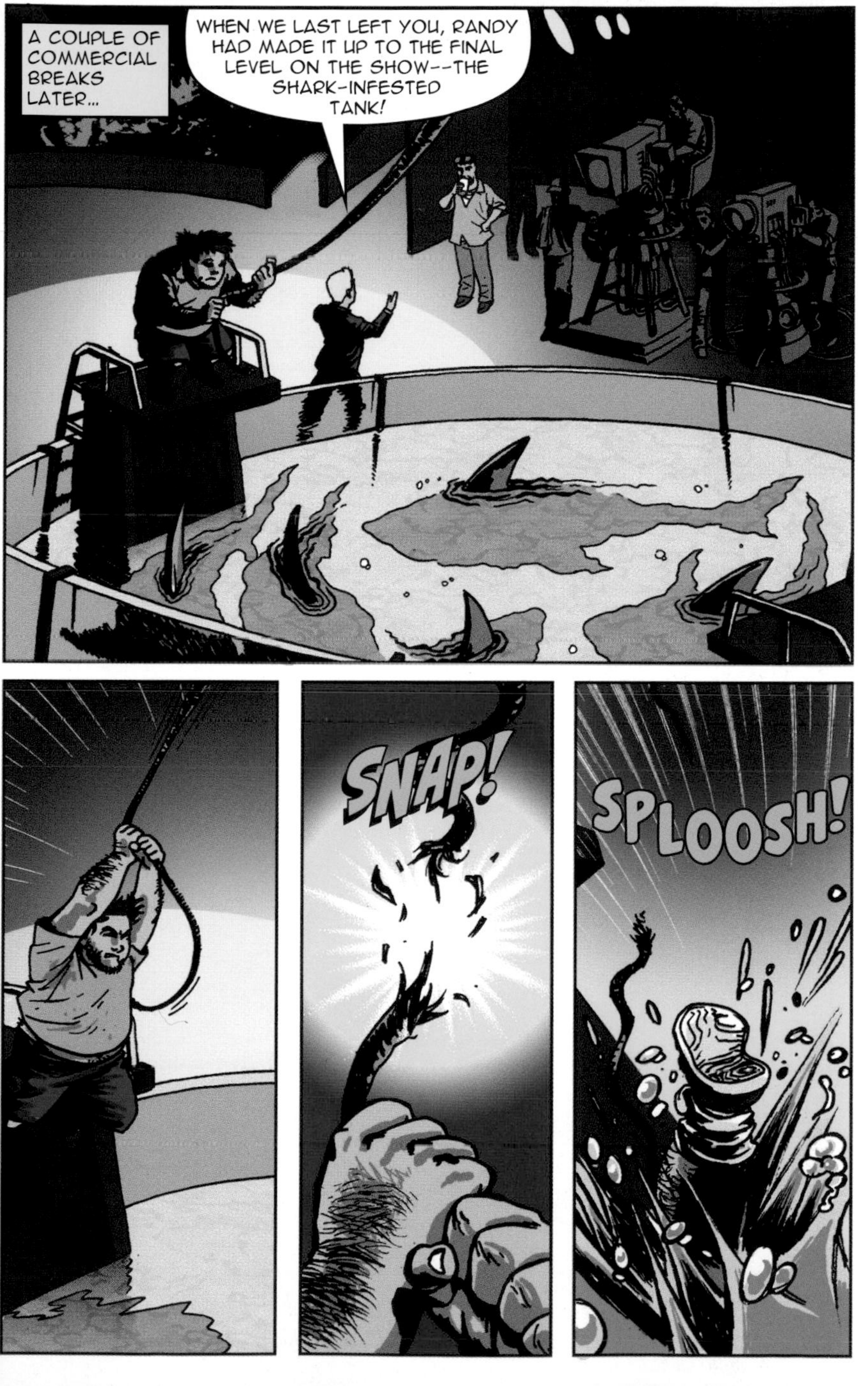
A COUPLE OF COMMERCIAL BREAKS LATER...
WHEN WE LAST LEFT YOU, RANDY HAD MADE IT UP TO THE FINAL LEVEL ON THE SHOW--THE SHARK-INFESTED TANK!
SNAP!
SPLOOSH!

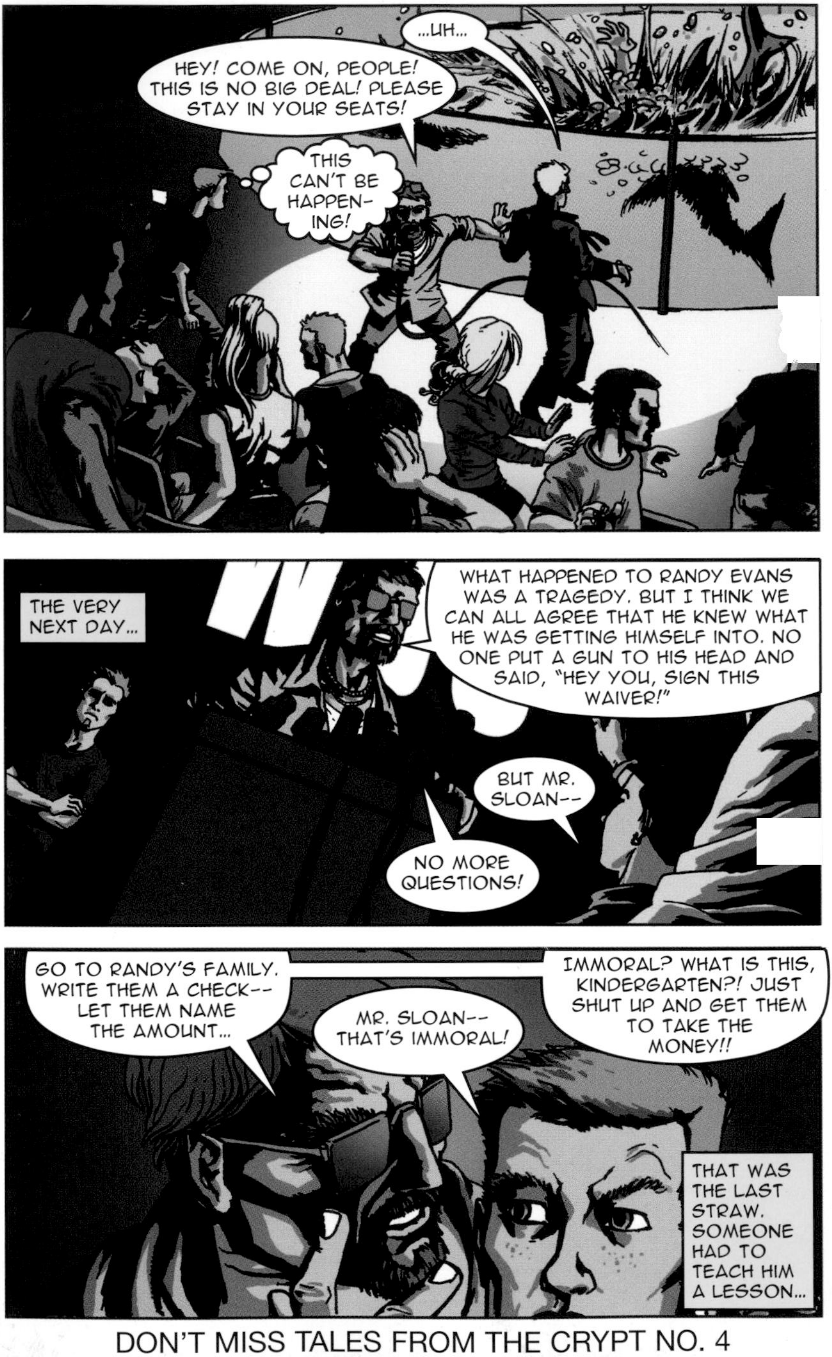
HEY! COME ON, PEOPLE! THIS IS NO BIG DEAL! PLEASE STAY IN YOUR SEATS!
...UH...
THIS CAN'T BE HAPPEN-ING!
THE VERY NEXT DAY...
WHAT HAPPENED TO RANDY EVANS WAS A TRAGEDY. BUT I THINK WE CAN ALL AGREE THAT HE KNEW WHAT HE WAS GETTING HIMSELF INTO. NO ONE PUT A GUN TO HIS HEAD AND SAID, "HEY YOU, SIGN THIS WAIVER!"
BUT MR. SLOAN--
NO MORE QUESTIONS!
GO TO RANDY'S FAMILY. WRITE THEM A CHECK--LET THEM NAME THE AMOUNT...
MR. SLOAN--THAT'S IMMORAL!
IMMORAL? WHAT IS THIS, KINDERGARTEN?! JUST SHUT UP AND GET THEM TO TAKE THE MONEY!!
THAT WAS THE LAST STRAW. SOMEONE HAD TO TEACH HIM A LESSON...

DON'T MISS TALES FROM THE CRYPT NO. 4
"CRYPT-KEEPING IT REAL"

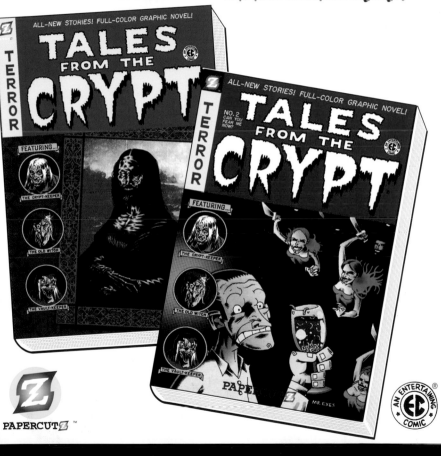

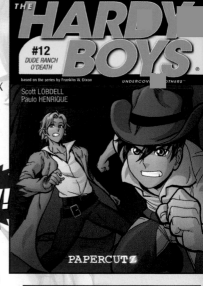

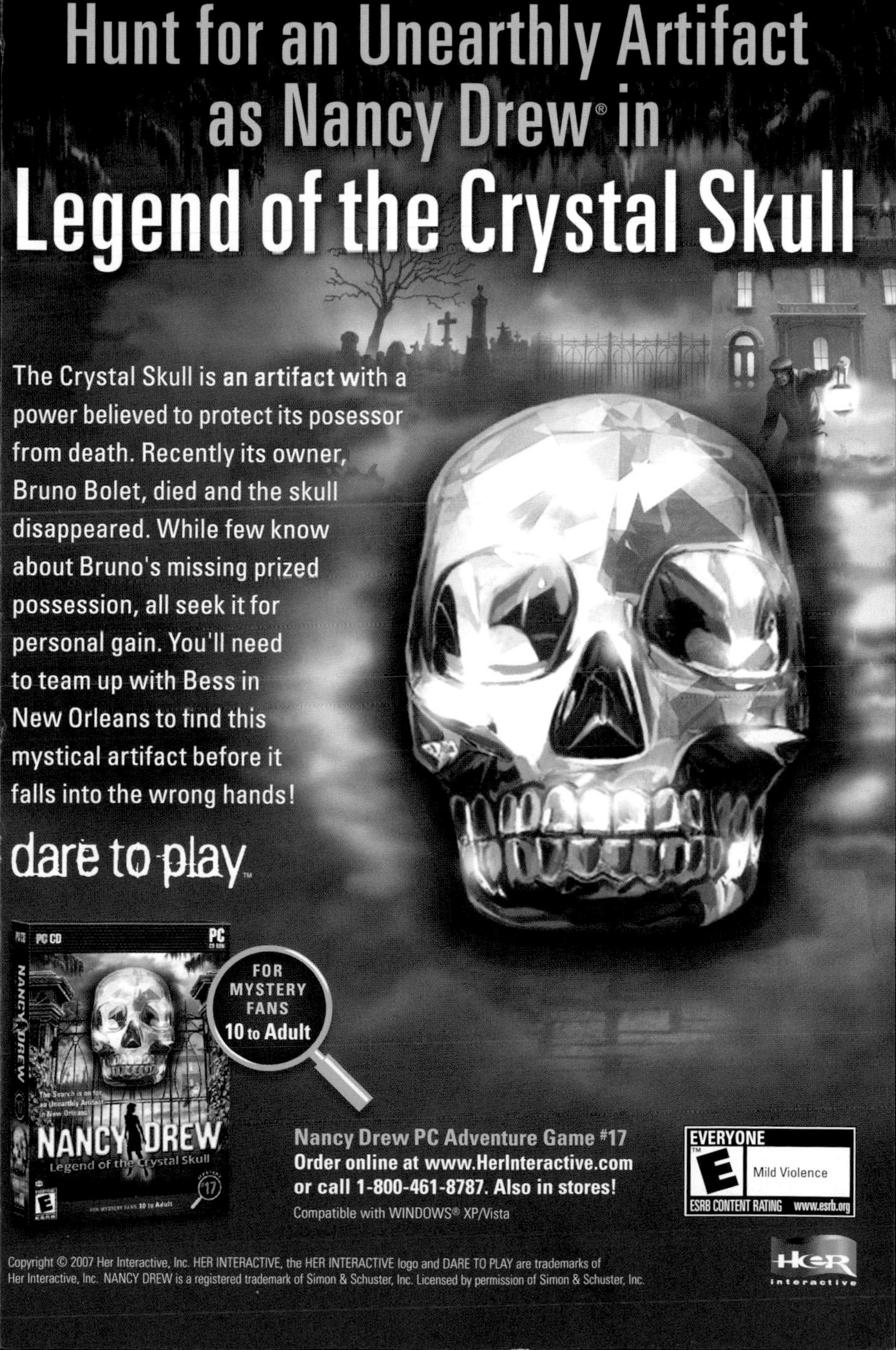
Hunt for an Unearthly Artifact
as Nancy Drew® in
Legend of the Crystal Skull
The Crystal Skull is an artifact with a power believed to protect its posessor from death. Recently its owner, Bruno Bolet, died and the skull disappeared. While few know about Bruno's missing prized possession, all seek it for personal gain. You'll need to team up with Bess in New Orleans to find this mystical artifact before it falls into the wrong hands!
dare to play™
PC CD
PC
NANCY DREW
Legend of the Crystal Skull
FOR MYSTERY FANS 10 to Adult
Nancy Drew PC Adventure Game #17
Order online at www.HerInteractive.com
or call 1-800-461-8787. Also in stores!
Compatible with WINDOWS® XP/Vista
EVERYONE
E
Mild Violence
ESRB CONTENT RATING www.esrb.org
Copyright © 2007 Her Interactive, Inc. HER INTERACTIVE, the HER INTERACTIVE logo and DARE TO PLAY are trademarks of Her Interactive, Inc. NANCY DREW is a registered trademark of Simon & Schuster, Inc. Licensed by permission of Simon & Schuster, Inc.
HER interactive

NANCY DREW

WATCH OUT FOR PAPERCUTZ™

If this is your very first Papercutz graphic novel, then allow me, Jim Salicrup, your humble and lovable Editor-in-Chief, to welcome you to the Papercutz Backpages where we check out what's happening in the ever-expanding Papercutz Universe! If you're a long-time Papercutz fan, then welcome back, friend!

Things really have been popping at Papercutz! In the last few editions of the Backpages we've announced new titles such as TALES FROM THE CRYPT, CLASSICS ILLUSTRATED, and CLASSICS ILLUSTRATED DELUXE. Well, guess what? The tradition continues, and we're announcing yet another addition to our line-up of blockbuster titles. So, what is our latest and greatest title? We'll give you just one hint -- the stars of the next Papercutz graphic novel series just happen to be the biggest, most exciting line of constructible action figures ever created! That's right -- BIONICLE is coming! Check out the power-packed preview pages ahead!

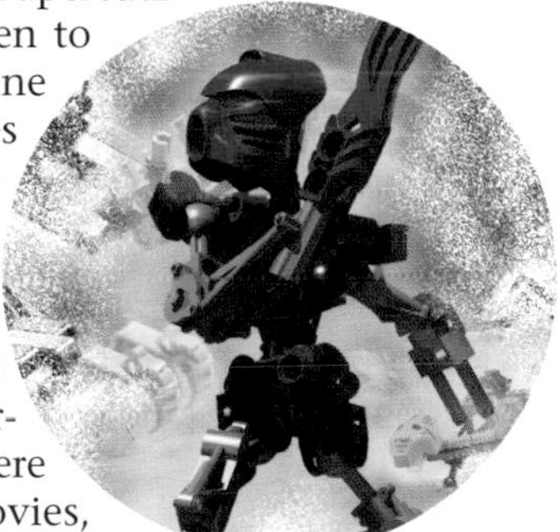

Before I run out of room, let me say that we're always interested in what you think! Are there characters, TV shows, movies, books, videogames, you-name-it, that you'd like to see Papercutz turn into graphic novels? Don't be shy, let's us know! You can contact me at salicrup@papercutz.com or Jim Salicrup, PAPERCUTZ, 40 Exchange Place, Ste. 1308, New York, NY 10005 and let us know how we're doing. After all, we want you to be as excited about Papercutz as we are!

Thanks,

Jim

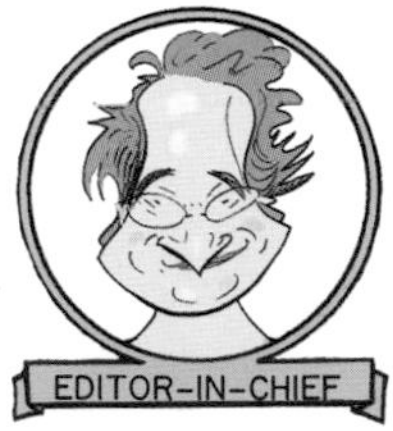
EDITOR-IN-CHIEF

Caricature drawn by Steve Brodner at the MoCCA Art Fest.

TWO DOZEN TEEN DETECTIVE GRAPHIC NOVELS NOW IN PRINT!

NEW STORY! FULL-COLOR GRAPHIC NOVEL
NANCY DREW
girl detective
#12
DRESS REVERSAL
BASED ON THE SERIES BY CAROLYN KEENE
PETRUCHA & KINNEY
MURASE & GUZMAN
PAPERCUTZ

You know, while it's exciting to be adding so many new titles, we don't want anyone to think we've forgotten any of our previous Papercutz publications! For example, can you believe there are now two dozen all-new, full-color graphic novels starring America's favorite teen sleuths?! Let's check out what's happening in the 12th volume of NANCY DREW...

Writers Stefan Petrucha and Sarah Kinney and artists Sho Murase and Carlos Jose Guzman present Nancy's latest case, "Dress Reversal." After showing up at River Height's social event of the year, in the identical dress as the party's hostess, Deirdre Shannon, things get worse for Nancy when she's suddenly kidnapped! That leaves Bess, George, and Ned to solve the mystery of the missing Girl Detective.

That's all in NANCY DREW #12 "Dress Reversal," on sale sale at bookstores everywhere and online booksellers.

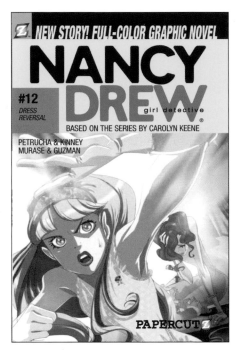

Behold. . .

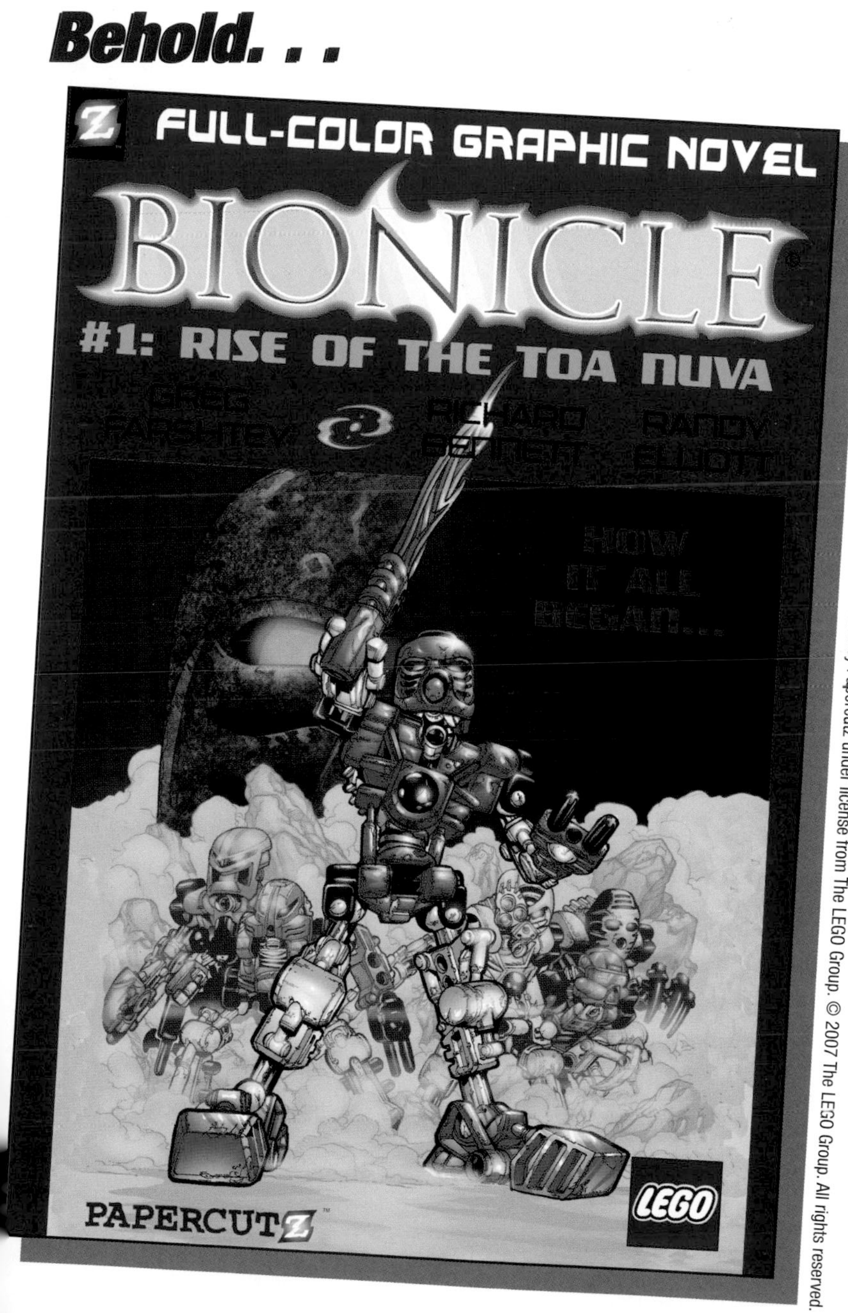
FULL-COLOR GRAPHIC NOVEL
BIONICLE
#1: RISE OF THE TOA NUVA
HOW IT ALL BEGAN...
PAPERCUTZ
LEGO

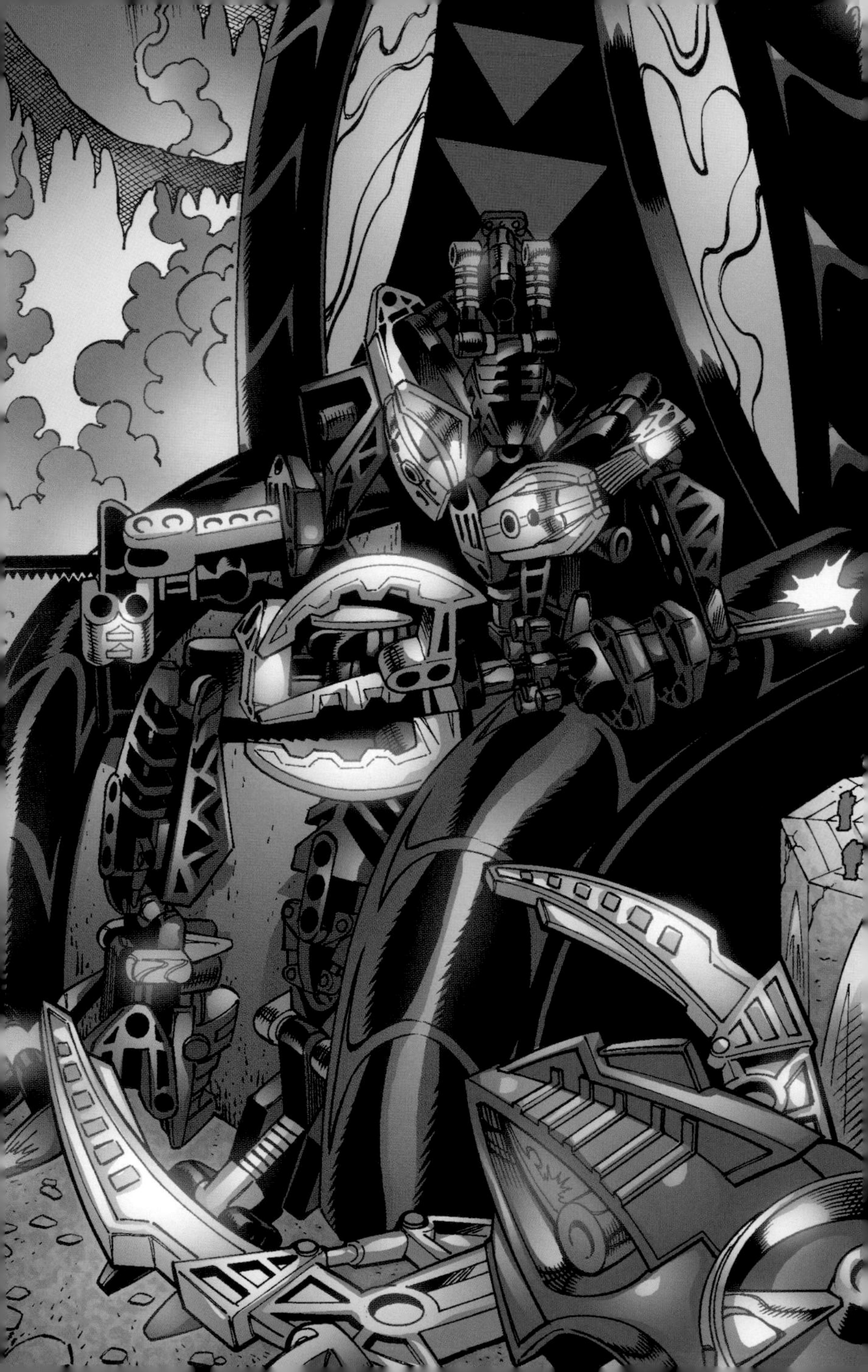

At the start of the new millennium, a new line of toys from LEGO made their dramatic debut. Originally released in six color-coded canisters, each containing a constructible, fully-poseable, articulated character, BIONICLE was an instant hit!

The BIONICLE figures were incredibly intriguing. With their exotic names hinting at a complex history, fans were curious to discover more about these captivating characters. Even now, over six years later, there are still many unanswered questions surrounding every facet of the ever-expanding BIONICLE universe.

A comicbook, written by leading BIONICLE expert and author of most of the BIONICLE novels Greg Farshtey, was created by DC Comics and given away to members of the BIONICLE fan club. The action-packed comics revealed much about these mysterious biomechanical (part biological, part mechanical) beings and the world they inhabited. A world filled with many races, most prominent being the Matoran. A world once protected millennia ago by a Great Spirit known as Mata Nui, who has fallen asleep. A world that has begun to decay as its inhabitants must defend themselves from the evil forces of Makuta.

The first story arc of the comics called "The BIONICLE Chronicles," begins when six heroic beings known as Toa arrive on a tropical-like island which is also named Mata Nui. The Toa may just be the saviors the people of Mata Nui need, if they can avoid fighting with themselves, not to mention the Bohrok and the Rahkshise early comics are incredibly hard-to-find, and many new BIONICLE fans have never seen these all-important early chapters in this epic science fantasy. But soon, those comics will be collected as the first two volumes in the Papercutz series of BIONICLE graphic novels.

These early comics are incredibly hard-to-find, and many new BIONICLE fans have never seen these all-important early chapters in this epic science fantasy. But soon, those comics will be collected as the first two volumes in the Papercutz series of BIONICLE graphic novels.

In the following pages, enjoy a special preview of BIONICLE graphic novel #1...

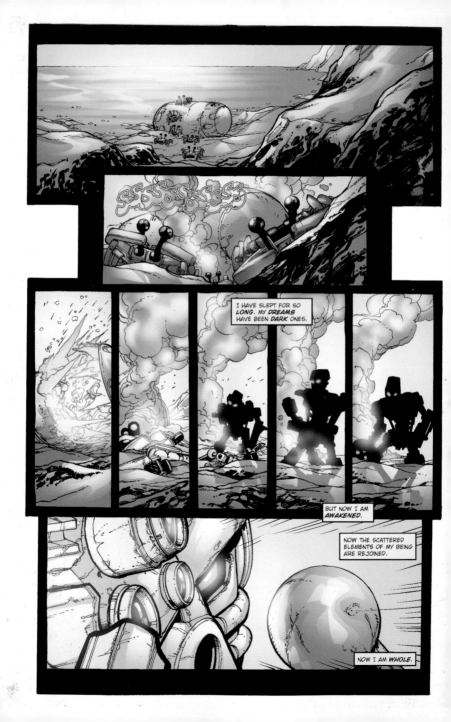

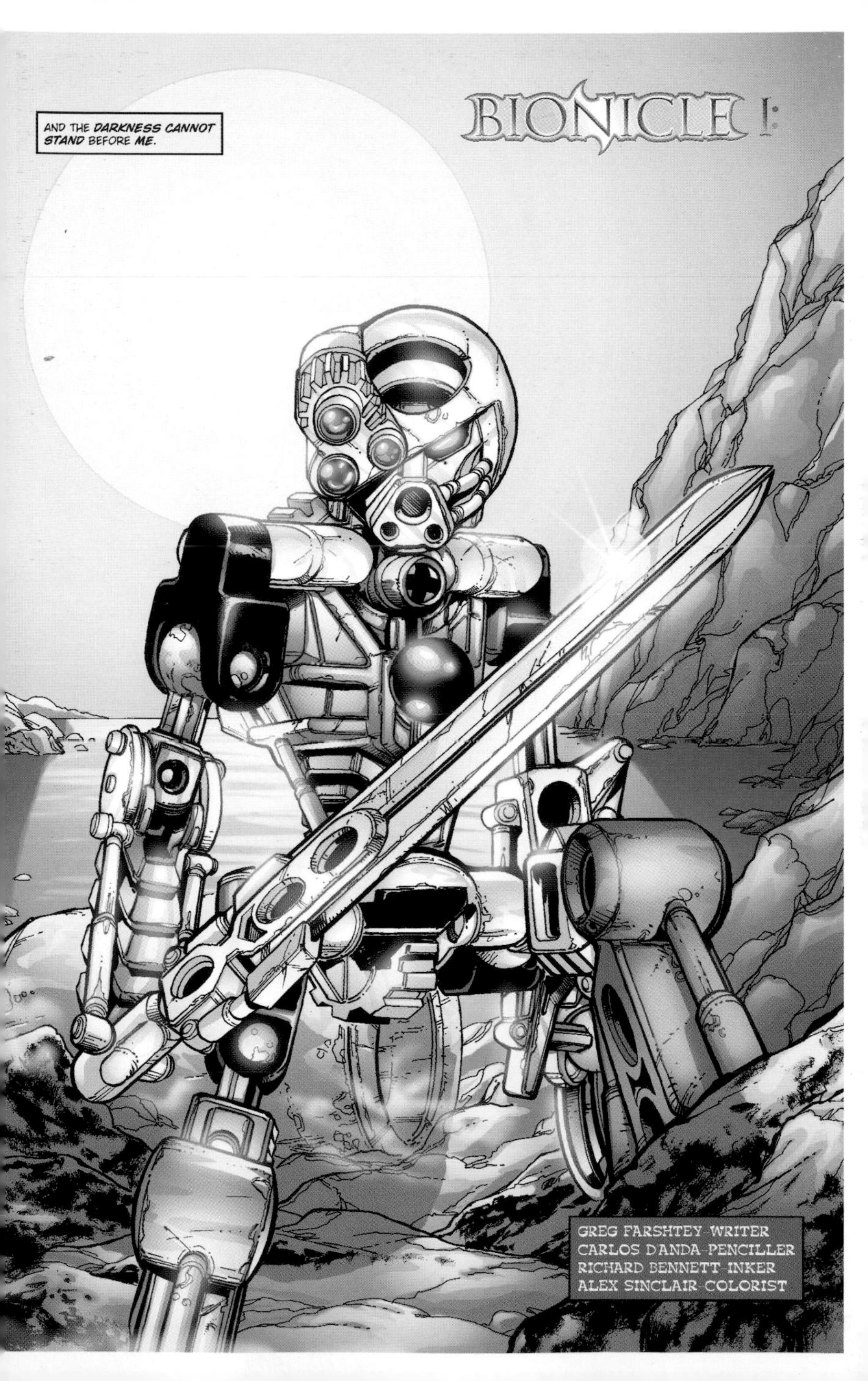
AND THE DARKNESS CANNOT STAND BEFORE ME.
BIONICLE I:
GREG FARSHTEY-WRITER
CARLOS D'ANDA-PENCILLER
RICHARD BENNETT-INKER
ALEX SINCLAIR-COLORIST

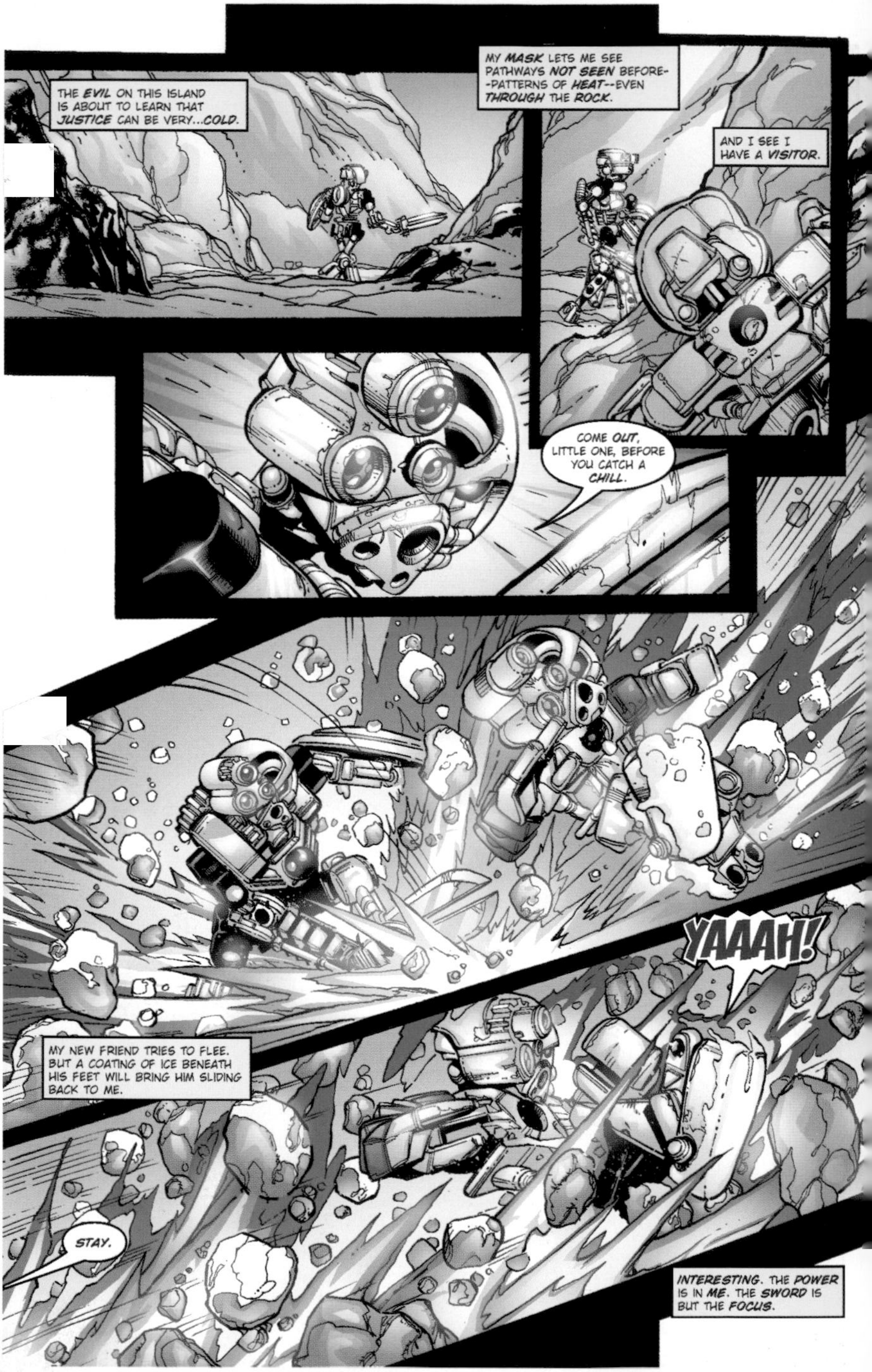
THE EVIL ON THIS ISLAND IS ABOUT TO LEARN THAT JUSTICE CAN BE VERY...COLD.
MY MASK LETS ME SEE PATHWAYS NOT SEEN BEFORE--PATTERNS OF HEAT--EVEN THROUGH THE ROCK.
AND I SEE I HAVE A VISITOR.
COME OUT, LITTLE ONE, BEFORE YOU CATCH A CHILL.
YAAAH!
MY NEW FRIEND TRIES TO FLEE. BUT A COATING OF ICE BENEATH HIS FEET WILL BRING HIM SLIDING BACK TO ME.
STAY.
INTERESTING. THE POWER IS IN ME. THE SWORD IS BUT THE FOCUS.

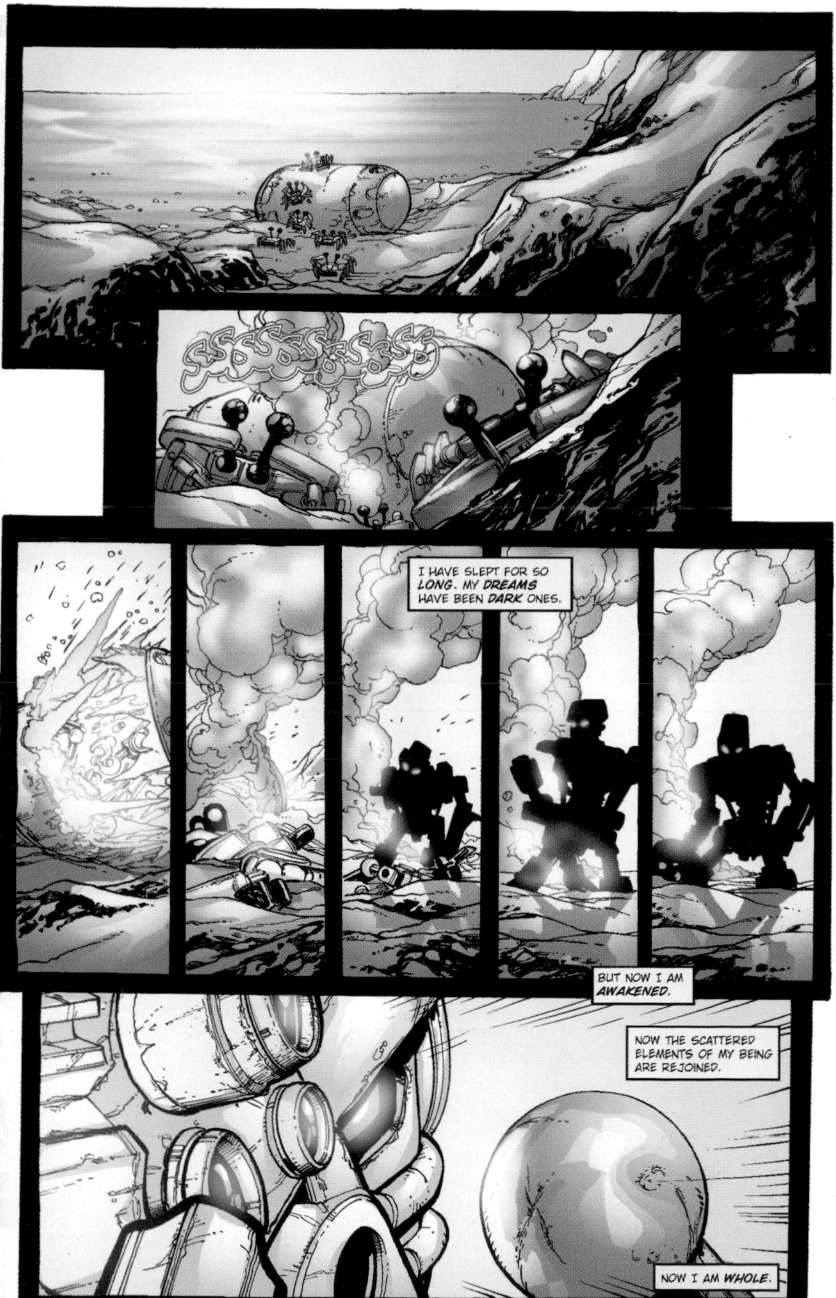
I HAVE SLEPT FOR SO LONG. MY DREAMS HAVE BEEN DARK ONES.
BUT NOW I AM AWAKENED.
NOW THE SCATTERED ELEMENTS OF MY BEING ARE REJOINED.
NOW I AM WHOLE.

A SPECIAL EXCLUSIVE

NANCY

DREW

girl detective

BONUS FEATURE IN #12!

Writing Nancy Drew becomes a family affair!

As all loyal Papercutz followers already know, Stefan Petrucha has been writing the NANCY DREW graphic novels since the very first volume. More recently he's been joined by Sarah Kinney, and together they've been chronicling the latest mysteries of our favorite Girl Detective. Some fans have asked how the two talented writers actually are able to write together? Do they sit side-by-side at their computer keyboard typing together? Does Stefan write one word, then Sarah the next? Well, that actual process will remain a mystery for now, but what we will reveal is that these two are not only co-writers, but they're actually husband and wife.

But here's where the plot thickens (whatever *that* means!)... turns out one of their daughters recently completed a very interesting project in school. Everyone in Mrs. Schreiber's third grade class had to write and draw a Nancy Drew comic, and Margo Kinney-Petrucha's charming Nancy Drew adventure has just been published in the Backpages of NANCY DREW graphic novel #12, "Dress Reversal"! That's right, not only do you get a great story by Margo's mom and dad, but she also wrote, drew, lettered, and colored a six-page story that's really a lot of fun! Take a peek at the excerpt on the next page -- we think it's great! You may want to pick up a copy of NANCY DREW #12 just to have the comics debut of Margo Kinney-Petrucha. She may be the next award-winning graphic novelist someday.

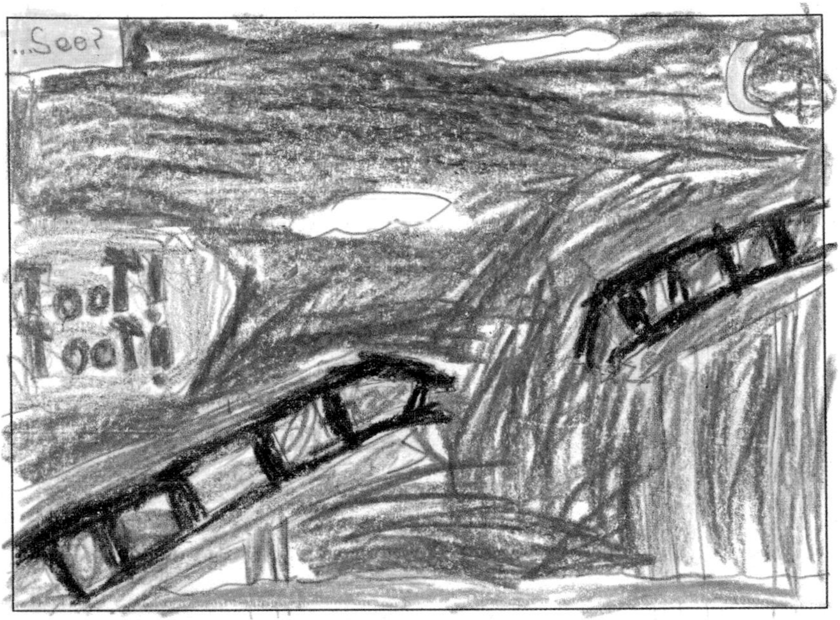
...See?
Toot! Toot!

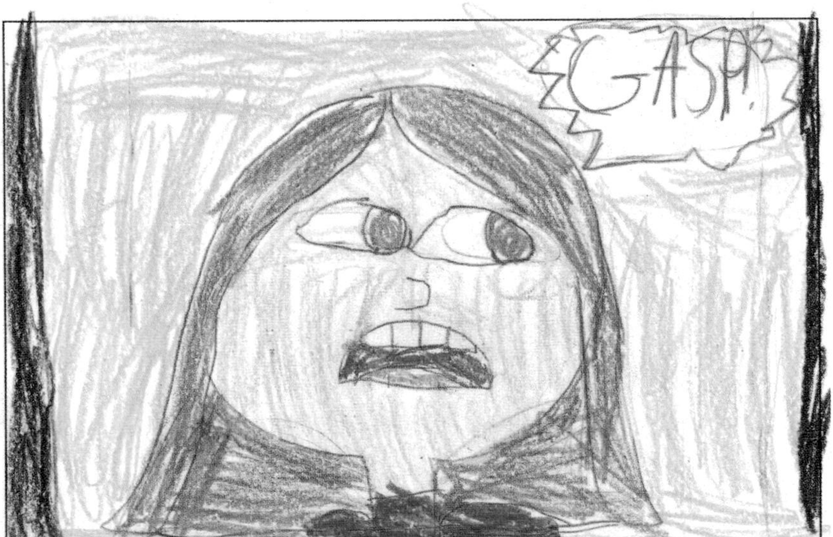
GASP!

ANNOUNCING THE WINNER
OF THE
"WRITE YOUR OWN NANCY DREW
MYSTERY" CONTEST!

To celebrate last year's Nancy Drew movie, we held a super-special writing competition at papercutz.com. We asked all you clever Nancy Drew fans to start their stories with the first page from our biggest Nancy Drew graphic novel adventure, "The High Miles Mystery." But what if instead of going off on the mystery in graphic novels #9 - 11, Nancy, and her best friends Bess Marvin and George Fayne went on a completely different adventure to solve a mystery dreamed up by YOU?!

We got so many wonderful submissions, that it was really difficult to pick just one winner. Ultimately, we basically took all our favorites, put them all in a hat, and picked one at random. So, without further ado, we here at Papercutz are proud to announce that the winner is...

AMANDA GONZALEZ!!

Congratulations, Amanda!

One of the unique aspects of Amanda's entry was that she wrote it in script form, similar to how Nancy Drew's graphic novels and movies are written, and not like the Nancy Drew books available from Simon & Schuster and Grosset & Dunlap. And now, let's all enjoy Amanda's story...

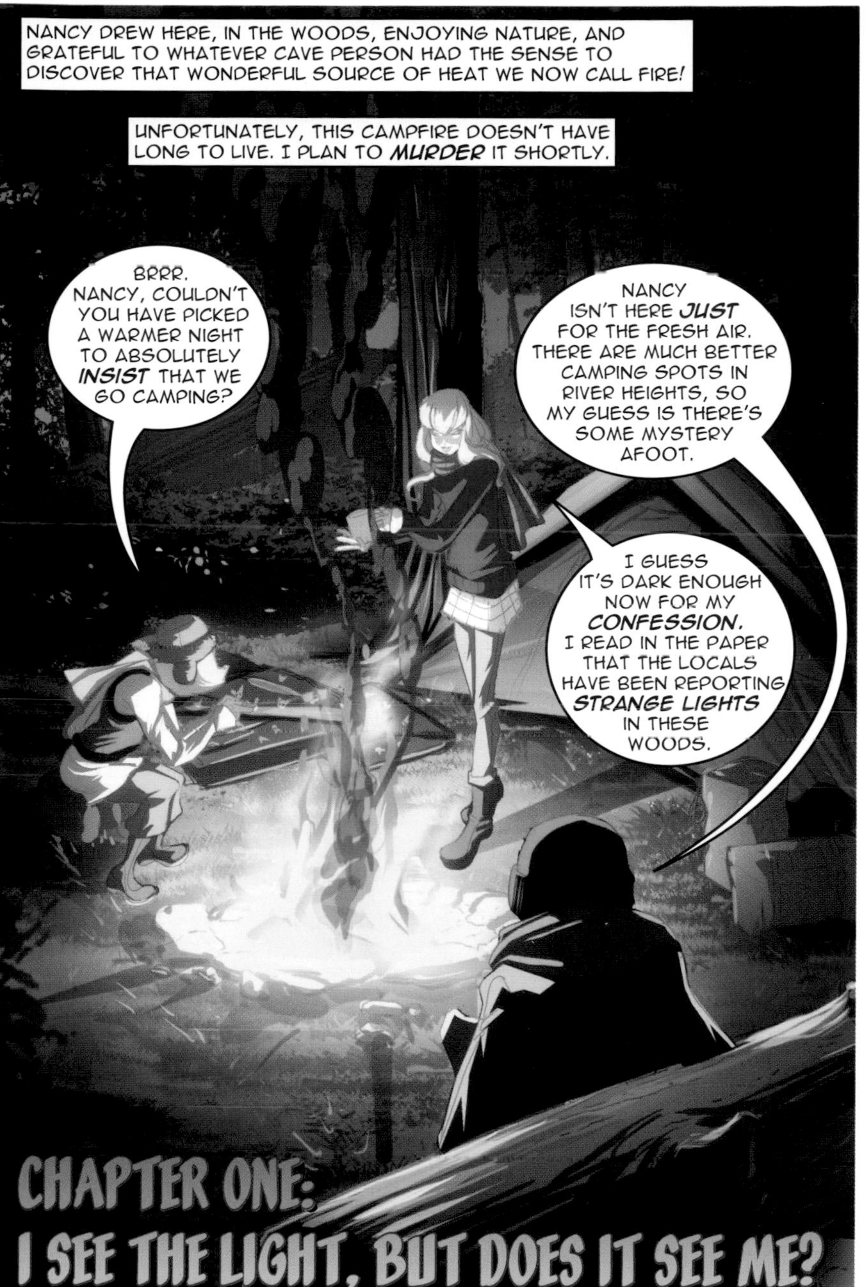
NANCY DREW HERE, IN THE WOODS, ENJOYING NATURE, AND GRATEFUL TO WHATEVER CAVE PERSON HAD THE SENSE TO DISCOVER THAT WONDERFUL SOURCE OF HEAT WE NOW CALL FIRE!
UNFORTUNATELY, THIS CAMPFIRE DOESN'T HAVE LONG TO LIVE. I PLAN TO *MURDER* IT SHORTLY.
BRRR. NANCY, COULDN'T YOU HAVE PICKED A WARMER NIGHT TO ABSOLUTELY *INSIST* THAT WE GO CAMPING?
NANCY ISN'T HERE *JUST* FOR THE FRESH AIR. THERE ARE MUCH BETTER CAMPING SPOTS IN RIVER HEIGHTS, SO MY GUESS IS THERE'S SOME MYSTERY AFOOT.
I GUESS IT'S DARK ENOUGH NOW FOR MY *CONFESSION.* I READ IN THE PAPER THAT THE LOCALS HAVE BEEN REPORTING *STRANGE LIGHTS* IN THESE WOODS.
CHAPTER ONE:
I SEE THE LIGHT, BUT DOES IT SEE ME?

The first page of "The High Miles Mystery," the basis for the contest.

Bess Marvin- Strange lights in these woods, are you sure about that, Nan?

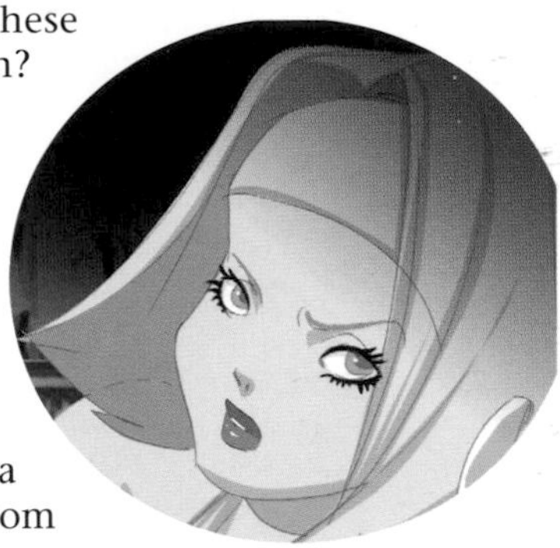

Nancy Drew- I'm positive Bess, it says so in this paper. One individual clearly said that it's not any flashlights because these lights were far too powerful and appeared to look 'mystical' in some way, they were 'purple, green, and blue colored lights that glowed in a strange way' that's the exact quote from the paper. Here take a look...

George Fayne- Oh, come on, Nancy, do you really believe all that nonsense? It's probably just some local kid playing a prank and reporting these strange lights that they made up. Or maybe it's aliens coming to get us all right here in River Heights, and they're after Bess and all the snacks she carries around in her backpack.

Bess- Stop that, George! Nancy, you don't think it could really be aliens, do you?

George- I was kidding, Bess! It's not aliens, there is no such things as aliens or any of that nonsense stuff.

Nancy- All right, you guys, enough arguing. I've called you both here on this "camping" trip to help me investigate this mystery and get down to the real facts of this case.

(The three of them go into the woods in search of these strange mystical lights. While walking with their flashlights, George trips and falls.)

George- Ouch!

Nancy- George, are you okay?!

George- Yeah, I'm fine. Hey, you guys, look at this.

Bess- Hey, it's some kind of strange light bulb-- and look there is a line attached to it that leads deeper into the woods.

(The three of them follow the line to the center of the woods where they find a tree that was draped with lots of different types of lights.)

Nancy- Shhh....do you guys hear that? It sounds like footsteps. Come on over here, we can hide behind these trees.

(The three of them hide behind the trees and wait to see who appears. It is Mr. Daniels -- the local owner of the Camping Supplies store in town. The girls continue to watch as he sets up more lights and starts to play a tape that makes sounds like an animal growling and walking.)

Bess- What in the world is Mr. Daniels doing? Look, he's turning on a switch over there. Hey, look, the tree just lit up with all those strange light bulbs and they look exactly as the man in the paper said: "Mystical lights of blue, purple, and green colors."

George- Yeah, and listen, the tape sounds like some strange animal moving around, making noise.

(The girls step out and ask Mr. Daniels what he's doing. George has her cell phone and explains to him that she is going to call the police if Mr. Daniels doesn't tell them the truth and confess to the locals that he is the mastermind behind the mysterious lights in the woods that was terrifying the locals.)

Mr. Daniels- All right, girls, you caught me. I was the one who submitted that story to the papers secretly. I made up the story and created these strange colored lights, along with the tape because I wanted people to spread the story around to other neighboring towns so

as to gain publicity. I figured with all the attention, news stations would be coming up to check out the story.

Nancy- And in order to check the story out they would have to wait till dark to come into the woods. But they can't get into the woods and go camping unless they have the proper equipment to do so. This means they would need to go to your

Camping Supplies store in order to get those supplies.

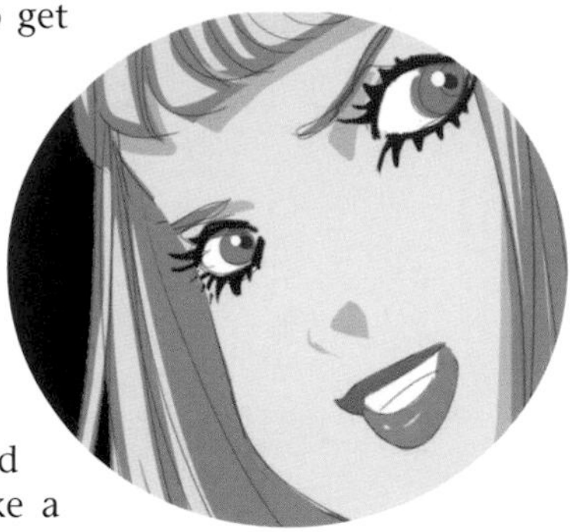

Daniels- Yes, that's right. It's just that business has been so bad these days. Nobody seems to want to go camping and all the kids are interested in these days is the mall and going to that new theme park outside of town. I figured with all the attention, I could finally get some business and make a profit. I apologize and I promise I'll tell the local paper that the story was all false and tell everyone the truth.

(The girls help to clean up the campsite and they all head back into town. And, as promised, Mr. Daniels came clean and told everyone in River Heights the truth. He wrote to the paper and told the police as well that he was responsible for having created the story and having set up the lights in the woods.)

Bess- Yes!!! We did it, you guys! We solved the case of the mysterious lights in the woods.

George- Yup! Now River Heights knows the real story behind this case. And the kids don't have to be afraid to go camping. Actually, I saw that Mr. Daniels's store is doing quite well, and there are more kids then ever before going camping. So, I guess it all worked out in the end.

Nancy- Good job, you guys, thanks for the help. I couldn't have solved this case without you both.

Another case solved by super sleuth Nancy Drew and her friends Bess and George!

THE END!